TENDER

TERRAWAY
BOOK NINE

MARY E. TWOMEY

MARY E. TWOMEY, LLC

TENDER

BOOK NINE IN THE TERRAWAY SERIES

By

Mary E. Twomey

COPYRIGHT

DEDICATION

To my readers.

I was set to end the Terraway series after book eight, but so many of you wrote in to ask for another novel. You shared with me your heartbreak, your own struggles, and your hopes and dreams.

This book is my love letter to you.
Don't ever think you aren't strong enough, powerful enough or important enough to make a difference in the world.

Without you, this book would never have been written.

ALLIE'S BUMP AND BLANK-OUTS

"I swear, if you make me mess up, I'll sic all the zombies in Sombi on you." It was a useless threat, since we all knew I had no control over the reanimated undead that roamed the icy region of Terraway's least traveled-to nation. This was a game of endurance and concentration—two of my fortes. Plus, it's not as if I could beat my beefy Puller in a round of arm-wrestling. I took my wins where I could get them.

"Is that so?" Mason scoffed, tipping my elbow just to make the entire tower of O-shaped cereal topple off of Allie's bulbous belly.

"You jag! I almost beat my record!" My sister giggled while I chucked the O's at Mason's face. I couldn't help but grin when he mimed falling over at the assault, acting as if anything could harm him. With his larger-than-life Matruculan strength, there wasn't much that could take him out.

Still, it was worth a shot. I flicked the cereal at his face, my smile widening with each dramatic groan I dragged out of him as he amped up the theatrics just to entertain Allie and me. "I stacked them twenty high! You're just sore I beat your record."

He combed his fingers through his hair. It finally grew out to just above his shoulders, and I loved the rugged lion-man look to him. Add his burly form to the mix, and I'm a goner, taken under by attraction to rival any teenaged girl with a crush. "I barely nudged you. You know nothing gives me greater joy than letting you win."

My mouth popped open in a scandalized gasp. As if I hadn't earned every obnoxious "I Win, You Suck" dance I'd treated him to. "That's it. Rematch. Allie, I hope you didn't have any plans tonight."

Graham tutted our childish competition when he entered Ezra's spotless living room, his posture erect, like the gentleman he was. His hair was never messy, which I think is sort of an extension of his entire being. Ever since Graham came into Allie's life, the messiness of her childhood was quickly replaced with an orderly, calm adult existence.

Gotta love a man in love.

Graham smiled adoringly at Allie, which made me love him all the more. He winked at her, and the solitary freckle near his left eye granted Allie a flash of playfulness to soften his professional demeanor. "As a matter of fact, she does have plans. I'm taking my wife out for dinner. Might be the only fine dining experience we get this month. We only have a day a week we travel Topside, so I'd like to make the most out of proper civilization."

I clasped my hands under my chin. "Say 'proper' again. You sound so very British when you do."

"You are a proper pain in my arse, October Grace." He said it with a tease on his lips, so I knew he was joking.

Graham was never parted from Allie for more than a handful of minutes. The more obviously pregnant she looked, the more he hovered. She was barely halfway through her pregnancy; I could only imagine how much more of a watchman he'll become toward the end. I loved watching them be sweet to each other. After all Philip put my big sister through, she deserved to be treated like a treasure.

My treasure. And I guess she was Graham's treasure now, too. I hugged her belly as I snuggled in next to her on the pure white couch. Mason came around and scooted in next to me, his bulk sinking the cushion and making my body nearly tip onto his lap, which I'm pretty sure was his plan. He draped his hand over my hip, tracing a lazy circle with his thumb. He was content to watch me fawn over Allie like the queen she's always been to me.

My spine turned to jelly when a swath of relaxation pumped into me via Mason's touch. He always thinks he's being subtle, but I can feel when he's pulling. I cast a stink-eye over my shoulder, but he shrugged it off. I knew he was worried I was going to get worked up over the sight of a pregnant woman, but it's been two years since I lost my baby. I'm not devastated when I see pregnant women who get to keep their little bundles of joy. I don't feel gutted at all.

I don't.

As if he could hear my internal pep-talk, Mason planted a kiss on the back of my shoulder and rubbed lightly up and down on my bicep.

Allie's voice is maybe the best sound in the world. "Honey, I'm not sure I should leave October Grace. Seeing my brother and sister one day a week is hardly healthy. To cut even *that* short?" She shook her head.

Graham narrowed his eyes at my triumphant grin, holding in his comment on what exactly "healthy" should look like. "Whatever you like, dear."

I drew hearts on Allie's belly with my fingertip, sending messages of love to her baby boy. We only just found out last week, and I was still geeked about it. "Sucks that you have to live in Terraway during your pregnancy. I mean, I get that it's healthier for you and the baby, but still. I just got you back, and I have to miss you all over again." My siblings and I had been through enough to where we felt no shame over our separation anxiety, and clung as tight as we needed.

Allie had been woken from her coma for barely over a year and a half, but much of that had been spent in Terraway, due to how quickly her and Graham got married and decided to start a family. It was fascinating to watch them dote and fawn and fall into gooey promises and blush-laced late-night kisses. He was so proper and precious to her, and she was amazed that a man could be so very kind. If I was limited to once-a-week visits for nine months so her baby could stay healthy, then I would deal with the separation (though not gracefully).

I rubbed my sister's belly and leaned into her side. "Lynna is a better cook than any old restaurant. What are you craving lately, Allie-Bear?"

Allie didn't respond but stared vacantly ahead, her eyes going out of focus.

She did that every now and then. She was with us, and then not. No one wanted to admit her brain had been severely messed with when she was violated by Sama, but the hallmarks of lasting damage were there. She'd bathed in the healing waters, which had healed a great many things wrong with her internal organs from years of cutting, anorexia and just plain neglect. The psychological wounds ran deeper, and though the healing waters were miraculous, my Allie still wandered off into the abyss in her mind far too often for it to be considered a cute quirk.

Graham stiffened, and I caught his eye. The tightness of his mouth told me that her brain-blanks weren't as few and far between as everyone was hoping. "Can I get you some water, sweetheart?" Graham bent at the waist to touch her ankle, bringing her back to the present.

"Hmm?"

"Water, Allison. Are you thirsty?"

"Thirsty?"

He squeezed her ankle that had somehow managed to stay slender through five months of pregnancy. I had looked like an overinflated balloon back when I'd been knocked up, while Allie looked like the picturesque mom-to-be that you see in magazines, shopping for organic produce and insisting on hypoallergenic baby carriers.

Of course, her personality couldn't be more opposite. Every baby gift was a huge celebration, with her waxing poetic about how much easier things would've been if she'd had fancy things like a stroller back when I'd been the baby she'd looked after. And she didn't understand the fuss over organic produce. When she first came to, it was all we could do to remind her not to dig in the trash for discarded scraps of food.

Yes, she'd come a long way, but her brain-blanks were the red flag that she still wasn't quite one-hundred percent. Every time she had one, panic and something maternal choked me around the throat until I could feel pressure building behind my eyes, just waiting for me to blink so my pent-up tears could go cascading down my cheeks.

"You don't have to go to the trouble. I can get myself some water," Allie replied with a gentle smile that matched Graham's.

Mason and I both moved to get up, as if the mere mention of a want electrocuted the couch to make our bodies act in Allie's favor.

Graham held up his hands to us. "Don't get up. She's my wife."

"She's partly my charge," Mason insisted. Though he was my Reaper, he was also one of Allie's four Pullers, so he felt the draw to watch over us both, down to getting the simplest glass of water. Death Omens had a hard job, reaping souls to keep the suns of Terraway running. If we didn't fulfill our roles, the entire underworld starved and withered. While the job was lightyears easier than it ever had been, with us only having to reap one soul a week to keep things afloat, the life expectancy for Omens wasn't all that long. The entire Vandershot/Manaul/Reese clan was determined Allie and I would be the first Omens to make it to our forties.

Grand ambition, indeed.

Graham waved for Mason and me to sit back down. "Stay just like that." Then to Allie, he mused, "I love to see you so relaxed. Your sister is good for you." Graham reached over and tucked an auburn curl behind her ear, and then flicked me hard on the nose for overruling his restaurant plans before moving to the kitchen.

Whatever. He had her all to himself six days a week in Terraway, with only Boston as the third wheel. My sister, my turn.

My phone buzzed in my pocket. When I pulled it out, Judge's warning flashed across the screen. *"Stay inside tonight."*

He's been doing that more often these past couple

weeks. Staying out of sight for the most part, but texting me warnings to stick close to Mason or stay away from windows. I wish I could say Judge was paranoid, but I know better than that.

I swipe back a quick, *"Will do. Miss your angry face."*

"Promise me, October."

I huffed at the screen. *"I super-duper promise."*

One day Judge will text me an emoji. For now, he's too old and serious for such things. But one day he'll be a goof like the rest of us, I'm sure of it. That'll be after he quits the drug trade he's been married to for the better part of his adult life.

I pulled out my hand sanitizer and wiped my fingers off. You have no idea how many germs lurk on phones, even one that's cleaned as often as mine. I'm just covert enough with my slight movements that I didn't divert Allie's attention from her husband.

Call me a creeper, but I loved watching Allie study Graham. The look of wonder whenever he did anything thoughtful struck me with equal amounts of joy and sadness. I was thrilled to see a man finally appreciate the perfect woman she was and dote on her so lavishly. Then my happiness crested when I realized that kindness and sweetness shouldn't be something that felt foreign to my amazing sister who'd helped raise me. What a terrible journey she'd had to endure to get to this point. She'd confessed that Philip had been sweet in the beginning when he came to her in her dreams, just as he'd been with me. But when she started resisting his advances, he turned violent.

Sama, I scolded myself as I snuggled back into Mason's body heat, stroking Allie's belly. Sama was the Mangkukulam who'd infiltrated her mind, and then mine, seeking out a Death Omen who could carry his offspring. Allie and I hadn't known what he looked like, so it was easy for him slip into our dreams and cozy up to us, pretending to be the perfect guy. He'd been Philip to me— a sexy romantic with a killer beach body and princely white-blond hair. He'd been a good listener, for the most part. That is, until he tried to have his way with me against my will. Then the whole listening part went out the window. Rapists are funny like that.

He'd been Thomas to Allie, coming into her mind before she knew anything about Terraway. He'd left her a comatose shell, giving me ample motivation to track him down for a good old-fashioned murdering.

Only I hadn't dealt the final blow to the man who haunted my dreams and orchestrated too many of my nightmares.

"Hey, are you alright? I felt a downward swing. Steeper than usual." Mason cozied in closer at my back, sliding the flat of his hand from my arm to my hip. He seemed to like that part of me in particular. He rubbed in slow, soothing circles, knowing exactly how to bring me back to the present.

I kept doing that, even though it had been two years since Finn had killed Philip.

Sama. Not Philip, Sama.

My stomach roiled, as it always did when thoughts of Captain Finn trickled back into my mind, creeping out of the dark closet in my psyche where I kept memories of him stashed. Most people hadn't understood Finn, but I got to see his softer side. I'd spent many nights with him curled around me while we slept. We'd fought together, killed together, listened to each other, and...

I swallowed hard, trying to shove the sight of Finn's smile away. It was too powerful, that cocky brush of happiness that came over his face whenever he saw me. The memory of it could yank me out of any normal moment, plunging me into the despair that comes when someone gives their life to protect yours, and you know it wasn't worth the trade.

I worked up a convincing smile, but knew Mason could feel my melancholy. He always knew how to sense when something was off with me, despite my best bravado and denial. "I'm totally fine. Just glad to have Allie back."

Mason didn't argue but slid his hand toward mine, acknowledging without verbally calling me out on my obvious tell that no, I wasn't actually fine. I hadn't realized I was scratching up the back of my hand until he brought it to my attention. He separated the offending fingers and laced them through his to stop me from hurting myself further. I hadn't realized I was doing it. Old habits die hard,

I guess. He labeled it "self-mutilation" which is just about the grossest description. I saw it as pain management. When my insides got backed up with too much sadness, clawing the skin off the backs of my hands dulled the ache I'd never been able to fully escape.

Finn had been my scandalous bliss but now he was my ache. If that was all I had of him, I wasn't ready to give it up.

Mason kissed the nape of my neck before he leaned over and picked the O's up off the floor with his free hand. I shuddered when he popped them in his mouth, grimacing at the floor germs he merely shrugged at.

"Dad, we're staying in tonight," Graham called into the next room. Then he cocked an eyebrow at Allie. "What's that grin for?" He looked down at his khakis and white button-down dress shirt, always the business-dressed professional, especially now that he was a full-fledged Puller for the most amazing woman in the world.

Allie had worn the constant look of wonder from the time she woke up from her coma, learned about Terraway, and was introduced to her handsome Puller, who couldn't get enough of her. "I hope I never get used to your accent. James Bond never sounded so good. Do you think our son will talk like you?"

Graham blushed in response, which is just about the cutest color on a man. I stinking loved them together.

"We can totally make that happen." I leaned closer to her belly and murmured in a terrible impression of a cockney accent, "Cheerio, bangers and mash, Helen Mirren."

Allie giggled as she kissed my auburn curls.

My phone buzzed with a text from Danny. *"Ana's still sleeping. Should I wake her up from her nap or let her sleep through dinner?"*

I chewed on my lower lip, wondering at what point I should let Danny sink or swim with this whole parenting thing. *"Wake her, or she'll be up all night. I put her down for her nap at one."*

"Can you come up and help me? She's going to throw a fit if you're not there."

I wanted to help. I love Ana, of course. Von and I lived at the mansion two weeks a month to help Danny raise her. The other two weeks were spent at my house with Mason, so I could get a double pull. *"I'm with my sister. You're her father. You can handle a bit of crying."*

Danny doesn't skip a beat with, *"You're her mum."*

I pocketed my phone and busted out my trusty hand sanitizer to expunge any germs from my fingers once more. Every time Anastasia Grace called me "mama," my heart melted for her. I've done everything for that little ballerina with a smile of gratitude on my face. This putting down of my foot was more to get Danny to grow up than Ana. As far as I'm concerned, that sweet girl can stay my little princess forever.

When Ezra moved into the living room, Allie sat up straighter, as if something in her needed to impress the parental figure. "Hello, D-Dad. Is it okay if we have dinner here tonight?"

Though the tired lines that had taken up residence around the edges of Ezra's eyes since Mariang's death didn't ever fade completely, whenever Allie, Ollie or I claimed him as our father, his smile couldn't be helped. His perfect British lilt made me wish my own slightly southern cadence sounded more regal. "Of course, princess. I wouldn't have it any other way. What would you like?"

Allie shrank at being put on the spot. Though it had been over a year and a half she'd known Ezra, she'd lived five months of that time in Terraway, sequestered from his adoration and sweetness. I remembered how often I pushed him away in the beginning, mistrusting any parental figure who claimed they could help me. Allie wasn't quite so visceral as I'd been, though she was often confused and bashful at the perks of her new life. Having Ezra as our dad? It was more than a perk; it was like winning the paternal lottery. "Ollie likes Mexican food, so maybe that for when he gets back?"

Ezra tilted his head to the side, taking in her inability to ask for anything for herself. So deeply was scarcity engrained in her that even after hefty doses of pure Ezra, she still didn't have the language to ask. "I can get Mexican food for Ollie. But what about you?"

Allie fiddled with the hem of her shirt, unable to look

at him when he focused his kindness directly onto her. "Whatever you want is fine. You know I'm not picky."

I gave Ezra a look and he nodded, not saying a word as he kept his eyes on Allie, waiting for a true response. It was a series of baby steps, drawing Allie out of the childhood we often still felt trapped in. Though Bev was long gone, the ripples of her abuse echoed through many of our choices.

Mason reached over me and pulled a portion of anxiety from Allie, knowing her triggers like a good partner should.

Allie fiddled with the hem of her shirt. "I mean, maybe if Lynna had extra pasta in the fridge, that would be nice. But if there isn't, don't go to any trouble. Never mind. I shouldn't have said anything. I'm speaking out of turn."

The corners of Ezra's mouth quirked upward. "As you wish it, Allison Mercy. Do we know when Oliver James is getting back from Sombi? I would've thought he and Levi would be home by now."

I pointed to the ceiling. "Levi's in the shower. He got back half an hour ago. But I didn't see Ollie with him. I don't think my brother went to Sombi. I thought last week before he left Ollie said he was going to hang with Langgam instead."

Ezra frowned. "Well, I know that's not accurate. King Langgam's in Lumipad, sorting through some political mess. Ollie told me he was going to Sombi with Levi."

I sat up straighter. "I thought Lumipad was off-limits to

the three of us." I motioned between Allie and myself and the absent Ollie.

"It most certainly is. That country's not nearly stable enough for a family of Omens to walk through. King Langgam knows how I feel about that. Excuse me."

Mason made a "yikes" face. "That's about as cross as I've seen him in ages. If Ollie's really in Lumipad with Langgam, he's in for a stern dose of 'I was worried sick about you, young man.'"

I stood, knowing the only thing that could pry me away from Allie was Ollie. "I'll go check with Levi. Maybe some wires got crossed." Before I could let my imagination run away with me, I scampered out of the flawless living room and up the steps toward my second dad's bedroom. Or, well, my first dad, since Levi was my birth father.

I knocked on the door, not hearing the water running. "Dad? Got a minute?"

Levi opened the door to the bedroom that was in the same hallway as the one I shared with my husband, but far enough down so that he couldn't hear our nighttime hijinks. That's the thing about mansions.

His long auburn and caramel-colored dreads were bound up in a leather lace, which Lynna had woven into a thick ball that somehow looked like an elegant nest at the base of his neck. He was dressed in simple jeans and a white button-down shirt, which, now that he was on two legs, was what he preferred. "For you? I've got all the time in the world."

"Easy to say when you're immortal." I smirked up at him, wishing I'd gotten even a portion of his height. He looked more like Mason in stature, where I wasn't nearly as sturdy. I leaned up on my toes, pecking his freshly-shaved cheek. "Welcome home. How was Sombi?"

He grinned, showing off his white canines. "Never a dull moment, as usual. Put down two dozen zombies before I came back. Didn't want to miss Allison's visit. You know how I love it when my three kids are under the same roof."

"She'll be happy to see you. Is Ollie in your room? I didn't see him come in with you."

Levi frowned. "I didn't take Oliver to Sombi. He was going to come along but decided to stay here instead."

"That's not what he told us. Ollie hasn't been here since we saw him leave with you." I tried to turn my back on my growing anxiety but the angst was petulant in its insistence that something was very, very wrong. I pulled out my cell phone and dialed my brother, who always picked up when he saw it was me. When the call went to voicemail, my mouth went dry. I held out my phone for Levi to hear the maudlin drone of Ollie's request for the caller to leave a message. My voice was taut with tension when I spoke into the phone. "Ollie, if I find out you ditched us to go somewhere you shouldn't, don't think I won't unleash my inner Bruce Campbell and come find you. Call me so I know you're safe." I ended the call, but didn't feel like the message got me any closer to my brother.

Levi's shoulder's bobbed. "Maybe he's just stepped away from his phone."

I swallowed hard, wishing I wasn't right about something being so very wrong. "I called Ollie during a job interview once. He stopped the interview and answered. The only time he doesn't pick up is if he can't." I spun on my heel and trotted to Ollie's bedroom, which was next to Levi's. "He's got to be in Terraway, where he can't get cell service."

"What are we looking for in here?" Levi inquired, his eyebrows bunched as he took my consternation upon himself, like a good dad does when his daughter's about to go off the deep end.

I shoved open the closet and peered up at the top shelf. "His backpack is missing. Ollie packed a bag and left without telling us the truth about where. He told Ezra he'd be in Sombi with you. He told me he was going to hang with Langgam, but Lang's been in Lumipad, where we're obviously not allowed to go."

"And he told me he was staying here with you all."

My mouth drew to the side. "Would he have told Von where he was actually going?"

"Seems unlikely he would confide in Von something none of us know, especially since Von's still in Europe."

"No stone unturned at this point."

Levi moved around Ollie's bedroom, and then called my name after I thumbed out a text to Von, and then to

Danny, for good measure. "Um, you might want to take a look at... Oh, no."

I was by his side in the next breath, our matching hazel eyes widening at the note in Levi's hand. When he read it aloud, the entire world stopped spinning.

"OCTOBER,

I don't want you to worry, but I went to Terraway to pick something up. I'll be back before you know it.

Stay close to Mason, Von and Danny while I'm gone.

Love,

Ollie"

2

LYING BROTHERS

"**N**o."

"You don't just get to say 'no' and have it be the definitive thing that happens." I bit back my childish urge to shout, "You're not the boss of me!"

Mason folded his arms over his chest. "Actually, since I guard you and you can't port down to Terraway without me, 'no' is exactly what I get to say."

"You're not the only one who can get me there. Dad!" I shouted, nearly losing my hold on my righteous anger when both Ezra and Levi responded. I loved when they did that. We were all congregated in the living room of the mansion. Arguing over the plan was getting us nowhere. "I need one of you port me down."

Levi was stalwart in his verdict, as usual. "Not a chance. You know the Ekeks and Manas aren't controlled. We all agreed at the family picnic this summer that you wouldn't set foot in Terraway again until Allison's baby is announced to the nation. That wasn't four months ago. I know you remember."

In lieu of arguing, I swiveled my attention to Ezra and unleashed all my persuasive powers on him. "Please, Dad?"

Ezra slid his hands into his khaki pockets. "Of course, my dear. Tell me which country Ollie's in, and I'll port you right there."

I opened my mouth and then shut it, taking in his compliant smile for the smug smirk of defiance it was. "You know I don't have any idea. He told us two different countries. Just take me anywhere in Terraway and we'll narrow from there. He's probably in Lumipad with Langgam."

"Probably, eh? Get me a definitely and we'll talk." Then he kissed my forehead, which infuriated me so badly, I nearly raised my voice at him. *Nearly.*

Allie had been quiet, but so attuned to her was I that her intake of breath was heard by only me above the conjectures and conversations surrounding Ollie's whereabouts. I turned to her, taking in her creased brow at the note that had been read aloud too many times to count.

I left the others to their futile planning. I knew that look. Allie was onto something but she didn't want to cause any waves. She'd always been afraid to take up space in her own life, so I took it upon myself to make sure there was room for her, whether she admitted she deserved it or not. Cupping her elbow, I led her into the kitchen so her concerns wouldn't be under the spotlight that constantly made her shrink whenever it was turned on her. "What is it?"

"It's nothing. I'm overthinking too much." But as she stared at the note, I think we both knew she wasn't being dramatic about a thing.

"Talk to me. If Ollie needs help, there's no theory that should be thrown aside. I'll listen. I always do."

She opened the paper again—a page with rough edges, torn from a notebook and folded in half. "Look carefully. Do you see something that doesn't add up?"

I pursed my lips as I stared at the hurried printing in blue ink. "Other than the fact that Ollie took off without telling us, to get something he didn't talk to us about? Not really. What am I missing?"

She cast around the kitchen, her shoulders loosening when she found the notepad magnetized to the fridge. It was Lynna's weekly grocery list. We all scribbled what we wanted, and the wonderful mother figure picked it up for us every Wednesday. "There. Ollie wrote this last week." She pointed to an item on the list, as if that proved her point (which I still didn't totally understand).

"Yeah? I guess so. Ollie eats like, two bananas a day. I'm not surprised he'd ask Lynna to pick up more."

"Look at the handwriting."

When my eyes combed over the familiar scrawl on the grocery list and then glanced at the notebook paper, I cringed at my major oversight. "This isn't Ollie's handwriting! Allie, did someone take him? Who? Manas? Ekeks? Who?" My skin felt cold, and a wave of dizziness swept over me. I gripped the counter to balance myself.

"Not Terraway. This one's on our world." She stroked the penmanship with a wistfulness that seemed utterly unbefitting the terror of this moment. "This is Darius' handwriting. See the angry slant? I'd know it anywhere. He used to write me love notes and leave them taped under the mailbox back when we dated."

Just like that, the cold inside of me shifted to fiery hot. Darius forged Ollie's signature? Nefarious McCray was pretending to be Ollie for... what? I whipped out my phone, my worry climbing more rapidly than I could quell it. "I heard them fighting last week," I admitted while the phone rang. "Ollie and Darius."

"About what?" Allie whispered.

"Ollie said it was too dangerous, but Darius said it was worth it. I thought..." I shook my head. "You know what I thought. I still think it."

"You think Darius was trying to convince Ollie to come work for him?"

"Every drug lord needs someone to be the money guy. Know anyone better at finances than Ollie?"

Allie shook her head. "No. Darius wouldn't ask Ollie to do that."

"He already did," I informed her, dropping the bomb on my sweet sister's head without warning her of the impending shatter. "People get real chatty when they assume I'm passed out."

Allie straightened, immediately going into mama mode. "When were you passed out?"

I winced, forgetting I hadn't told her that. "I over-reaped on accident." I held up my hands when her nostrils flared.

"Again?"

While I knew she would never yell at me, her disapproval was far worse, even at a whisper. "It snuck up on me. Honest. I was out with the guys and reaped just by bumping into too many people. It was awful. Found out the next day that there was a mass-shooting at the club."

Allie covered her shriek with her thin hand. "Why didn't you tell me?"

"Because you're not supposed to get worked up during your pregnancy! I shouldn't be telling you this now, but I'm not thinking clearly. Point is that Darius did ask Ollie to go work for him and Ollie said no. Now Ollie's off on this vague mission and left us a note that's not actually from him but from Darius?"

She hung her head. "So much for the McCray-Reese truce. It was going so well."

"Darius left a note for Ollie so we wouldn't go looking for him. This is what they do when they..." I didn't want to say it out loud, but the phrase "make someone sleep with the fishes" came to mind.

Allie was resolute, her nose in the air. "I don't believe

Darius would hurt Ollie. What you're implying is... They're like brothers!"

My tone darkened. "No. *Judge* is Darius' brother." Before my feet could explain themselves to the rest of my body, they were carrying me toward the exit. The glow of Lynna's pristine kitchen was suddenly too pure for the menace that was roiling inside of me.

Allie's pitch rose in worry. "October, no. Don't do anything."

I stopped, my hand on the door. "All I'm going to do is chat with Judge. See what's what. Buy me some time, will you? Tell the guys I'm running to the grocery store to get you peanut butter and pickles, or whatever it is you might be craving."

"October, wait! Darius would never hurt us! Darius loves me!"

I can tell she regrets her words the second they leave her lips. She covers her mouth at the sound of the scandal we never talk about. It's no secret Darius still carries a flame for my Allie. She broke it off years ago because she thought she was going mad when Sama started to take over. She didn't want to admit to Darius that she was crazy, so she ran away, severing all ties and leaving him without any closure.

She shakes her head and sucks in a breath. "Us. Darius loves *us*."

I did my best not to sound like a jerk or like a child who was mouthing off to her mama. "Every day that

Darius asked me to take messages to the prison for him was a day that he hurt me. Every time he begged me to come treat the wounds he gave the people in his organization who turned on him, he hurt me. He had no problem putting me in the thick of harm's way, and I highly doubt that twice-a-month family dinners took Ollie off his list of possible assets." I opened the door, knowing I didn't have a huge window of escape. "I'll be back after dinner, hopefully with answers. Enjoy the pasta and tacos."

My heart did its best to harden against Allie's quiet pleas for me to stay, but her softness wormed through, finding the cracks in the armor I still donned when going up against Judge. He was the older brother who'd abandoned me, but against all odds, found his way back into my life. If something was off, Judge would know about it.

The trick would be getting him to confess before things got ugly.

3

A GRIM WELCOME

My house was on the way to Judge's, so I stopped by for a few minutes. There was the shred of hope that Ollie was just chilling here under the radar, but after a quick check of all the rooms, my heart sank yet further.

I hadn't been home in a week, and inhaled the aroma of the carpet cleaner that always served to center me. Von and I lived here two weeks out of the month, giving us a little space to be married. He was in London this week though, helping his mom pack up so she could move to the mansion for good. Lavinia Vandershot swore up and down that she was only moving to be nearer her granddaughter and forthcoming grandson, which we all understood was code for "shacking up with my hot high school sweetheart." She also mentioned wanting to keep an eye on her boys, since they lived here now, with the exception of Alton, who resided with his girlfriend in Sussex.

I didn't say a word about it, even after I'd walked in on Ezra doing the very polite nasty with Von's mom last month when she'd flown in for a visit. I mean, lock the door or something. Sheesh. The two hadn't noticed my intrusion. So Ezra and Lavinia continued sneaking around, since the charade of secrecy seemed so very important to them.

But we all knew. It gave us a little giggle. They were so careful around us, as if the idea of Ezra being with anyone other than Bev would be traumatic for Ollie, Allie and me.

My phone chirped in my pocket, but I ignored it. Mason had been my shadow while Von was away, and I knew he was pissed I didn't pick up the phone on my way over here the four times he called.

Make that five.

Getting back inside Terence my Taurus, I drove over to the ritziest area on the wrong side of the tracks. I gripped the wheel as my car rumbled through the area where we'd grown up, inhaling the anxiety that clawed at my insides. I scratched at the back of my hand, my stomach tightening when too many foul and desperate memories slammed into my chest. I didn't want to hear Bev's deeply southern cadence yelling while she banged me over the head time and time again with the back of her hairbrush. I'd gotten sick again because she hadn't paid the heat bill. If I didn't get well enough to leave the trailer before her disgusting flavor of the month came over for a booty call, things were really going to start getting unpleasant.

The back of my hand bled, and finally I was able to shake off the sound of Mama's voice.

The ghetto was worse, but you had to go through it to get to Judge's ridiculously large house, which was just on the outskirts of the city. It was near enough for him to be close to the action, but not so near that crackheads could commit to the effort of walking to his house and cause problems. You had to be intentional about finding Judge, which didn't deter me one bit.

I pulled up to his statue-lined security gate that was meant to keep out riff-raff like me. The stone carvings turned my stomach. What most no doubt assumed were just creepy depictions of three-foot-tall fantasy fiction characters, I knew were actually goblins frozen in a state of panic while the entire race spontaneously turned to stone and died.

I hadn't meant to commit genocide. Titus had been King of the Goblins, and wanted the sagrado stone for himself to keep the other countries in peril. He'd gone after Mason, so in a state of panic, I cracked him over the head with the heavy rock. I'd forgotten he'd used the *tahi* charm to tie his life force to his people's. Good use of the spell during times of famine. If the king ate, the others wouldn't die of starvation. It was a dangerous tightrope he walked, though, because when he tried to harm Mason, my Bruce Campbell rip-tear-kill mode turned on, and I didn't consider the vast consequences of my actions.

King Kabayo collected the statues of the Goblins, decorating his kingdom with them to show all of Terraway that their pesky enemy was vanquished. When Judge heard the story, he grew fascinated with Goblin history, and even asked Kabayo for several dozen statues. Now they belonged to him, lining his security gate with gnarled fingers, saggy potato-shaped faces, open mouths and beady eyes that never closed.

I punched in the code Judge had given me a year ago when I'd first visited him with Von. I used it often enough when I swung by with Danny. With Mason. Sometimes Boston. Ollie, most recently. It's like the guys didn't want me hanging out with a well-known criminal. Judge and I spent most of our evenings together playing Monopoly, like true gangsters.

I frowned when the gate didn't open. The keypad gave me an angry buzzer sound instead of the pleasant chime that should've let me on through. I whipped out my phone and dialed dear old Judge, my sneer sinister when he answered. "Hey, Judge. I think you have something that belongs to me."

"Now's not a good time, baby girl." The velvety timbre of his voice always brought me back with a jerk of emotions I still hadn't fully reconciled. He would never be the man I wanted him to be, though he'd come a long way from being my nemesis.

Until tonight.

"You know, I don't really think that matters. I'm not going home until you give my brother back."

"What?"

"You heard me. Send Ollie out or tell me where he is. Then you can go back to your regularly-scheduled illegal activities."

I waited for his response but was granted the chime of entry instead. I sat in my car once more and pulled through, parking in such a way that my plates wouldn't be visible to cops. They no doubt frequently took snapshots of the place.

It wasn't Judge who came out to greet me, but Terence and Big Mike. Their guns were out and pointed at the ground, readying to shield me from impending gunfire. I glanced around but saw nothing unusual in the twilight.

Terence nodded once for me to come quickly, so I drew my wooden baseball bat from beneath my seat (a good "just in case" accessory for me) and followed the men inside. Though Terence was an armed ex-con, he was a safe place for me. When I'd been his nurse in lockup, he'd protected me more than once. Even now as we walked into the enormous home with legit parapets, he positioned me so I was between him and Big Mike, shielded from the street and whatever dangers lurked in the dusk.

I began to wonder if this really was a bad time.

When we reached the safety of the house, I heaved a

gust of relief. "What the crap, T? What are you buried in this time?"

Despite his giant stature, Terence was the quiet one. He holstered his weapon and jerked his chin toward the stairs. "Up there." He was always doing that, saying slightly less than the bare minimum.

I remembered my fury and glowered at Big Mike as the goon locked the front door behind me. "You seen Ollie around?"

To Big Mike's credit, he didn't look like his usual "I've got too many secrets" self. His eyebrows rose slightly. "Ollie's missing?"

Suddenly the word "yes" felt stuck in my throat. My brother was my constant. I never had to worry about where Ollie was because he was never into any terribly dangerous shenanigans.

Except when he went zombie hunting in Sombi with Levi, Mason and the guys.

And except when he ventured to Dagat to visit the Mermaids and train with the Kataw soldiers. That was pretty dangerous, too. Don't think we didn't have words about that.

I looked up into Big Mike's eyes that always tried to remain stoic, hoping I could siphon off some of his composure. When his gaze locked in on mine, I could see he didn't have much serenity saved for himself tonight.

When I took in Terence's demeanor, it wasn't much better. I noticed beads of sweat dotting his forehead and upper lip. His roundish face looked a little worn, which wasn't like him.

"Terence?" I asked, wondering if he'd let me take his temperature.

Big Mike spoke when Terence defaulted to silence. "Judge is in his saferoom. If you're here, that's where you'll stay. Up you go, kid."

I chewed on my lower lip to keep my burgeoning questions tucked away for the moment. Terence was breathing hard, worried beyond what a simple night-in-the-life called for. Terence mopped his forehead with a bandana from his pocket and motioned to the stairs. I could tell he didn't want me around to witness the moment of supposed weakness.

I dashed up the steps, calling out Judge's name when I couldn't remember where the saferoom was located. I knew it wasn't in his bedroom. He was too smart for that.

Judge came out of a door down the hall wearing gray dress slacks and the lavender button-down I'd bought him. The sleeves were rolled to his elbows, revealing the gold watch he'd purchased when we'd gone shopping together a few months ago. I'd told him it was just plain too flashy. I think he bought it purposefully just to get under my skin.

Judge had his shoes on while walking about his own home, making it clear that this wasn't a place that would ever grant him rest, beautiful as it was.

His black eyes narrowed at me, his full lips pulling into a taut line of disapproval. "You'd better have a compelling reason to barge in here with a baseball bat, baby girl. This is a bad night for a drag-out between the two of us."

"Good. I was hoping to catch you on a bad night where you're already disagreeable." When he didn't scoff at my sass but held his firm stare steady, I gave up my bravado. "Where is Ollie? What did you do with him?"

4

SAFEROOM

Judge's eyebrows rose with affront. "What did *I* do? Why would you think I'd mess with Ollie?"

"Did you hurt him, Judge?"

His nostrils flared as he pointed at me in accusation. "I've done a lot of things you have every right to be mad about, but I've never laid a hand on your brother. I wouldn't cross a line like that."

I wanted to be angry, to fight further to uncover... anything, but I could see the truth in Judge's response. Suddenly I wasn't the woman with a baseball bat on a mission of vengeance; I was a scared little girl fresh off the little league field. I was lost in the world, searching out a safe harbor.

And I'd landed here, of all places.

Judge softened at my slumped shoulders but then stiffened at the sound of gunfire outside. His eyes widened and he snatched at my hand, yanking me into a nearby room and bolting the door. "Get inside. There's a panel on the wall next to the bed. Pull at it, and you can hide in there."

"Judge, what's going on?" I glanced around the room I'd not been in before. Though the lights were off, I could still see well enough. It was an ordinary guest room with no carpet. The bed with a rubber sheet over the mattress made the hairs on the back of my neck stand on end. I shuddered at the implications I didn't want to consider. The bare walls and bars on the windows, even though we were on the second floor, didn't give me that feeling of security the iron rods were intended to instill. I knew Judge well enough to understand this was a room meant for pain and fear, the latter of which was rapidly seeping into my pores.

"Just some problems at work. Nothing more." Instead of releasing me to go behind the panel, he kissed my forehead, holding me to his chest so we could breathe together for a few beats. His heart was pounding more furiously than the steady thrum he usually held to. His ebony arms squeezed me tight.

Over the years, Judge had showered me with presents I didn't want, because he'd bought them with tainted drug money. He was always generous with his money, generous with his time when it came to me. But it wasn't often Judge let me near his fear. I could feel the angst in his embrace, so I stayed in his arms, centering him as best I could. I palmed his spine, smoothing slowly up and down as I pressed my ear over his heart. "Hey, it's alright. Tell me what we're dealing with, and we'll figure it out." Or more likely, I'll call the cops, and *they'll* sort everything out.

"They took Darius."

"Who did?"

He motioned toward the window. "I know it was them."

I frowned up at him. "Are you sure? Did they admit to it?"

He scoffed. "Criminals aren't as forthcoming as you might think. And before you spout off something witty like, 'you would know,' you can save it. I'm not in the mood."

I chuckled, despite the grim circumstance. "Ollie's missing. He left a note that he was picking up a surprise for us. But he's gone. He said he'd be back by now in the note but he's not answering his phone. Allie realized the note was written in Darius' handwriting." My voice turned quiet when I realized how far off the mark my assumptions were. "I thought maybe Darius got impatient waiting for Ollie to come work for him."

Judge touched his finger under my chin to lift it so I could see his steely gaze in the dark. "Baby girl, I know you love your brother. I wouldn't let Darius take him from you. And Darius loves Ollie. He wouldn't hurt him. You should trust me more than this. We've come a long way in the past year or two. I'm disappointed in you that it's all devolved so quickly."

My chin quivered but I refused to let any moisture fall from my eyes. Though I was constantly disappointed in Judge's choices, it was rare I felt the gravity of his disapproval. "I'm sorry."

"You should be." He's angry. I can see it, feel it radiating off of him. I hurt my Judge with my assumptions. "You have no idea what I've been through this past month. What's the point of trying if I'm always the bad guy?"

His words don't make much sense to me. "You've been mostly MIA lately. I mean, you showed up for twice-a-month family dinner at Ezra's, but you barely said a word. What are you talking about? What have you been through?"

In typical Judge fashion, he doesn't give me all the information, but keeps me guessing. "Things are changing around here, but none of that's going to matter if I'm always the villain to you. You have to open your eyes, baby girl, or you're going to miss the best parts of me. Maybe even the best parts of you. Don't be like everyone else. Don't always see me as a bad man."

I swallow hard, but he won't let go of my chin, so I'm stuck still gazing up at him, giving him full perusal of my shame and fresh agony. "Then where's Ollie? Why did Darius forge a letter from him?"

Vulnerability shone through Judge's all-consuming control. "I don't know. I'm guessing the two idiots took off together." He swore, leaning his head back against the door as he stared at the ceiling. "I really thought it was

Santori. I sent a pretty clear message that now I realize was unclear if he didn't have Darius to begin with."

"Did you check Darius' room? That's where Ollie's note was."

"Of course I checked his bedroom. I also called his cell phone, if that's what you're going to ask next."

I leaned up on my toes to peck his cheek. "Go tuck yourself into your panic room. I'll be right back."

"Where are you going? Stay right here."

"Just want to see Darius' bedroom. If they're missing, I need clues."

"You need to stay hidden. Coming out here at night was dangerous enough. Did you not hear the gunfire?"

"I need to find Ollie!"

Judge hugged me tighter, pressing my cheek to his chest. He smoothed his deadly fingers through my auburn curls in an attempt to soothe us both. "We'll find them, baby girl. I won't let anything bad happen to Ollie. I know that would destroy you."

I gulped, feeling in my gut that something was terribly wrong.

Judge had endured enough chit-chat. "Behind the wall with you. Now. I don't want to hear any more arguing about it." He didn't release me but kept his arm affixed around my back as we walked toward the panel. Upon closer inspection, I realized that it folded over the wall almost seamlessly, leaving no trace of our hiding place unless you knew to look for it. Judge had suggested installing a panic room in my house, but I'd refused, thinking he meant something big and bulky in the corner that could be confused with a port-a-potty.

When he opened the panel, inside was a shallow cavity —about two-and-a-half feet deep by five feet wide. The only sign of hope was a bare bulb affixed to the ceiling, which Judge didn't turn on. "This feels ominous," I commented, wary of stepping inside. I knew the second the door closed us in, there would be no room for denial. Ollie was missing, I was smack in the middle of Judge's empire, and there was no way out, except through gunfire. "Judge?" My fear couldn't be masked in my tone.

He moved me toward the far corner and stood with his body guarding mine, closing us in the dark space. With his gun drawn, he clutched me to him and kissed my forehead once more, which I'd learned was his habit when he was anxious. "Quiet, baby girl. I'll keep us safe."

I knew I shouldn't sink into Judge's hug, indulging in the promise I was certain he couldn't keep. But Judge's promises were too beautiful to deny that night. While the house was peppered with gunfire, I held my Judge tight, worried more about Ollie's absence than the bullets that threatened to end us all.

5

GUNFIRE ASIDE

It was nearly fifteen minutes before the gunfire and yelling died down, and through it all, Judge and I held each other. There were many times I'd needed him in my adolescence, longed for him to welcome me into his home and his arms, but he'd remained distant and cold. Then he'd wanted a spot in my life when I was already grown and frozen over from years of wishing he would come back to me. Things weren't perfect between us now, but I treasured the rare gift it was to be able to let myself feel scared, trusting he could handle my weaknesses when I finally set them loose.

"Distract me," he whispered. "I've been worried sick that Santori had Darius. Haven't been able to think of much else. Now that I know Darius is just hanging with Ollie, I feel a lot better."

"Gunfire aside," I amended.

He shrugged but still pressed me tight to him. "Nah. That doesn't bother me. Too used to it, I guess. Big Mike always handles things without too much of a mess. Plus, he's got T now. I'm only worried because you're here. Speaking of which." He pulled his phone from his pocket.

"What are you doing, ordering a pizza?"

He clucked his tongue at me. "Making a quick call." He kept his voice low, even though it was clear the action was entirely outside the house. "Hello, sir. This is Judge. October came to my house without her Pullers." He paused for Ezra's relief. The sound was mingled with indignation that matched my own. "It's a little chaotic at my place right now, but I'll bring her back to the mansion as soon as the trouble clears up. No, sir. I mean, Dad. I keep forgetting that's how we do things." He gripped the phone tighter. He always tried to remain stoic, but each time Ezra insisted on Judge calling him "Dad" I caught a fresh slice across his heart. He'd never had cause to use that word growing up. It seemed Ezra was determined to redeem us all. "No, Dad. It's nothing I can't handle."

It was so bizarre to hear Judge be all polite. He rolled out his best manners for Ezra, who'd invited him into our Terraway life with open arms.

I slid out of his grip when Judge ended the call, though there wasn't far for me to go. I folded my arms over my chest and glared at him. I wasn't sure he could see my eyes through the darkness to get the full effect of my frustration, but I aimed my scowl in his direction all the same.

"Don't you have some sort of cement shoes policy against snitches? That was unnecessary."

"I don't know everything about your other world, but I do know that you can't go sneaking off without Mason and that husband of yours."

"You know Von's name."

"And I have yet to use it, so I'm winning." He ignored my scoff. "An entire nation depends on your safety and Allie's. If something happens to you, a world dies. You get that, right?"

"Yeah, I get it. But if something happens to Ollie, I also die."

He held up his hand. "I actually respect Ezra. I ran what I thought was a big organization. It takes a lot of work to spin the plates how I do. But to see the responsibility on Ezra's shoulders? I'm not trying to make his life harder. He's been good to me. We understand each other. He's the only man who's ever asked me to call him 'Dad.' If you went missing, he would call me. I'm just paying him the same respect."

"I owe you something that'll piss you off."

"Come to my house with a baseball bat. That should do it."

My brain caught on something strange. "You said 'ran,' like you don't run a big organization anymore."

Judge was silent for a few beats. "What if I told you that's why I've been hanging back these past few weeks?

What if I told you all the noise outside right now has something to do with that?"

A flood of emotions climbed up to strangle me around the throat. "What are you talking about?"

"Too many things you've been too stuck in your ways to see. You've been begging me to change for years but when I do, you still only see a black man not doing his part to rise up."

I guffawed at him, angry, shocked and horrified that he had the gall to basically boil me down to being racist. "First off, don't you talk to me like that. I'm not a mind-reader. I'm also not someone who looks at you and sees 'only' an anything. What are you talking about? You changed things? What's different? It still smells like gunpowder around here."

"I stopped it all. Closed up all my not-so-legal business dealings three weeks ago, and it's been hell ever since."

My mouth fell open but no words were brave enough to tumble out.

6

THE WRONGS WE NEVER MEAN TO DO

"Are you serious?"

Judge exhaled his frustration. "You know, you've been on my case for years to do exactly this. Then when I do it, nothing changes. You still think every problem you have is my fault. I didn't hurt Ollie. It sucks you think I would ever do something like that."

"I'm sorry, Judge. You're right. I've been unfair."

If I was stunned at his revelation, Judge was equally bowled over at my apology. "Did you seriously just say that to me? Are we the kind of people who apologize to each other? Don't break our perfect track record. I like us how we are, for the most part."

"No, you're right. I wanted you to stop all this but I never offered to help you. I never actually believed you would ever listen to me. You're really out of the drug game?"

Judge huffed his frustration at me. "Yes, and that's exactly what we call it. The drug game."

"No more cocaine?"

"Nope. Cleaned everything out. Let everyone go. All my legitimate businesses are going to have to sink or swim based on honest profitability."

My heart was swelling and bursting over and over again while my mind tried to keep up with the rapidly-changing world. "I'm so proud of you, Judge. This is amazing."

"Yeah? Well, it's actually not. It's hard and dangerous and awful. Most of my people didn't take the news so well. There were lots of fights we had to end the quick way." He paused for my wince. "Santori's scooping up most of them, which means we haven't actually done a damned thing to make the city better. There's practically the same amount of feet on the ground, only the money's running in one direction now—away from me. Santori should be sending me a fruit basket or something. Instead he's here shooting up the place, as if I didn't hand him the keys to the kingdom on a golden platter. He's trying to make it look like this is something he took from me."

My brain scrambled to keep up. "How can I help? Do you guys need to stay with me until this all blows over?"

Judge was quiet, and I'm sure he was trying to find a tactful way not to scoff in my face. "I'll let you know if it comes to that."

"I've got news for you, pal. Gunfire outside means it might be time to find a new address."

"Quit sassing me and come here. I've been on edge for weeks. And I told you to stay indoors tonight. You 'super-duper' promised."

"I'm indoors now. What safer place could there be than with you?"

Judge's chuckle found me in the darkness. He reached out and took my hand, sliding me toward him again so I could rest my cheek against his chest. Every hug still felt like making up for the lost years when we'd let our anger and distance get the better of us. When we shut up enough to let the silence speak, real tenderness surfaced. "There. That's much better. Not sure if I'm calming you down or myself, but either way, this seems to be the thing that fixes it all. We wasted a lot of time not doing this. Fools, the both of us. Pushing each other away when we've always been better together."

I breathed deeper when Judge held me. My lungs took in the scent that reminded me of childhood, even when it was covered in cologne and the trappings of adulthood. "I'm worried about Ollie. This isn't like him."

"I know. It's like *you* to run off without backup or explanation. Ollie's far more responsible. Must've been important for him to take off like that. It's Darius I'm worried about. At least you got a note."

"We'll find them," I reassured us both.

We stood just like that, savoring the embrace we'd

needed but had been far too stubborn to ask for. We were the same animal in that respect. We didn't hold back affection now that we sensed the other was in need, since we'd done the withholding dance for years. Our brothers going missing definitely qualified.

The street went quiet, though the sounds were pretty muffled, so it was hard to tell for sure if the ruckus was gone. "Are they…"

"Shh. Big Mike or T will come and get us when it's all clear."

We waited ten more minutes before the door opened, bathing us in fresh-ish air. Terence was sweating even more than he'd been doing earlier, but worse was the blood that oozed down his arm. He was breathing hard and fumbled with his gun as he fished around the equator of his overlarge belly for his holster. "Santori's people are gone. Big Mike's outside cleaning up the bodies now."

When he turned on his heel, my voice sharpened. "Just where do you think you're going, young man?"

Terence's footing was unsteady as he shifted to face me. "I'm going to help Big Mike. Did *you* want to move dead bodies?"

I narrowed my eyes at him and pointed to the bed. "Sit, Terence. Judge, where's your first aid kit? I'm guessing you won't let me take him to the ER."

"He'll be fine," Judge said dismissively. "He's had worse."

"And if he goes to the hospital now, then he'll live to

have even worse some day soon, I'm sure." I peered at the blood that was pouring far too fast for a quick fix. I swore, grabbed the sheet off the bed and put pressure on the wound. "Judge, he needs a doctor."

Judge's lips tightened. "Are you or are you not a nurse?"

"Are you or are you not deaf? This is... Judge, as a nurse, I'm telling you he needs to go to the ER."

Judge stomped off down the hall and came back with a first aid kit by the time Terence and I agreed he would at least sit down on the bed. Of course, he only agreed after he walked smack into the wall. "Oh, that... Yeah, maybe I'll sit down. Okay, Nurse Gracie."

"Easy, sweetheart. Here, let me help you." I touched his non-bloody elbow with the intention of leading him to the edge of the bed, but the second I made contact, I gasped when I felt the one thing that terrified me to my very soul. Ice shot through my fingers and up my arm when Terence's soul leapt from his body into mine. "Terence? Terence?" I panicked and tried in vain to rub the soul off my hand and put it back into his body. "Terence, no! Judge!" I screamed, my knuckles icy from the reaping I hadn't meant to perform.

7

FROZEN SCREAMS

At my distress, Judge ran to me, flinging the kit onto the floor, his gun drawn. "What?"

Though Judge now knew all the terminology, I didn't have the words to explain it. I pointed, making good use of my joints before they became too stiff to move. Already I could feel the poison of the foreign element inside of me, swirling around in my veins as if that was the natural order of things. "Terence! He... The bullet wound must be... It's too late."

Judge's nostrils flared. "It's not too late. You've barely looked at him. I'll take him in, if there really is no other option. I won't let my brother die. Obviously." Then he turned to Terence to take in the scope of his brother. Terence was breathing too heavily for a man whose biggest job at the moment was sitting upright. Judge cupped his shoulder. "Hear that? I won't let you die, T. If October says I need to take you in, then that's what I'll do."

"It's too late," I repeated, showing him my hands as if admitting to him they were dirty. I already knew as much, but tonight they felt positively filthy from all the many sins I was steeped in. "I... I didn't mean to. I can't control it."

Judge threw his hands in the air, exasperated. "What? What happened in the twenty seconds I was gone?"

My chest felt cold, though if it was from the reaping or from the terror, I couldn't tell you. "I reaped Terence."

The only noise Terence made was a helpless bleat of fear.

It took Judge a whole five seconds to process the finality of it all. "What? No! No, you didn't. Undo it! Put his soul back in him!"

"You know it doesn't work like that! Terence is dying some time in the next little bit. His soul's corroding inside of me." I stumbled forward and gripped Judge's forearm. "I need Mason to pull it out. Please, call Mason!"

But Judge was in a world unto himself. His brother had been released from prison but was now on death row by the cruel business of this unnatural selection. He'd been safer behind bars than out in the open with Judge. My fingers felt thick and fumbly when I pulled out my phone and turned it back on, cursing as I tried to fat-finger my contacts list.

Judge was tending to Terence, which was as it should be. I wanted to help, to give him any sort of comfort, but I couldn't move much more than the Tin Man as my limbs started shutting down. The ice in my veins was painful now, freezing me over as I put the phone to my cheek, praying that none of this was actually happening. "Mason?"

I couldn't even flinch at the yelling that greeted me—so iced over were my shoulders.

I sliced into my boyfriend's tirade with a panicked, "Mason, I reaped Terence by accident!"

He stopped his rant short, his angry swearing turning to nervous cussing. "We're already on our way. Ezra, how many minutes does your GPS say?" Then Mason said in a soothing voice, "Five minutes, *hani*. Just five minutes and I'll get it out of you."

But I'd heard Ezra say they were still half an hour out. I whimpered as my jaw felt corroded from the cold, too stiff to do more than mumble now. "Mason," I whispered, scared and worried that this was all going far worse than I'd ever imagined.

"Are you sitting down?"

"No. I need to help Terence! He needs to know how *The Three Musketeers* ends!" I'd been reading him a chapter at a time after our twice-a-month family dinners. The visual hit me like a ton of bricks: me on the white couch in Ezra's living room with Von snuggled on my right and Terence on my left, his eyes tracking the words as I read them aloud. Ezra was in his recliner, and Ollie, Judge and the guys were usually strewn about the living room in various stages of stuffed from Lynna's amazing meals. I tried never to bring attention to the fact that Terence had a hard time with academia, but everyone knew that when I read, a spot next to me was always reserved for Terence. "He needs me," I eked out.

Mason brought me back to reality. "No, you need to sit down or you'll fall. Listen to me. We've been through the drill dozens of times. If you get separated from us and accidentally reap, you call us and sit or lie down somewhere out of the way."

Judge's phone rang but he didn't answer it. He was too busy tending to his brother. He had the roll of gauze out, though I couldn't tell you what his plan was, other than to wrap it like a messy spiderweb around Terence's entire arm with the bullet still lodged in there.

I tried to bend my knees but they weren't cooperating. I could tell Mason was trying to be calm for me, but every now and then he'd pull the phone away from his ear and shout, "Would you go faster? Red lights are a suggestion in these types of situations."

Soon my fingers were too frozen to hold onto the phone any longer, and it slipped from my grip onto the carpet. I heard Mason shouting my name but I couldn't get to him, and he couldn't come for me fast enough.

Terence met my gaze with something I'd never seen in his eyes before. Fear was an odd color on him, turning him from big-man-at-the-ready to a little boy lost at the carnival. Terence was never scared, but there it was, plain as day, smack in the middle of the night.

I wondered if Terence had ever gone to the carnival. Mama McCray had been wonderful, but she'd had her hands full—a single mama raising three boys on her own in a not so great neighborhood. Did he think about his mama often? Was working for Judge his life's plan, or did he have grander ambitions? I'd never asked him what he wanted, only warned him not to go back to Judge's empire. Now it was too late.

"I'm here," I mouthed, not knowing what else to say. I couldn't tell him it was okay or that I would make it better. Terence was well-trained in spotting a lie a mile away, so I offered him the only true thing in my possession: love.

Knives were stabbing into my skin every time I breathed. The movement of my ribcage felt like my bones were serrated, grating on my joints. The minutes ticked away as the pain built and Judge's panic grew. The rubber sheets were slathered in Terence's blood, which dripped in crimson ribbons onto the wood floor, staining the brown with pure and utter death in action.

Judge helped Terence to stand, using his body as a crutch to get his younger (but much bigger) brother down the hall. He was finally caving and taking Terence to the hospital, but we all knew it would be too late. Still, it spoke to how much Judge did love his family that he would break his stalemate on taking his people to the hospital if it might get Terence the help he needed. Judge finally did the right thing for his brother, but as the front door slammed shut, I knew with fresh heartbreak that it was too late.

And there I stood, alone in the room, hoping I didn't fall over, but unable to get my knees to bend. Minutes ticked by as tears began to roll down my cheeks. The silence of the giant house was the only witness to my pain when the knives sliced with better precision, seeking out every hidden nerve to saw their song of torment into my body like bows on violins. The corroding soul inside of me wept to be returned to Terence. I wanted to save him from the fear we all felt when our final hours drew near. I wanted to hold his hand, to offer some comfort in his last moments. But I was frozen to the spot, stuck in my terror that was only broken up by grief.

It wasn't until the door downstairs opened that I realized I couldn't defend myself. I was in Judge's territory, fresh off a gun fight, and I couldn't lift my hand to defend myself. Panic amplified my agony, sending torture through every muscle so that each locked down completely.

"October?"

The sound of Big Mike's voice ripped a cry from my lips. "Help!" I begged, wishing there was never a time where I was helpless. How I hated my job when moments like this arose. I didn't relish the idea of constantly needing Mason and Von with me every time I left the house. I didn't like the fact that there were problems I needed someone else to help me solve. It spoke against my "I'm fine" nature to constantly need pulling. As much as I liked to think I'd made peace with the job, moments like this one set me back from my Zen-like ideals.

Big Mike burst into the room, breathing heavily from the fight, coupled with running up the stairs. I made a mental note to do a bit of cardio with him. "October, it's okay." He had his phone to his ear, his eyes casting worried glances at my frozen form. "She's in the house. What do I do? How do I get it out of her?" He nodded and then set the phone down, nearing me with his hands up to prove their innocence. We had trust issues still, but since Judge had precious few secrets from his gargoyle, Big Mike had been coming to family dinners and knew all about Terraway. "Mason said you need to lie down. I can be careful but I don't want to make things worse for you. Where does it hurt?"

"Everywhere!" I worked out through gritted teeth. "Go ahead. It's going to be awful either way."

Big Mike winced at my scream when he touched my skin, backing away and shaking his head. "I don't know how to get you off your feet if I can't touch you!"

"Go on, Michael. It's fine. Just ignore my screaming. I can't help it. Quick, please!"

Big Mike swore in a steady stream when he picked me up and carried me to the bed, too afraid to move me to a different room.

My skin screamed as Terence's blood that was spread out all over the rubber sheets stuck to my clothes and hair.

Pain was one thing, but being slathered in germs and bodily fluids brought my panic to new heights. I tried to squirm off the bed but that only dipped me further into the remnants of Terence's bullet wound. I couldn't hear Big Mike any longer over my howls of terror and agony. I wanted nothing more than to run far, far away from here, straight into a shower, and then straight into a dark room where I could howl my agony over life's unfairness into the void. I could feel Terence's blood on my neck, slipping under my collar and touching my spine.

Terence's blood sticking to my arms.

Terence's blood painting my hair.

Big Mike fanned me with frantic, jerky motions, since he couldn't think of anything else to do. In truth, there was nothing he could've done that would help, other than get me off my feet and watch over my body until Mason ripped the soul out of me. "Go be with Terence," I worked out between howls of agony. "Tell him I love him."

"Am I allowed to leave you like this?" Big Mike and I had never been great friends, but we had an understanding: we were in it for the McCray boys.

"Terence shouldn't feel alone when he dies. There's nothing more you can do for me. Only Mason can help me now. Go!"

Big Mike wasn't a fan of screaming women, so he didn't need another prodding to leave the room. Beneath the agony, I was grateful Terence had one more person with him.

But I wanted to be there. I wanted to hold Terence's hand and kiss his cheek. I wanted to do all I could to save him, even if I knew it was a done deal. I wanted to help him, but at the end of the day, his soul would be used to fuel the suns of Terraway, giving the underworld enough stability to last a whole week.

I didn't want Terence's soul recycled like that. He had so much more I hoped he would do with it. I never wanted this life for him. Now that his days were coming to an end, I wondered if I'd done all I could to drag him away from Judge's world.

Terence was dying. As I screamed and then devolved into hyperventilation atop the bed, Terence was fighting for his last breath, drawing it out so he could add just one more inhale, and hopefully another after that.

8

RED AND YELLOW

ason's face was blurry. When I saw him hovering over me, I couldn't feel relief. In fact, I couldn't feel anything but the pain. Even after he'd ripped the soul from my body, agony still echoed through my veins. My heart was on perpetual breaking mode, wondering how the world dared continue to spin without Terence in it.

All of that duress paled in comparison to the unending scream that resounded in my brain. I'd been trying to get away from the germs but now I was bathed in their tiny microorganisms. My mind was a blur, checking out to the point where I couldn't lift my arm to indulge in the freedom of movement my body was finally granted.

I had Terence in my ear. Terence between my fingers. Terence sticking to my ankles. Terence all over my cheek. Terence down my collar and seeping down my back.

My body went... somewhere with... someone. I couldn't hold onto any details, save for the last vestiges of Terence that had drenched my flesh in bacteria and death.

I was laid on a cold tiled floor but I couldn't be upset at yet more germs added to the mix; I was at my max capacity, so everything felt like white noise. The pain in my joints paled in comparison with the horror that played on repeat in my head. My body was limp, and moved at the will of whoever was in charge while my brain took a hiatus.

So checked out was I that I didn't even notice I was naked until the I felt a warm, hairy body press against mine. Mason was saying... something to me as he lifted my noodly form off the tile and stood under the spray, shielding me from the brunt of the heat. He sat me down in the tub and then turned to the side, letting the steamy water hit me in the face.

My brain went fuzzy again and minutes later, I realized I was sitting in Mason's lap in the shower while the water pulsed over my chest. His lathered fingers on my scalp reminded me that I was still alive, though I hardly felt it.

My mind went blank again, but came back a few minutes later. Hard soap was running up and down my spine because Mason knew exactly how to bring me back to myself. When I was cogent enough to start clawing at the backs of my hands, he tsked me gently and scrubbed between my already clean fingers with the soap. "Easy, now. Deep breaths."

Wherever my eyes roamed on my body, Mason tracked it and glided the soap over the area. Over and over again, he scrubbed spotless parts of my body, paying special attention to my back and arms. We'd come a long way to where I could be naked on his lap. I was happily married to Von, but Mason had officially been my boyfriend since about a month after the wedding. I'm not sure how our arrangement would work otherwise—I was so tied to them both.

Mason waited until my body finally relaxed against his before he put the soap down, heaving a sigh of relief. The hot spray bathed us in privacy enough to where my tears held more grief than embarrassment. Mason didn't judge me while I sobbed into the crook of his neck. "I don't know Terence's favorite color," I admitted. "I don't know how he likes his eggs, only that he ate whatever they served in lockup because that's what was there. I never asked him what he preferred, though. I don't know which book he wanted to read next, or if he has any friends outside of the McCray organization and us. I reaped him by accident!"

"I know, *hani*. There was nothing you could've done to save him. It was just his time."

"A gunshot wound isn't someone's time. That's some lowlife forcing time's hand!"

Mason considered my words with a nod. "Fair enough. Terence died without pain. How about that? That's a good thing to do for a person—to take away their pain."

I wanted to argue further but quieted under the hot

spray. In my heart, I knew that even though Mason was trying his best, there was nothing that might make this all better. No pretty bow on top would undo the fact that Terence had been given a second chance at life, and he died in a very predictable manner. He'd saved me when Pistola stabbed me back when I worked at the prison, but I couldn't rescue him now.

I knew I should care that I was naked, but I couldn't bring myself to fuss about anything other than Terence. I sank into Mason's arms that promised to be strong when I couldn't lift life's burdens off my chest. His hair was darker with the water, hanging in ribbons that framed his face. The thick tresses had grown to a shag that I knew would eventually become dreadlocks when it was long enough. Since his strength was tied to his hair not being cut, I relished his waves in whatever state they came to me. I held onto the ends of his hair and wept on Mason's shoulder as the shower pelted at my grief.

We stayed like that for the next twenty minutes—naked and unashamed. His steady pulling took my grief down to a slow stream of tears that didn't overwhelm my existence with the agony I knew was lurking on the horizon.

"Big Mike went to the Emergency Room to see what help he can offer Judge and Terence," Mason informed me once I was lucid enough to hear him. "Ezra and Levi are downstairs cleaning up the mess. As soon as you're feeling better, we'll go on home."

"I want to sleep in my own bed in my own home tonight. Can we make that happen?"

"I thought you might say that. It won't be just the two of us, but sure. I can't imagine Ezra or Levi letting you out of their sight after the stunt you pulled."

"Should I pretend I'm sorry when we get out of the shower?"

"Pretend all you want, but never do that to me again. We were in the living room at the mansion making a plan to track down Ollie, and I go into the kitchen to find you gone. I'm not impervious to heart attacks, you know."

"I'm sorry."

Mason scoffed. "You'll have to pretend better than that for Ezra and Levi." He turned my chin so I was looking up at him, unable to ignore his angst over his charge going MIA. "Don't ever do that to me again. Where you go, I go."

His words were too beautiful to brush off, so I closed the gap between us and kissed the mouth that said such lovely things to me in my hour of darkness. Mason and I kissed at least a handful of times a day, indulging in the colors and sounds that came when an Omen kissed someone from Terraway.

A low rumble resounded in his chest, reminding me that Mason was very much a man. Hues of red and yellow danced across the insides of my closed eyelids, swirling over the night that felt scraped across my chest. The pounding of the shower water over us was accompanied by the sound of flutes. Sometimes the tunes were happy and light. Sometimes they were playful and mischievous. But tonight, the flute was somber and sad, letting the sorrow be what it was without adding too many frills. The music filled my entire being, shifting my body in Mason's arms so we could more thoroughly indulge in our alone time. He was a soothing balm for my soul—not enough to truly heal all that was broken, but enough to sweep me away from the reality that could turn all too grim on a dime.

We tried not to be rough with each other when we drew out the LSD-like effect that always happened when his tongue found mine. "I love you," I breathed between kisses, feeling his tongue multiply and dash all over my skin. "I'm sorry I ran."

He gripped my backside, his fingers trying to be gentle and desperately failing. "You should be." His tongue tasted like red and desire, and I couldn't get enough. I wanted to be far, far away from the devastation of the night. Mason's kiss was just the ticket to sweep me away. He cried out when the euphoria licked at him, spurring us into a frenzy of more, and still more. His calloused hand caressed my breast, and I nearly lost my mind.

Von never minded when we kissed. Sometimes he even wore this contented look when he watched us dote on each other. The hazards of the job were that Mason was part of our marriage, and as odd as that looked to the outside world, we hadn't been able to find a way around it, not that we were trying all that hard.

It wasn't until my dad's fist pounded on the door that

we startled out of our lust-filled haze. "If you think I don't know exactly what you're doing with my daughter, you're wrong."

Mason's spine stiffened, and he scrambled to get me to stand from his lap. It was hard to break out of our haze, so he steadied himself against the tiled wall before answering a breathy, "We'll be out in a few minutes, Dad."

Levi had insisted Mason call him "Dad." They were both Matruculan, and took to each other far easier than Levi had warmed to Von. Those two still bickered all the time, though I think that's how they preferred things.

Mason and I stood before each other, naked as the day we were born. Our eyes took in every glorious inch with a small smirk that was totally inappropriate, given the gravity of the evening.

Suddenly I felt the need to apologize for my wider hips and the softness of my stomach, as if Mason didn't understand that having a baby changed a woman's body.

Sensing my growing angst, he drew me into a one-armed embrace, my body flush against his so he could kiss me once more—soft and sweet. "I do love you," Mason said quietly, trailing his other hand down the curve of my hip. "Never do that to me again."

9

LOSING JUDGE

After like, a hundred lectures and a threat from Ezra that he'd make me wear the *karsel* bracelet and put me on house arrest, Levi, Mason, Ezra and me settled in for the night at my house on Lenoy Avenue. My body was exhausted from the agony of the soul corroding inside of me for far too long. I was also wiped from the emotion of losing someone close to me. Big Mike called in the middle of Ezra and Levi's shared tirade, confirming that Terence had died on the way to the hospital.

That was the only thing that excused me from the lecture of never leaving my Reaper's side ever again, so long as we both shall live. Mason held up his hand to put an end to it all, and made to draw me into his arms for a hug I couldn't handle. I gently pushed him away and moved into my bedroom, collapsing atop the mattress in a pile of sorrow.

I went back and forth in my mind, thinking up different ways I could've saved Terence from a life lost at the tail end of Judge's empire. I called Darius, asking him to come home. His voicemail wasn't the place to leave a message like "your brother's dead," so I kept my greeting simple and vague. Turning on my phone welcomed a litany of messages I'd missed but none I wanted to hear.

It wasn't until Allie's soft coo from the other side of the door caught my ear that I bothered lifting my head from the comforter. "October? Sweetheart, I'm coming in."

It didn't matter that I'd locked the door. Too many of them had keys to keep any semblance of privacy. But I didn't mind Allie's intrusion, provided it was only her. "I don't want to talk about it," I insisted as she walked quietly into my room with Graham.

Allie sat on the side of my bed, rubbing her belly. Then she stopped the motion and stared into the void she drifted into all too often. I watched her with a nurse's eye and a sister's worry. Her concerned face was completely blank. I counted off an entire minute before the panic in me welled to the spilling point. "Allie!"

She startled at my volume. "Huh? Oh. October." Her lashes opened and shut twelve times before sympathy registered on her face once more. "Honey, are you alright?"

I nodded, though I'm not sure how truthful she expected me to be. "Did you need something?"

"I just thought you might like a cup of tea. Ezra's brewing some now."

"No, thanks. Tell him I'm already asleep."

Ezra called from the living room, "If you're asleep, then I'll save the offer of tea for the morning."

Mason had pulled to the point where my body felt limp, but it was still mostly functional. I wanted to scratch the backs of my hands but I couldn't commit to the effort. Allie seemed to understand this, and placed her hand atop mine, nixing that idea right quick. Graham sat on her other side, and for a while, no one spoke. It was too sad to talk about, too awful to try and make sense of. Terence was dead, when he'd gotten his life back only a year and a half ago.

When my phone rang, I didn't move to answer it. Instead, Allie picked it up. "Hello? No, Judge isn't here." Then she scrolled through my call list before replying with, "He hasn't called her, no. I'll tell her. I'm so sorry about everything, Big Mike. Please let me know how we can help, other than keeping an eye out for Judge if he shows up."

Allie set my phone back down, the lamplight casting a warm glow on her pinched and beautiful features. "Big Mike can't find Judge. If Judge calls you, let him know. He's worried."

I shifted my hips atop the mattress, blinking up at the ceiling. "I know where he might be."

Graham stood. "Then tell me, and I'll go find him."

Allie helped me sit up, though I wanted nothing more than to lie down for about a hundred years. I noticed a slight twinge of discomfort on her features that she tried to hide. "Judge won't go home with you even if you do manage to find him. I'll take Mason. Besides, Allie needs to get back to Terraway. She's in pain but she doesn't want to say it out loud."

"I'm fine, October," Allie insisted, but Graham wasn't about to take chances with his wife or his son. I loved that about him. He had a singular focus: if it wasn't good for Allie, he wasn't interested.

Graham put his hand on Allie's elbow. "We said we'd go back to Terraway after dinner, and it's well beyond that. You know it isn't good for the baby to be Topside for very long. We'll swing home and pick up Boston, and then return to Terraway."

Allie hung her head, her voice trembling with emotion. "I don't want to leave my family. We just lost someone precious to us. Plus, we still have no idea where Ollie is. I can't just leave when my brother's missing!"

I was about to tell her that's exactly what she needed to do, but Graham was gentler. "Ollie's not missing, for one. He or Darius left a note saying he'd be back. This whole thing got dreadfully out of hand. So he's a day late coming home. That's no reason to risk our son's life by staying Topside too long."

"I don't want to leave things like this."

Graham straightened. "If you think I'll jeopardize your life or our baby's, you're wrong. Mariang *had* to carry her baby Topside, and she died because of it. I'll not see you go the same way, nor will I see our son go the same way Sept..." He caught himself too late. Graham paled, his eyes locking in on mine with palpable regret. "I misspoke. Forgive me, October."

I waved my hand like it was all no big deal, as if it didn't punch me in the gut every time anybody mentioned my dead daughter's name. "Graham's right. Allie, you need to be in Terraway. I'll have Ezra send word the second we find Ollie. If Judge will allow any sort of funeral for Terence, I'll make sure you're there."

Allie sighed, knowing she was outnumbered. "Oh, fine. Promise you'll stay with your Pullers from here on out?"

"I super promise."

Allie kissed my nose and exited the bedroom, leaving me to convince my body to get up and move. Judge was lost but I knew where he could be found.

It was a chore to get to the hallway, so when Mason found me with half a burger in his mouth, I didn't protest his hand on my elbow. I'd resented needing someone to lean on in the beginning, but now I didn't fight the process as much. I couldn't decide if that was me maturing or just plain giving up.

"Going somewhere?" Mason asked.

I pointed toward the front door. "Judge is missing. Big Mike can't track him down."

"And you can?"

I glanced up at him. "Of course I can. Come with me?"

"What are the chances of me talking you out of this?"

When he took in my stalwart expression, he conceded. "Alright, fine. But take it into consideration that Judge might not want us to go looking for him right now. He isn't exactly in a good place."

"Noted. Dad? I don't guess you'll let me go off with just Mason, will you?"

Levi crossed his arms over his broad chest. "You guess right. You're barely strong enough to walk. I'm not about to let my baby go off in the dead of night to search for a drug lord who's having a bad day. I'll leave a note for Ezra for when he gets back from porting Allie, Graham and Boston back to Terraway. He just left with Graham and Allie to pick up Boston."

Mason led me to the front door and leaned me against it, taking in my labored breathing. "Maybe I pulled too hard. Sorry about that. I was worried about the soul being inside of you for too long." He bent down and even went so far as to slide my shoes on for me, tying them up so I didn't have to bend over and bother with the laces. He waited for Levi to turn around before he pressed a kiss to my knee, sliding his palm up the back of my thigh. It was a small thing, that simple touch that tied us together, but it anchored me just enough so I didn't float away.

My fingers reached down to feather through his hair. "I love you," I whispered. Mason stood and laced his fingers through mine when my dad joined us.

The drive was short but Mason made it eventful. He was still newer at driving and took potholes at a run, which gave me mild heart palpitations. Terence my Taurus groaned at his callous treatment. Since we arrived at our destination in one piece, I didn't complain, but rather made a note to drive the next time. I'd been on the phone with Danny and Anastasia through part of it, and I can only hope she didn't hear my bitten-off cussing when Mason ran a red light.

The moon shone down on the ghetto that had once been part of my childhood. Of course, back when I'd been a little girl, the neighborhood hadn't been quite as bad as it was now. Many houses had missing or broken windows. Too many had eviction notices posted. The overgrown shrubs announced to the world that this was an unredeemable neighborhood.

I didn't like the idea of anything being beyond repair, but this place didn't give me much hope. The shutters had been white and cheerful, once upon a better time. Now they were broken, faded, and some were missing altogether. One window on the familiar house was boarded up, which, if I remembered correctly, had been Darius' bedroom. The siding was filthy, and I tried not to notice the bullet holes along the left portion next to the front door.

It had looked so big when I'd been small, but now the three-bedroom ranch looked... sad. And that wasn't just because my very favorite drug dealer was sitting on the stoop, head in hands while his elbows leaned on his thighs.

"How'd you know he'd be here?" Levi asked.

My voice was quiet to respect the somber nature of the night. "Judge misses his mama. He's like Ollie, in that he wanted to take care of his younger siblings. He just did it wrong, is all."

Mason kept his hand in mine when we walked from the car over to the house.

Judge didn't look up when I approached but motioned for me to have a seat next to him. "How'd you find me?"

I didn't answer, just sat down and wrapped my weighted arm around his shoulders. At my simple touch, his body collapsed in on me.

A horrible sob unleashed from Judge's lips that were already slick with tears. "I didn't take him to the hospital fast enough!"

I knew better than to argue with such utter brokenness. So I held him, giving him what no one else could—a safe place to let his guard down. Though I wanted to get him clear out of Dodge, I held him until his sobs turned into hiccups. It was only then I realized that Mason was pulling for Judge, his hand on the man's shoulder.

"Let's get him home. He'll stay with me until the..." I was about to say "burial" but I didn't want to push Judge over the edge. "Judge will stay at my house for a while." He'd been my safe place when I was little; I decided it was time to return the favor.

Judge didn't protest as I led him into my car. I'm not sure he even knew what was going on as we drove away.

Levi was cautious about letting Judge into our home, but all in all, it was my call. Still, my dad hovered the second Judge crossed the threshold.

I led Judge into Ollie's bedroom, guessing Ollie wouldn't mind a visitor if he wasn't home yet. It had been my bedroom before life and misfortune had taken my daughter away from me. Ollie gutted the place and rebuilt, redecorated and redeemed the broken bits of the home that housed some of my worst memories. Still, I could picture the carnage, despite our best attempts at moving on.

The moment Levi and Mason moved to the kitchen to talk privately, Judge reached for me in the lamplight, his hand gripping my arm with purpose. "Did it happen? Can you feel my soul?"

I blinked at him. "Have you been drinking?"

"My soul. Did it go into you yet, or do you have to touch the dying person for longer? I don't want to feel it when I die."

I pursed my lips. "A person's soul only goes into me if I touch them within a day of them dying. A simple touch is all it takes. I didn't mean to reap Terence, Judge. Honest."

"I know, I just... Take my soul. I don't need it anymore."

My eyes widened with alarm. "Honey, no. You're not going to die tonight. It might not feel like it now, but we'll make it through this."

His gaze was heavy with too much life piled atop his back. His next words came out slow, delivering a heavy heartbreak that threatened to shatter me where I stood. "What if I don't want to live through it?"

If I'd thought Terence's corroded soul inside of me was painful, it was nothing to Judge's quiet admission that he thought his next logical step should be to off himself. Dread and devastation washed through me at the thought of the world without my Judge.

I couldn't think of the right words because panic and denial were warring with my tongue. It wasn't until he pulled his gun from his pocket and pointed it at his temple that I screamed. I wasn't a woman in her home anymore; I was a little girl watching her superman come undone. "No, Judge! Stop!"

Tears poured down his cheeks. "Turn away, baby girl. You don't want to see this, and I know I don't want to feel this. Remember that I'll always love you. When you find Darius, tell him... Tell him I'm sorry." He drew a stuttering breath in time with all the air leaving my lungs. "It'll be painless," he told himself, pressing the barrel to his temple with agony glistening in his eyes.

There was so much training I'd had to go through in order to work in the prison, but all of it flew out of my brain once the image of Judge with a gun to his head burned itself into my psyche.

It was a thing of luck that Mason and Levi darted out of the kitchen at my shout. Mason gasped but Levi didn't hesitate. He ripped the gun from Judge's hand and held it out from himself like it was a diseased rat. "Can I just chuck this somewhere?"

"No. Give it here." I gently took it from my dad and moved into the backyard, shooting all six bullets into the tree, punishing nature for humanity's many crimes.

My cheeks were slick with sorrow when I came back inside. I moved the kitchen chair to the fridge and stashed the gun in the tiny cupboard above it to keep it from sight and from being easily accessible. My sobs were audible now, and as Mason helped me down from the chair, his arms around me understood that there was no going back from something as terrible as this.

10

MY HUSBAND

I slept fitfully with Judge in my arms and Mason at my back in the bedroom I usually shared with Mason and Von. We didn't rise with the sun but slept the morning away, content to let the day be gloomy and not face the whole thing at all. Big Mike and Sherita were taking care of the details as best they could. Ezra stayed in touch with Big Mike to make sure our family could help in whatever way they would let us.

But truly, there wasn't much to be done. Cremation was scheduled, there would be no funeral, and a cleaning service was scrubbing the blood from Judge's house. Sherita dealt with closing down Terence's accounts and all of his personal affairs. For all the impact Terence had on my life, his entire existence was closed out in the span of a day. Sherita even went through his clothes and donated them, so Judge didn't have to deal with that step in the process, either.

I held Judge in our shared grief until the afternoon, when someone let themselves into my home without ringing the doorbell. "October? Where is she, Dad?"

My heart stuttered in my chest at the sound of Von's voice. Mason kissed the back of my shoulder before he got out of bed to greet the missing piece of our eternal trio. The slap of their bro-hug warmed me faster than pretty much anything else could, and though Judge was still snoozing in my arms, I wanted to run in all of my agony into the living room to greet the man I loved. Still, I held tight to Judge, knowing he needed me to stay with him.

Von stood in the doorway, keeping his chain store cup of coffee out of our bedroom to respect my rule of no food or drinks in my room. My white carpet was precious to me, and he respected my neurosis with all the kindness of a devoted husband. "I see I didn't need to fight through the jet lag with this." He held up his coffee. "I didn't realize we were hosting a slumber party. Room for a fourth in there?"

Mason clapped Von on the shoulder. "Take my spot. I need to stretch my legs and get some fresh air. You good on blood?"

Von pointed to his golden eye that was more than halfway blue. "Had a bag on my way over here just to be safe."

"Good man." Mason made to leave but paused on his

way out. "Oh, I took a shower with your naked wife. Then we made out."

Von's good-natured grin couldn't be tempered. His angular cheekbones and black messy hair refused to be softened. The world would truly be a tragic place if Von was tamed by even the smallest degree. "Well, naturally. I assume you were a gentleman?"

"Of course." Mason explained the devastating day all in hushed tones, so as not to rouse Judge. Though, Mason had been pulling pretty steadily, so I'm not sure much could wake him at this point.

"Terence is truly…" Von touched his mouth with three fingers, then whispered, "dead?"

Mason nodded. "The whole thing is awful. He…" Mason sighed and pointed to Judge. "Watch him, okay?"

Von's brows creased with mild concern, the dimple in his left cheek undetectable. "Him? Aren't we to watch her? That's the usual gig, right? Until death do the three of us part?"

"Watch him," Mason confirmed, and then left with Levi to go on a run in their Matruculan forms. Maybe that was one of the reasons those two bonded so well. With my dad as Sandy the dog and Mason as a wolf, they could share a worldview not many of us could. All in all, I was glad they had each other.

Von stood in the doorway, leaning against the side with a lackadaisical look to him, as if making the whole universe brighter simply by being part of it was no big thing. He thoroughly enjoyed the effect he had on me, and basked in the attention my eyes paid him. "I missed you," I whispered.

His gaze fell to Judge. "Always say that to me while you're holding another bloke in your arms. I'm back, love. Mason called and said you ran off, so I caught the soonest flight out. Sorry for the delay. Apparently people don't understand our love well enough to schedule more frequent flights."

"What a silly world."

"Indeed." His eyes softened as he took in the scope of my lazy state. I was usually up and out of bed by seven, so I couldn't imagine how strange I looked still being in bed midday after a night and morning of crying. "It's been a long one, yeah?"

Though Mason had already told him as much, I felt the need to confess the awfulness I'd been part of. "I reaped Terence. I didn't mean to."

"Did you mean to run away from Mason? Because it sounds like that's the only thing you can hold yourself accountable for, yeah?"

I nodded, but the guilt still weighted my insides. "Terence is dead."

Von moved from the doorway only a moment to put away his coffee and then came into the room, setting his leather jacket on our dresser. This used to be Ollie's room, but the king-sized bed was big enough for Mason, Von and me to share. Or in this case, Judge, Von and me. "I take it we have a new bedfellow?"

"You take it right." I smoothed my fingers down the silk of Judge's cheek. Everything in me knew to be tender to him. I held the life he hadn't meant to let spin out of control in my hands, giving him rest for his weary soul. My words came out wrapped in a choked whisper. "He tried to kill himself last night, so we're on suicide watch until further notice."

Von froze, processing all the new information. "Wow. I leave the country for a measly week, and everything goes into the toilet. I'm here now, love. Did you want me to watch him so you can move about?"

"No. I don't mind. I'm a little out of it myself, dealing with it all. Bed seems like the best place to be, other than wherever Ollie ran off to."

"He's still not back yet? Ezra filled me in on that little nugget. That's not like him, yeah? You, Allie and Ollie keep tight tabs on each other."

I explained the note and the filled in the rest of the details he'd missed while helping his mother move out of her home in London over to Ezra's mansion.

"Bollocks."

"I know, right? It's not good, no matter how you slice it."

"No, not that. I have no doubt Ollie will come straight

home with Darius, wherever the two of them are. It's just that I had this very tawdry strip tease worked out, but this hardly seems the time to test it out on you."

I sniggered at his inappropriate humor. "Probably not the best time, but I'll take a rain check. The one you did in my imagination several times before everything fell apart was deliciously X-rated. I hope the real deal lives up to the hype."

"Are you quite certain it's not the time for us to reconnect?"

"I'm sure. Not until Judge can handle… anything."

"Okay, but just so you know, it had plenty of this in it, which I know you love." He did a feminine shimmy for me, to which I fanned myself. He yanked his red t-shirt over his head and laid it out over the dresser, unbuckling his pants without flourish.

Well, not *no* flourish. I mean, it's Von.

He changed and climbed into bed with me in nothing but navy flannel pajama pants, letting loose a contented groan at finally being able to relax on a mattress instead of an airline seat. "Remind me never to leave this bed again."

"I'm glad you're home."

"You should be. I'm very charming. Is my ring still on your finger?" He picked up my hand to examine the small iceberg he'd planted there.

"I tried trading it for some magic beans, but they wouldn't take it. Said it wasn't big enough."

Von laughed airily through his nose. "Off with his head, whoever he is. If it's not large enough, then perhaps I should have a neon sign made for you that flashes the words 'Von's Eternal Bride.'"

"Way ahead of you. I already had one made up while you were away. Only I misspelled it, so it reads 'One's Eternal Free Ride.' I got quite a few men opening doors for me. Can't imagine why."

He propped himself up on his elbow and gave my lips a light kiss, respectful of the fact that I was holding a slumbering man and dealing with fresh grief as best I could. "I missed you terribly. I'm sorry it took so long. Mum's got a lot of stuff. But she's here now. She insisted her things be moved into a bedroom near Anastasia's room, but I think we all know where she'll end up." His eyebrows danced suggestively.

"Good for them both. Ezra smiles more when she's around."

Von slid open the drawer of the nightstand and fished out a cinnamon stick from the tin where he kept his spare stash. He chewed on the end while he thought aloud. "How about you? I'm guessing not many smiles are going to be happening any time soon."

I shook my head.

Then Von did the perfect thing. He rolled onto his side and spooned me, kissing the nape of my neck. "That's alright, love. I'll hold you until it doesn't hurt so very badly."

"That might take a while," I admitted, my throat dry from too much crying.

"Then perhaps I'll be the luckiest man in the world, and you'll let me hold you forever." Von feathered his fingers through my hair, and for the life of me, I fell in love with him all over again—a hazy glow through my grief.

11

JUDGE'S MELTDOWN

*T*hree days later hadn't seen much change in our house. Ollie and Darius were still missing, I was still anxious to find them, and Judge was still beside himself. He slept most of the day and tossed next to me at night. Mason had taken it upon himself to comb through Sombi to make sure Darius and Ollie hadn't gone on an impromptu zombie hunt there, and came back with zero signs of them, which was nothing short of devastating.

"Sherita called again," I informed Judge from my spot on the couch when he came out of the bathroom. He rarely left the bed, and though he was too proud to admit that he didn't want to be without me, his hard stare whenever I left the room for too long said it all. I'd ventured as far as the living room this morning, which I could tell he wasn't thrilled about. He wanted his grief private and contained to my bedroom, which he realized I was no longer inside.

"Sherita doesn't need to call. She doesn't need to hound me. A man's not allowed to take a week off when his brother dies? When his brother dies in his arms in the back of his car?"

I waited for Judge's temper to subside marginally. I knew how to be tender with him, even when he'd reached the stage in his grief where he was determined to be a prickly porcupine. "I don't think Sherita's trying to hound you. I think she's worried about you, sweetheart."

His lips pursed as his temper swung. "Don't call me 'sweetheart.' I'm the adult and you're the child. I'm not your little doll. I'm allowed to take time off of work. I built all my businesses so they can run without me seeing to every little detail. Now that my empire's been significantly pared down, there's even less I should be bothered about right now."

I didn't speak at first but let his words crackle in the air between us. I was grateful Levi was in Dagat looking for Ollie and Darius to see if they'd run off to have some fun with the Mermaids. My dad would've snapped at hearing Judge speak to me like that. But I understood. Sometimes I was a jerk when I was wounded, too. I folded my arms over my chest and leaned my hip against the arm of the couch. "Is that how you want to talk to me? I call you 'sweetheart' and you suddenly feel the need to prove to me that you're nothing like sweet?"

He shrugged. "I don't care about any of it. I don't care about being nice. I don't care about the business I flushed down the toilet for nothing. For nothing! This was supposed to make things safer for my family but it didn't! I don't care about Terraway or regular earth. I don't care about what we're going to do with Terence's ashes, and I certainly don't care about you and your opinion of me."

Judge winced at his own words but didn't take them back. He stood taller, puffing out his chest as if he had a right to go around breaking people's worlds so he didn't have to admit he had a heart that was capable of rupture.

Von was listening from the sofa, turning the page of the newspaper without looking up at us. "You got this, Peach?"

I didn't take my glare off of Judge. "Uh-huh." Judge had been working his way through the stages of grief, but seemed to be stuck on "anger" a little longer than all of humanity might've liked.

"I want my gun back."

I chewed on my lower lip before speaking. "For what?"

"I'm going on a walk."

I motioned to the front door. "By all means. Go for a walk. This is the kind of neighborhood you don't need a gun in order to walk through in broad daylight. Foreign concept, I know."

Judge sighed his frustration. "Give me my gun, October."

"Give me a break, Judge."

He stalked past me but paused when the scent from

the kitchen reached parts of his psyche he was trying too hard to close off. "What's that smell?"

I waved him into the kitchen. "It's your mama's applesauce. I wanted some comfort food."

All the venom in Judge's being gusted out of him at once. "You made the applesauce?" His voice sounded instantly younger, tinted with wonder I'd been hoping was still rattling around inside of him somewhere.

I waited for him to put his face over the pot and get a good whiff of the stuff his childhood had been made of. When I answered, I kept my tone light. "Oh, I didn't make this for you. I don't cook for people who don't care about me."

His head turned so he could throw me a wounded stare. "Do I need to say I'm sorry?"

"I don't need you to lie to me, no."

"Good. Then let me have some applesauce."

"Oh, no problem. I got you some already, in case you kept acting foolish." I stood and plucked out a jar of the crappiest generic brand applesauce the store had to offer from the cupboard and sat it down in front of him at the table. "This is yours."

His mouth tightened. "Very funny. I get your point. I've been an ass."

"Don't sully the good name of the noble donkey with the awful behavior you've been touting around here."

He stepped back and crossed his arms over his chest. "How am I supposed to act, huh? Tell me what you want from me, October. My brother's dead and my other brother is missing. Everything I've built is gone." He bunched the fabric over his chest in his fist. "My whole life feels like nothing! All of it means nothing!"

I leaned back against the counter, my expression calm as I gave his grief the space to spread out in the air. It had been bottled up inside of silent tears for far too long.

"Do you have any idea how hard I've worked to get our family to this point? We had nothing growing up! Hustling was the only way to put food on the table, so that's what I did." He jabbed his finger down on the kitchen table to punctuate his point. "It was the only way to feed you, if you recall from over there on your high horse. We didn't have extra food to go around when you three came knocking on our door. Mama did what she could to take you all in because she was a saint of a woman, but I'm the one who picked up the groceries. *I'm* the one who made sure the heat stayed on."

"That sounds hard," I offered, unsure what the right thing to say might be. Since I didn't have any words that might fix it all, I reached for the only balm I could think of. "I'm listening. Tell me more."

"Let's talk about the time in high school when Ollie and I applied for the same job, bagging groceries at Pete's Market. I got passed over for reasons I'm guessing you can figure out. You act like I didn't try to do right by my mama and get a real job, but I did. I tried over and over again, but for some reason no one saw past my color. Eighteen interviews in one week. Fifteen the week after that. On and on with the same results." Then he held up his hands, his eyes narrowing as sarcasm creased his tone. "Not that I still remember details like that from so long ago. Not like they still burn me."

Von froze on the couch, sitting in my eyeline from my position in the kitchen, pretending to read while my mouth fell open in horror. I guess I understand that discrimination happens. I mean, I know it's real. But to think of that happening to Judge made my skin feel cold and clammy.

"When I got my driver's license, my score was higher than Ollie's on our test—both written and on the road. Do you want to know how many times Ollie's been pulled over? Zero times. Do you want to guess at how many I've been pulled over?" He shook his head, as if I was the profiling cop who has nothing better to do than make boys afraid of the people who should have their backs. "I can't remember the last month that went by that Darius or I haven't been pulled over for Driving While Black."

Tears stung my eyes. I didn't want any of this to be true. I wanted to plug my ears and sing songs about unity and holding hands so loudly that the whole world would have no choice but to stop being a raging butthole and just be kind already.

Instead, I listened, which seemed to be all Judge was requiring of me. I couldn't fix his world, but I could at least respect his pain enough to hear his agony while he bled. I could stay with him until it didn't hurt quite so much.

Judge motioned to the framed pictures of Ollie, Allie and me on the living room wall. "You put Ollie up on a high horse because he never hit the streets. Well, good for Ollie. Good for all the men who found a way to take care of their mamas and their brothers and their sisters. I'm not a good man, October! Is that what you want to hear?"

Tears that I'd been holding back out of respect for Judge's pain burned the backs of my eyes, adding too much pressure to a conversation that came preloaded with the stuff. "No!"

"Do you even know what redlining is?"

I nodded mutely, bunching my toes to keep from running into his arms to stop his justifiable hurt with a hug. There are times for blunting the ache and times for giving it permission and space to breathe.

"Mama's credit was good enough for a home loan. We had more than enough saved up for a down-payment. But bank after bank denied us. Do you know why?"

I was afraid to nod.

"Because they want to keep the black man exactly where he is! They wanted to keep my mama in the ghetto. They wanted to keep Darius in the hood. They wanted to keep T in a school that didn't give a shit if he ever learned to read. They wanted me to be small so they could sit on their white hill of privilege and feel like big men." He slammed his fist into his chest, his eyes so wide, he looked like he might never be okay again. "I will not be small!" he raged, his shout making me startle and shrink against the counter. "So I built an empire even the cops are afraid of. The cops who pulled me over, locked T up, and made Darius afraid—they know they don't belong in my world. They've been trying for years to prove to me that I don't belong in theirs. I built something so big that I paid cash for my house. I won't ever grovel and make them feel big. My mama deserved better than what she got and *I'm* the one who gave it to her. So the next time you look down your privileged nose at me and tell me you're disappointed in my choices, you can save it. I'm disappointed in the whole damned world."

I saw the tired and strangled mark of Ollie on him. But the difference was my brother had never taken his lot in life out on me, though I'd brought far more responsibility on Ollie's shoulders than I ever had Judge's. Still, I listened to Judge's pain as it rang in my ears. I didn't argue that hey, I had a crap childhood and adolescence too. His pain didn't erase mine, so I didn't feel the need to prove the validity of my scars to him. Judge's story was tragic in its own rite, and the kindest thing I could think to do while he bled was be there so he didn't feel the need to bleed alone, trapped in a sadness that not enough people cared to understand.

I cared. I cared very much if my Judge was hurting.

His pitch rose the more he trusted in the fact that I wouldn't try to curb or reframe his pain to make it more palatable for the cheap seats. "I deal with the cops, with Santori's people, with unreliable dealers—all of it! It all falls on me. Do you know how many families I feed with my empire? Do you understand how many men out there are just like me, who wanted to buy their mama a house in a nice neighborhood but got redlined into the ghetto? Do you have any idea how many people depend on me because I'm their only shot at getting out?" He touched his forehead, and a flash of unexpected guilt mingled with anger on his features. "I can't take a few days to mourn my brother without Sherita nagging me, asking where I'm at!"

I tilted my head at him, wondering where the touchiness about Sherita was coming from when he was on the track to rail against the man. She'd been his assistant for years and he'd never said a bad thing about her. He spoiled her with trips to the spa, expensive jewelry and nice meals.

I took a shot and picked at the thread to see just how far Judge could unravel. I was already in tears, so I pretty much had nothing to lose. "Sherita's the problem now, eh? Now she cares about you too much? Nobody cared enough about you growing up, and now Sherita's a nag because she's worried about you? Make up your mind."

Judge shot me a morose look that broke through a portion of his venom. "She's pregnant, okay? Is that what you want to hear? Sherita's pregnant, and she's keeping it."

My mouth fell open and my tears turned full-stop. "Is the baby yours?"

Judge mimed laughing, and then devolved into pure

sass. "Like you haven't known we had a thing together for years."

I held up my hands. "I had no idea. I mean, I hoped, but I didn't know for sure. She's pregnant?" My countenance lightened with the news as I swiped at my cheeks. "Judge, that's exciting! Why didn't you tell me sooner? I would've sent her something to say congratulations. No wonder she's worried about you."

But Judge looked as if this was the opposite of good news. "She's keeping the baby just to torture me! Now she's got me for life, owing her things I never agreed to." His eyes were wild with the confession. "I don't know how to be a dad! I just got my brother killed, and I can't even find my other brother. Can you honestly see me with a baby?"

I quirked an eyebrow at him. "Um, yes?"

"Be serious."

"Well, you're acting like one right now, so I assume you understand how to relate to someone with your emotional IQ." Yes, I was being a brat, but to be fair, he started it. "Sherita isn't trying to torture you. She's having your child, Judge! Grow up!"

His face soured. "Grow up? What, like you're all grown because you've been pregnant once? You've never raised a kid, October. You have no idea how hard this is going to be. You've never been a parent!"

It was the gut-punch that pushed me one inch too far. Suddenly I felt myself toppling over the edge of the composure I'd fought so long to maintain. Like it didn't kill me every time Anastasia called me "mama." Like it didn't slice me open every time I saw Allie's pregnant belly. Like my daughter's death on the day of her birth was something one was just supposed to be cool with and get over. Like because I was cheated out of the parenting aspect, I somehow never was a parent to begin with.

Judge was in pain, so he needed me to suffer, too.

Von was off the couch in the next breath, jerking Judge with both fists on his collar. Though Judge was slightly taller, Von had gone from stoically invisible throughout our fight to now a mess of deranged and confrontational. "Choose your next words very carefully."

Maybe Judge would've apologized, but threats only made him dig his heels further into the mess he'd created. He spat in Von's face, sealing his eviction notice.

My husband only smiled in response, cruelty teasing his features with a playfulness only Von could pull off. His words came out slow and sinister, ringing down my spine with a warning that my worlds were splintering in two, yet again. "That's good. Push away the only person in your life who loves you enough to look after you. Push away the only woman you trust enough to cry in front of." Then, with strength he'd acquired because nature deemed it necessary for him to be able to protect me with consider-able muscle, he shoved Judge so hard, my stunned friend careened back three steps. "Push her down so far that she's nothing to you. Right now, I don't care about the bullshit you Americans put each other through to excuse yourselves from the burden of kindness. I care if my wife is disrespected in her own home. Tell me what a big man you are now, talking to her like that."

"Von," I cautioned, knowing he'd been just as wounded by Judge's words as I was.

"No!" Von shouted, and cleared the gap between them so he could shake Judge with his temper. "Why should he get a child and not me? How does he get off complaining about the gift I'd kill for?"

I was so sick with grief, I had to fight my way through my knees buckling. I didn't want to think about the doctor we saw this summer. I didn't want to remember the test results. I didn't want any of it. I wanted pure, sugary denial, which is what Von granted me most days.

When I moved forward to touch his back to soothe him, he angled his chin over his shoulder to show just how hurt he truly was. "We were parents, no matter what anyone says. We were parents for a few glorious moments, and that's the story that'll stay with me. Like being in the military. Once you're in the military, you'll always be part of that family."

"Agreed. You're a great dad to Penny and Anastasia. You were a Superman dad to September, too." When Von looked like he might take a swing at Judge, I coiled my hand around his bicep. "Let him go, Von. He's miserable, and he's trying to get us to join him. There's enough to fight the world about. Let's not turn on each other."

It took a few beats, but I breathed easier once Von

turned away from Judge, who sank to the linoleum while Von pointed down at him with disgust. "You'll not speak to my wife with such contempt, especially not in her own home, and never in front of me."

Judge kept his chin lowered but granted Von the satisfaction of a nod, which I knew was as good as we were ever going to get to an apology.

"Come on, babe." I tugged on Von's arm, leading him away from our source of contention and out into the fresh air, where our anguish could breathe a little easier.

12

BABY MAMA DRAMA

The next night, Von and I took Ana to the pediatrician. After she was declared the healthiest, sweetest, cutest baby girl in the universe, we took her and Mama Vandershot out for lunch. After we returned Ana to Danny in the afternoon, we went to Judge's house to meet up with Sherita and pack up a few things for him.

Even after the altercation, Judge still didn't want to leave my house. Glutton for punishment, I guess. His apology consisted of ordering me a nice new jacket, which I promptly burned right in front of him.

That was the first time he smiled. Just like that, we were back to being us—whatever that looked like these days. Still, Judge didn't want to leave my house, so Von and I took it upon ourselves to take care of him like the parents inside of us knew how to do.

Sherita wasn't far enough along to look pregnant, but

the sheen of sweat on her forehead told me she was elbow-deep in morning sickness, for which I did not envy her. Von packed up a few of Judge's things while I sat with Sherita at the kitchen table. I listened to her while she broke down over Judge's breakdown, the ups and downs of her pregnancy, and the creek she and Big Mike were stuck up with Judge refusing to deal with... pretty much anything. The empire he'd built had been freshly disbanded last month, so there were still shifting pieces and conversations that needed to happen. "He needs to come back and put things back how they were. He's crazy if he thinks he can walk away from it all. Talk to him. Make him see reason."

"See, that's where I can't help you."

Her eyes grew wide, framed with lashes slightly darker than her milk chocolate skin. "You're not going to help me?"

"I'm not sending Judge back into the cesspool he's created for himself, no. I want your baby to have a stand-up daddy. Don't you?"

Her mouth firmed with defiance. Her wardrobe was silk and looked expensive. Her fingernails were painted to perfection, and her hair looked like she'd just had it done. She always looked adult and polished, and tonight was no exception. "I want Judge to be Judge. I don't need him to fish a halo out of his back pocket. I love him just as he is."

"So do I, but 'the way he is' has made him miserable. 'The way he is' got Terence killed." I knew it was cruel to say, but I laid it all out on the table for her to examine. "Your baby deserves better than gunfire outside his or her bedroom window."

"You can't keep him from his baby!" she shouted, startling me and bringing Von running down the steps.

I held up my hands. "I'm not keeping him at all. He's staying with me as long as he'd like because he helped raise me. He took me in when I was a kid, so I'm returning the favor. I owe him that much. But he's free to go whenever he likes. He's messed up right now, Sherita. I'm hoping to send him back to you with his head on straight, so he can do right by you and the baby."

She shook her head, as if I'd told her nothing of value. "He's obsessed with you, you know."

I raised my eyebrow, wondering just how bad the baby hormones were hitting her. She'd always been perfectly nice to me before. "Is that so? Wow. That's actually a new one for me."

"There's not a thing about him I don't know. Not a tracker I don't order or a gift I don't send out." Then she fixes me with a venomous glare, as if I'm the man who got her pregnant and left her high and dry. "Two-hundred-fifty-five-thousand-three-hundred-sixty dollars and seventeen cents."

"Excuse me?"

"That's how much Judge has spent on you over the years since I came along. Tracking devices, a private detail following you, jewelry, a refrigerator, new clothes, a breast pump." She leaned forward angrily. "A breast pump! Look me in the eye and tell me that the man who buys you a breast pump isn't obsessed."

My mouth fell open in horrified confusion. "That's what you think? You think Judge has it bad for me? He's twelve years older than me, you know. He's practically my brother, which is why he cares. He's my family. That's why he got me a refrigerator when my home was vandalized and trashed. We look out for each other in crazy stalkerish ways that don't make sense to anyone because *neither of us* make much sense to anyone! Our families only had each other for a very long time, so when there's a need, we rush in to fix it. That's all I'm doing right now for him." I sat back and placed my palms on the flat of the table, reining myself in and scolding myself for raising my voice at a pregnant woman. "Congratulations on your pregnancy, Sherita. No matter how this conversation is going right now, I really do like you, and Judge loves you. He's just messed up in the head right now. But rest assured, I'm very much married, and Judge very much isn't barking up my tree. Woman-to-woman, I'm sorry if I've done anything to make you think it was any other way."

At this, Sherita paused, and then broke down in hysterics, the poor thing. "It's not you! I don't know what's wrong with me! It's these hormones. I was in the grocery store this morning and screamed at a stock boy because they were out of the milk I like. Then I sobbed like a crazy person and they asked me to leave the store!" She shook her head at herself when I stood and plucked a napkin from the drawer and handed it to her. She dabbed at her eyes. "I know he's not lusting after you. You're the fifth woman I've reamed for taking Judge away. It's the fact that I'm pregnant and alone, and I didn't even need a tracker to find him. I knew he'd be with you, and not with me. I know I'm making more of it than it is, but it hurts."

I switched to a seat nearer to Sherita so I could put my hand close to hers. I debated touching her fingers, but she blew her nose into the napkin, so I decided against infesting myself with germy mucus. "Look, I want him to go back to you. I'm doing all I can to push him in that direction. But his brother just died in his arms, Sherita. Judge isn't going to make good decisions for a while." I sat back, running my hand over my face while Von watched the exchange with wide eyes from the entryway. "In the meantime, what help do you need from us?"

"Help from you?" She scoffed, though not unkindly. "You're just a kid."

I nodded, tempering my words as best I could. "That may be true, but if I'm old enough for you to feel threatened by me, then I'm old enough for you to lean on when life gets tricky. I trust you've got my number?"

She nodded as she stood. "Tell Judge... Tell him nothing." She blanched with remorse. "Oh, don't tell him I accused him of wanting to sleep with you. Don't make me sound crazy."

I raised my hand to stave off her worries. "Never. Have

a good night, Sherita." I waited until she exited before my shoulders slumped. "That totally sucked."

Von slung the backpack filled with Judge's things over his shoulder. "You handled it all masterfully." He leaned over to deliver a kiss just deep enough to drain the last of my tension from my altercation with Sherita. "I think I've got something that might cheer you up."

"Is it a unicorn? Because I think I deserve something magical and mystical for not shoving her."

"Even more spectacular than a unicorn, if you can believe it."

"Is it your smile?" I teased, drawing out the smirk I adored.

"Even better than that." Von grimaced. "I think somewhere Danny just vomited at our cuteness. Totally worth it." He withdrew a piece of paper from his jeans pocket and dangled it with a wicked grin. "Tell me I'm the best shag of your life."

"Hands down. Though, you're the only shag of my life, so the competition's not all that steep."

"Fair enough. I'm so very grateful you and Mason are still in the kissing phase of your relationship. I'm working my way up to actually being worried about your answer someday." He kissed me two more times, lazy and luscious, just how I liked it. "Tell me you constantly lust over my arse."

"Fortnightly," I admitted, fanning myself. "I walked smack into a telephone pole the other day because I was picturing you shaking your groove thang in a slow mambo."

"Mm. Did your fantasy go something like this?" Of course Von pulls me out of my chair and starts up a tame mambo. Of course Von knows *how* to mambo. His hips always tantalized me; I love the way we feel when we're fused together in any sort of dance. Even while wearing a backpack filled with Judge's things, he's still smooth and lithe in his movements, seducing me as easily as breathing.

"Exactly like this, only you were more naked, and we weren't here." I motioned around Judge's home.

"Mm. I was naked. What were *you* wearing?"

My breasts were pushed up against him, my stomach taut and my hips moving where he directed. This wasn't my first dance with Von, after all. "I was wearing baggy pajamas, eating popcorn while you shimmied for me."

He closed his eyes in a hiss of feigned lust. "Don't tell me they were flannel. You know that's my undoing."

I leaned up on my toes while we danced and whispered in his ear my very sexiest, "Smelly. Dirty. Red. Flannel."

He tugged on my hand and led me toward the stairs. "That's it. I must have you now. Judge won't mind if we use his bed. He's got a thing for you, after all. He'd probably be all for it."

I mime-barfed through laughter that bubbled out of me as I shook my head. "Gross! He's like my brother. Okay,

okay. Enough seduction. What's my present you found me?"

In true Von fashion, he bent down on one knee to present me with my gift. After all, a present with no flourish isn't an occasion. Von makes everything an event. He beamed as he presented me with a piece of paper. "I've brought you garbage, my eternal love."

I sat down and leaned my elbows on the table. "You know the old standards like flowers and chocolates? They're still good." I reached into my pocket and pulled out my hand sanitizer, cringing that I've just touched hands that had been digging in the garbage.

He unfolded the scrap of paper and smacked it on the table, sliding it toward me. "This is better. People leave all sorts of things in the rubbish bin. Darius' bin was particularly fascinating." He ran his finger down the list of the names, and only then did I realize Darius had made a list of the countries in Terraway, with a few crossed out and one country circled. "I think I've just scored us a lead on Ollie's whereabouts. Fancy a trip to Hayop?"

13

SINGLE BED

"Whatever. I'm going." My stubborn streak, I'd learned, was only matched by Ezra's. You wouldn't think it to look at the man, but he could be a real pill when he insisted on ridiculous things, like my safety.

"I think we've established that you're going to go to work with Von or Mason, and that's the name of that tune."

Von and Mason were busy talking about the best routes to take through Hayop as they sat on the stools at the kitchen counter. Though the mansion had plenty of space, they were both wary to let me out of their sight. Something about me being a flight risk. Such drama queens.

With my fists on my hips, I narrowed my eyes at Ezra,

gearing up for round three. We'd been going around and around this all day, and I was determined to win.

Unfortunately, so was Ezra.

"Is Hayop dangerous?" I challenged, my chin raised. "I'm not pregnant, so no one in the land of Matruculans is going to try to attack me so they can eat my baby."

Ezra pinched the bridge of his nose. "Hayop isn't dangerous, but whatever it is that Ollie's involved with was clearly something so treacherous he didn't want you near it. I've already alerted King Carter to keep an eye out for Ollie. Patience, my dear."

"Patience? Are you freaking kidding me, Ezra?"

Von shushed me as only he could without incurring my wrath. "Darling, Ana's asleep upstairs, and so is Judge. Let's not wake them."

"Sorry." I hadn't meant to raise my voice, but something about Ezra's totally calm demeanor got under my skin faster than most other things could.

It wasn't until Von's mom meandered into the kitchen that I stood straighter and assumed a less aggressive tone. "Did I miss something exciting?"

Lavinia Vandershot was the picture of poise at all times. Despite the brewing rumble in the kitchen, she was composed. Her black waves were pulled back in a full bun, showing off the angular cheekbones she'd passed down to her eldest boy. There was a clarity to her voice that I was apparently lacking, if I still hadn't convinced Ezra that he was being a butthead. I blame his upper hand and her decorum on that British accent.

"No, ma'am," I muttered.

Ezra made to reach for her hand but caught himself, freezing and looking around guiltily before he slid his hands into his own pockets. As if we all didn't know they'd been hooking up for like, nearly two years. Ezra cleared his throat. "October Grace is worried about her brother's disappearance, though there doesn't seem to be any foul play afoot. Oliver left a note, took a friend and went to Terraway on a personal errand. October is overreacting, and wants to go track him down herself."

Lavinia Vandershot sized up the sternness of my chin as if that's all she needed to come to a conclusion. "You know where he's at in Terraway?"

I motioned to the note, which I still hadn't touched, since it had been found by Von in a trash can. "Best we can tell is he went to Hayop, so that's where I want to go."

Lavinia nodded once, and I saw a bit of the same stubborn streak I clung to with such ferocity. "Very well. Ezra, last I heard, Hayop was in a state of peace. Has that changed?"

"No, but…"

I stood taller, loving the direction this conversation was taking. Ezra could say no to me all he wanted, but he squirmed at denying Lavinia Vandershot anything.

"King Carter is King Mason's brother. I trust we would

have the utmost security and comfort for the Omen in Hayop?"

Ezra balked at her but it was Von who spoke up. "We? So you're going on missions to Terraway now?"

"Is that a problem?" Lavinia was shorter than Von but when she glared at him, she looked whole feet taller. Maybe that's because Von shrank marginally under the weight of her authority. Either way, it was totally cute to see my lassiez-faire husband clench up so tightly.

Von tried to regain himself but his voice was higher in pitch now and his movements restrained. "Of course not. I was going to suggest the same thing. Family trip to Hayop. What could be better?" Then, so subtly I barely caught it, the corners of Von's mouth quirked. "I trust we can tell Mason to have his brother book a single bedroom for you in Hayop's castle?"

Ezra whirled around to open the fridge, as if overcome with hunger all of a sudden.

Lavinia's tone turned sharp as her cheeks flushed. "Of course I wouldn't require anything other than a single bed. I don't know why you'd suggest otherwise."

"I think you know why," Von teased, traipsing on the line all of us firmly pretended we couldn't see, so we didn't dare cross it. Leave it to Von to dance along the forbidden edge with a smile on his face. "Now who would Mum want in her bed these days? I mean, two years. You'd think we'd all assume by now you'd prefer a double bed."

With her eyes wide, her posture rose impossibly

further. "Von Vandershot, I'm sure I don't know what you're talking about. You'll stop this nonsense this minute!"

"Then I still have fifty-nine seconds to discuss the thing that's got you all twisted for some odd reason?" Von paused to let out a devilish chuckle. "You're all flushed, Mum. I can't imagine why. No favorite son of yours would want you sleeping in a single bed you'll be begging to share with..." he paused a solid three seconds before "Anastasia" tumbled out of his mouth, deflating Lavinia in the next breath.

"Oh! Oh, yes of course." She gusted out a laugh, her hand on her breastbone. "Yes, please. Mason, if you don't mind, I should like my granddaughter to sleep with me, if she likes."

Mason had been watching the whole exchange with his sandwich still half-raised to his mouth. "Um, sure. Of course Carter can get you whatever you need. We're really doing this, then? We're going to Hayop? Bringing Ana and the whole family?"

Before Ezra could pull his head out of the fridge to answer, a little voice that had stolen my heart over and over again called for me.

"Mama?"

I relinquished my hold on Von's hand and trotted out of the kitchen, through the hallway, past the entrance, toward the living room and to the base of the stairs. "Baby doll, what are you doing out of bed?"

"Mama, up," she said by way of explanation, holding her chubby little hands out to me.

I didn't need to be told twice. I ran up the steps and scooped her in my arms. Her silky black hair was just long enough to be put into pigtails, but the braids I'd fashioned always fell out by morning. I kissed the button nose of my round-faced angel. Mariang looked up at me through the aqua eyes of her daughter, and I was struck anew with love for the girl who would never know one of the sweetest souls in all of Terraway or Topside.

14

DANNY'S GIRLS

I shot Anastasia a look of scolding that neither of us bought. "I think it's bedtime, little treasure. Past bedtime, actually. Where's daddy?"

She pointed toward the base of the stairs to where Von was standing like Romeo beneath Juliet's balcony. "Do you need help, Peach?"

"Daddy, song." Ana begged so pitifully, I didn't know how Von could be expected to say no to her.

Von flitted up the steps in record time, resisting the urge to take her from my arms. "You want a song? I think that can be arranged. Where's your other daddy? He doesn't sing near as well as me, but he's got to be around here somewhere."

"Daddy sleepy," she complained, clinging to me. I loved the feel of her arms around my neck, declaring to the world that I was her safe place.

"Oh, that silly daddy," I tsked, moving toward her bedroom.

She whined and pointed instead to Von's and my room. "No! Mama sleep!"

I turned toward Von with inquisitive eyebrows, but Von shook his head. "Nice try, tiny mastermind. You know that when Uncle Mason's here, you can't stow away in our bed. You can sleep in your crib or with daddy."

"Daddy," she ruled, her eyes fixed on Danny's door.

I kissed Von's shoulder. "I'll go get her water cup. Sing your song without the flourish, or she'll be even more awake than she is now."

Von scoffed. "I can't believe you'd ever want me without flourish. I don't think I come any other way, love."

"You break it, you bought it. If you insist on being entertaining, you're staying up with her tonight." I handed off Anastasia Grace to Von and moved to her bedroom to grab the beloved blankie Allie had fashioned from one of Mariang's favorite dresses. She'd made two, in case we ever lost one. I often worried what might happen if we couldn't locate Ana's pink silk blankie. At this point, I was fully prepared to send her to college with the thing.

I thought Von would pull away to rock her on his hip, but he followed me into the baby room and leaned in for a kiss. It wasn't deep enough of a swoon to whisk me away to our makeout place, but just enough to remind me how much I truly did love Von with all of his theatrics. Then he sang to Ana while I fished out her nighttime props.

On our way down the hall toward Danny's room, I cracked the door to Ollie's bedroom, where Judge was crashing. He'd drunk far too much when we'd brought him here, since he was too beside himself with grief to go back to his home. Though Judge and I were still a bit touchy with each other, given the state of our tempers, we both knew I wouldn't abandon him when he needed me.

By the tearstains down the side of his face that the hallway light illuminated with its faint glow, I guessed that Judge would be needing me for quite some time. I realized how sacred I held that truth, counting it a privilege to look after my family, no matter the state in which they came to me.

A wave of agony tightened my stomach when I pictured Terence as I remembered him during his last day on earth. I didn't tell him I loved him. I'm not sure he heard me the other times. Did he understand that I cared how his life turned out? Did he feel appreciated? Did he know that I loved him for fixing my bike when I was little? For letting me read to him, sharing whole imaginary worlds together?

Maybe he didn't know I loved him at all.

I shut the door, unsure I would ever be ready for the grief that had Judge firmly in its clutches. I moved down to the other brother who was further along in his battle with grief.

"Danny?" I whispered, cracking his door open. "Danny, it's your night with Ana, and the crib isn't cutting it."

Danny was technically on baby duty, but Ana usually found her way into our bed every other night when we stayed at the mansion two weeks out of every month.

Yes, the math added up that Von and I had to be sneaky and really try to get moments alone. Neither of us were all that thrilled with our marriage being so thoroughly invaded, but Ezra was firm that double-pulling was necessary in helping me live longer, so Mason slept with us two weeks a month while we lived at my house on Lenoy Avenue. During the other two weeks... Danny just plain wasn't ready to be a full-time parent. Some days Danny wasn't equipped to do even the normal things, like take a shower or remember to eat. To entrust him with a baby worried everyone. So Von and I took care of Anastasia Grace during the half of the month Mason was in Sombi. She slept in our bed many of those nights so Von could pull for us both in his sleep.

Taking care of Danny had somehow fallen to me, since I was pretty much the only person he communicated with in more than just grunts and glares.

It was a broken system, to be sure, but it was holding, however tenuously. Von had joked with no bite or resentment whatsoever that he was the husband, Mason was my boyfriend, and Danny was my wounded, three-legged puppy. He was not wrong.

When I opened his bedroom door, Danny groaned and rolled over to face me, his eyes refusing to open. "Danny,

Anastasia's awake. She wants to sleep in here tonight. If that's not cool, you'll need to put her back to sleep yourself. I need you to give handling stuff like this more of an honest effort."

Danny shifted under the covers. His room was military-clean, but that was mostly because he didn't fiddle with much. He didn't have any hobbies, interests or passions. He was stuck in his abyss. I was the only one who refused to leave him alone—for better or worse. "Bring her on in. I'm too tired to reason with a two-year-old."

I set down the water sippy cup and the blankie, taking in Danny's short dark hair and the grump lines across his forehead that only grew more pronounced when he was roused in the night. He always looked tired now, no matter the time of day, but I suppose some things can't be helped. I'd taken him to get his hair cut so he looked presentable for his mama. Danny didn't even have the wherewithal to care if his hair touched his ears, which he'd always been a stickler for.

When Von came in with Ana at the tail end of his song, he laid her down in the bed next to Danny and kissed her forehead. "Goodnight, my little raspberry."

Yeah, it was impossible not to fall in love with Von.

When I made to leave, Danny reached up and gripped my hand but locked eyes with Von. Before he spoke, I knew what he was going to ask for. "Ten minutes?"

Von nodded without hesitation. "Of course, little

brother. Whatever you need. If October has ten minutes, that's fine. It's up to her." He kissed my shoulder and brushed his hand across the small of my back. "I'll be downstairs, Peach."

I waited for Von to exit, the room growing quiet as Ana burrowed into Danny's side, her thumb finding its way into her mouth. Everyone like, super has an opinion about kids sucking their thumbs, to which I unblinkingly replied, "This baby lost her mama on the day she was born. She can suck her thumb until she goes to Harvard, if that's what gets her through."

I was still feeling my way through motherhood. And learning how to talk to people, apparently.

"You doing okay, Chief?" I asked Danny in a whisper.

"If you're going to make me talk, then forget it."

"Well, with an invitation like that, what woman wouldn't want to climb into bed with you?"

"Shut up and get in." He patted the empty spot on his other side.

I folded my arms, unwilling to respond to such a degrading offer. "Try again."

Danny harrumphed, though we'd been through this exchange enough times for him to understand how he should talk to me. "Please," he whispered, blinking up at me with actual vulnerability shining through his emotional blockades.

The sheets smelled of Danny, which wasn't a bad thing, but I didn't like that I knew what his sheets smelled like at all. About a dozen times a month, Danny invited me to snuggle in his bed, usually with him and Ana. Being so connected to Mariang as he'd been, living the single dad life was a transition he was still in the process of making. The nights were hard for him, so he often asked Von if I could rest with him for a little bit, just to calm his nerves. That had been one long conversation. The Vandershot brothers had tried pulling for Danny, we'd gone through options of nightcaps, sleeping pills, tea, but the only thing that calmed him down so he could sleep through the night seemed to be... me. Though I wasn't Duwende, somehow I'd become Danny's Puller, quieting the turmoil inside of him when nothing else would.

I pried up the covers and laid down on my back, the outside of my thigh touching his. "Long day?" I asked quietly. It was both unnatural and normal as breathing to lay in bed with Danny.

"It was fine. Less eventful than yours. Still no word from Ollie?"

I shook my head, swallowing the lump in my throat.

"He'll turn up."

We started each night together the same way—with the outside of our thighs touching. Then Danny would snake his arm under my shoulders, tipping me on my side to cradle me closer. He never relaxed fully until my nose was touching his neck, the sharp edge of his jaw resting against my forehead. Then he could finally indulge in the deep breathing that meant he could get some real sleep.

It was weird, to be certain. Weirder still when my hand knew it belonged on his sternum. Danny and I had seen each other through too many highs and lows to be able to leave each other to weather life's storms alone. Not many understood Danny, but I did. Or, well, I tolerated him better than most, which I think counts as understanding.

"Oh, that's much better," he sighed, his eyes darting to his daughter to confirm she was asleep. It was the cuddle that relaxed him, for sure, but it was also the fact that he pulled for me in these quiet moments. He needed the job, even though his position had abandoned him. "You're all wound up about Ollie." His arm moved slowly over my back, and I could feel him pulling the cleverly masked anxiety from my entire being. "Are Von and Mason completely dropping the ball?"

"No, they're upset about it too. We're doing the best we can to concoct a plan without losing our minds to panic."

"You're an Omen," he reminded me, as if I didn't know. "Their stress should be secondary to yours. I'll talk to them. Get them refocused so they remember the point of the job."

"No need. I'm not fragile."

Danny touched each of my fingers that rested atop his sternum, going down the row until he'd stroked the tension out of each one. His voice was low and had a slight rumble to it whenever he laid with me like this. "You're not invincible, either. I'll take care of it."

I didn't know if I should be confiding in Danny, who

was basically about as emotionally mature as a slug. But in the quiet of the bedroom, my worries spilled out into the dark. "I reaped Terence," I confessed, though he already knew as much. Still, I felt the need to confess it over and over, admitting to the world that I was a terrible person, capable of stealing the soul from a human.

Danny's hand rubbed up and down over my ribs. He didn't respond, but pulled a fair amount of agony from me the moment my words hit the air.

"Judge tried to kill himself!" I whispered. Though I'd been composed and focused on Ana and our trip to Hayop minutes ago, as soon as I confided in Danny, I felt embarrassing pressure building up behind my eyes. My lashes slammed shut, as if that might hide me from the agony that swarmed when the mental image of that awful night plagued my mind.

Danny pulled again but it wasn't strong enough. When I moved my hand off his chest so I could scratch my skin, he caught my fingers and replanted them where they belonged over his heart. "Not like that. Easy, honey. Don't you know that I'm here?" He waited for my sullen nod and the extra close snuggle I couldn't stop myself from indulging in whenever he called me sweet names in the dark. "That's right. If I'm here, you don't bleed."

"It feels better when I do," I choked out, my hands begging to be scraped at. "It hurts too badly to think about it all."

He sent another dose of pulling into my body,

siphoning off the edge I was constantly driving myself towards. "I'm not going to let my girl hurt herself tonight. Tonight, you talk instead of bleed." He only ever spoke to me so sweetly under cover of darkness. In the quiet of the night, Danny saw right through me. He pressed his lips to my forehead. "There's more. I can feel it building."

"I don't know where Ollie's gone!" At this, my tears spilled over onto his jaw. "He would never leave me like this. He knows it would make me crazy. And Darius would never ignore Judge's phone calls. Something's wrong!"

Danny's fingers lazily traced up and down my wrist that rested atop his heart. "If something's this wrong, I'll help you fix it. If you're going to Hayop, I'll come too."

"You don't have to do that," I protested through a sob.

"Yeah, I do. It's my job to protect the throne." Only it wasn't. Danny froze at his knee-jerk statement but I didn't call him on it. That *had* been his job when Mariang was his charge. Now he was retired. He pulled again and again until my shoulders relaxed and my tears finally tapered off.

The sound of Ana's steady baby breaths soothed us both for a few beats. Danny loved to have Ana on one side and me on the other. "His girls," he called us when no one else was around to witness the cuteness. He scooped Ana on his left and me with his right arm, inhaling the top of her head before turning to do the same to me. I felt his chest swell, as if he'd been holding off taking in a full breath until we were both within reach.

He leaned in and slowly kissed my lips three times—a

thing he did in lieu of saying goodnight or thank you. Of all the things I never thought I'd learn about Danny, I now knew that he relished slow kisses. Everything else about him was abrupt and harsh, but his lips were soft and took their time, introducing me to swirls of brown that danced behind my eyelids, then sparkled with flashes of glittering bronze as they cascaded downward.

Yes, Von knew. Yes, Mason knew. Neither of them dared take away the small concession Danny had asked of his life, because some days, I was the only person who could coax Danny out of bed.

The bronze didn't tease, but gave us what we wanted—comfort and something solid to hold onto. My hand rubbed over Danny's chest, drawing out the baritone noise of contentment I treasured. That deep purring sound made me feel like perhaps not everything broken in the world would always remain so very hopeless.

That was our pattern: three slow, long, tender kisses that lasted several minutes, his soothing moan, a kiss to my nose while we blinked away the brown and gold psychedelic lightshow, and then sleep.

"Goodnight, honey."

"Goodnight, Danny."

Then Danny settled into his pillow, and about two minutes later, he was snoring softly.

I'm not sure any therapist would bless our family with the label of "healthy," but when we'd been through all that we'd endured, we scrambled for anything that might get us closer to being functional. I'd learned that sometimes functional was the most you could hope for. It was one notch above bare-bones survival.

I snuggled into Danny's chest, wishing far more for him than this. Far more for him than me.

15

KINGS AND LIARS

"I'm not sure how you talked me into this. I have people out looking for Ollie right now. There's absolutely no reason for us to be in Hayop."

Ezra's stream of regret hadn't let up the entire time during our trip down to his, Levi's and Mason's homeland, but that didn't dampen my Matruculan Reaper's spirits. Mason breathed in the air with a deep sense of satisfaction that radiated from his smile. His chest was barreled more than usual with the pride that came from showing us around his childhood home. "Ezra, you'll be setting up in here. I'm sorry I couldn't swing more rooms, but some of them were already booked. Would you mind sharing with Lavinia? I can have them send up a second mattress."

Ezra paused his rant, his movements careful. "Oh, um, yes. Of course. I shouldn't mind that at all, if that's alright with you, Lavinia."

Mama Vandershot did a good job of attempting to compose her excitement. "Not at all. Happy to accommodate."

I sniggered quietly to Von. As if the King of Hayop didn't have a million rooms available for Ezra, who ran the council. Our "Parent Trap" wasn't exactly subtle, but it did the trick.

King Carter was... pleasantly ridiculous. He was loud, goofy and winked with the smarm of a man who knew he was in his prime at the ripe old age of thirty-one. "Mason, you should wear the robes with our family crest when you go out. It's not every day the King of Sombi returns to his home. And with the Omen, the future Omen and their entourage? I can't think of anything better. When you wanted to arrange this, I admit, I thought you were joking."

Mason's grin hadn't dimmed since we'd crossed into his childhood home. "I missed my dear baby brother. Tell me you've planned a feast for us. Tell me there'll be dancing and music and all the things I've missed about this place."

Carter slapped his brother on the back but shook Levi's hand with a respectful bow. "Absolutely. And anything you need, please do let me know. We're honored to have Hayop's Immortal staying with us."

Levi stood with his chest barreled and his spine straight, taking Mason's spot on my left when Mason moved down the hallway to greet one of the servants he recognized. "Thank you, King Carter. I'd like an update on any leads you might have as to the whereabouts of my son."

"Ah, yes. Business talk. We almost made it through the tour of the sleeping quarters, but alas, now we're to have the serious talks." At Levi's narrowed eyes, Carter sobered marginally, which looked like a real strain for him. The crinkles around the corners of his slate eyes begged to be put to use smiling whenever levity drifted off his face. "No, sir. There's been no sight of Oliver, but I've got several soldiers searching the nation. Are you certain he came here?"

Judge had been silent that entire morning, buried in his grief as we shuffled him from our home to Ezra's, and now to Hayop. He didn't seem to care much where he landed, only that we were together and moving closer to finding Darius. When he spoke up, I craned my head to study the oddity. "October, I need to talk to you. Any of these rooms good for some privacy?" he asked Mason when my Puller trotted back to us, making a point not to ask Carter about his own palace, but addressed Mason instead.

Mason shrugged. "Sure. This one's yours." He aimed his thumb toward the room next to Ezra's.

Judge met my eyes and jerked his chin for me to join him. The entire palace had a rustic but lavish theme. It was hard to put it into one category. Everything was hand-hewn wood with iron fixtures throughout. The ceilings were covered with light blue paint embellishments and accents of gold, giving a sense of artistry to the roughness. It felt like it was trying to be an enormous hunter's fort, but for a really posh nature enthusiast. There were branches twisted along the crown moldings with gold grape clusters drawing your eyes upward.

Judge had business on his face, so I'm guessing he hadn't been distracted by the grapes hanging from the ceiling. I trotted into the bedroom with Von by my side, shutting the door behind us. "What's up?" I asked lightly, though I could tell a storm was brewing behind Judge's dark eyes. It was the most animated I'd seen him in days.

Judge's upper lip curled at the sight of my hand in Von's. "What's up is that you should know by now when someone's lying to your face. You're twenty-five years old, October. You seriously didn't catch that? This Carter guy knows where Ollie's at. There aren't any soldiers out looking for him."

My mouth fell open. "What are you talking about? Carter's not on trial, here. He's a good guy. Hello, he's Mason's brother."

Judge shrugged, letting me know that none of that mattered. His intuition trumped all other logic. "I don't care about that. All I care about is that this fool thinks he's slick enough to lie to our faces. I only pulled you in here because I don't know all the rules for Terraway. Can I get the information out of him my way, or do I have to like, ask Ezra to beat it out of him?"

"I love how much faith you have that Ezra's soul is as

damaged as yours. Ezra wouldn't beat the information out of someone."

Von shot me a look that suggested I had no idea what I was talking about. "Ezra doesn't hesitate to get the job done—whatever job it is. You say Carter's lying? Let me bring Mason in."

Judge sighed. "Yes, let's bring in the brother of the liar. That'll go over great."

Von tilted his head at Judge. "Well, it's not going over at all unless Mason okays it. I would never forgive him if he started in on my brothers without me knowing every step of it. Mason and I have no secrets. We share everything."

Judge narrowed his eyes at me, looking so harsh that I flinched. "Yes, including some things that shouldn't be shared."

Von ignored Judge's dig and ducked his head out. "Continue on the tour without us, everyone. Official Omen business. Oy, Mason. In here."

"Daddy, up," Ana called to Von, whose tone turned syrupy on a dime.

"Of course, my sweet raspberry. Daddy's here." He arrested Ana from Danny's side and hoisted her in the air. "Danny, do see that Mum gets settled in, yeah?"

He scowled, looking very much like Frankenstein's monster. "Alright. But if something's off, I want in on it. I'm still a Reaper."

Von nodded, swallowing the lump in his throat. "Of

course, Danny. If anything's amiss, you'll know about it first thing."

Von ushered Mason in, then shut us in the room, meeting my eyes while he cradled Ana on his hip. He caught Mason up with a few succinct sentences, at which Mason scoffed. "No, you can't forcefully interrogate the King of Hayop."

Judge, if you can imagine, took the firm limitation smashingly. The two went back and forth, which I had no interest in paying attention to, since Mason had home court advantage.

The sound of Von's song was a welcome distraction while Judge and Mason kept arguing. "Daddy's sweet princess picks ten roses, then gives them each a sniff." Then he counted to ten, kissing her nose after each number. "Daddy's sweet princess picks ten daisies, then gives them each a sniff."

I listened through seven more flower varieties, which Ana giggled through. There were so many things I wanted to say to him, but we were always surrounded by half a dozen other people. When he finished his song, I was glued to his side.

"Darling, stop it with those bedroom eyes. Can't you see there's a child in the room?"

I couldn't wait. I kissed his lips, drawing him from reality just long enough to remember the good parts of the life we shared with so very many people.

"If you're finished making out, there's actual business to discuss," Judge groused.

Von smirked. "Oh, well if you're waiting until we're finished, then perhaps we don't have to hurry. Come, Peach. Let's have a good, long snog. Judge will wait."

I brushed my nose across his, and then did the same with Ana, who was accustomed to both her daddies kissing Mama.

Then Von pulled back and smirked at Mason. "She needs to be kissed, Mason. Do your duty, Reaper."

Mason went from frustrated with Judge to smirking at me. He gave me two small kisses, which was just enough to reconnect us.

When I sensed Judge was about to blow, I turned to face him, stepping away from Ana, as if that might help distance her from any unsavory talk about to go down. "Alright, let's get to the heart of it. Why do you think Carter's lying?"

Judge glowered at me. "Um, sight? It was plain as day!" When I didn't accept his sass for an answer, he harrumphed. "If you think I'm going to explain how I know things it's taken me years to understand, we don't have that kind of time. Not if we want Darius and Ollie back. Mason's being difficult. Would Ezra let me force the truth out of Carter? That's all I need to know."

I shook my head. "Not on a hunch, no. We can talk with Carter and see what comes about, but nothing more than that without actual proof."

Judge groaned. "Your way is going to take forever."

"Yes, but my way keeps you out of jail. I've seen you interrogate people without force, and it works just fine."

"Then what's the plan? You know this guy better than I do." He met my gaze with determination, which was the most clarity I'd seen in his eyes in days. His depression was still there, but his willingness to plan something showed me he wasn't all for throwing in his last chips at life any time soon. That was the hope, at least.

I turned to the door, wondering what the right move was—trust or interrogation. My eyes closed as the verdict came out with a heavy sigh. "I think we'll need some liquor."

16

ELEVATED STATUS

"Why are you grinning? We're about to accuse a king of lying to us." Judge walked with Von, Ana and me down toward one of the receiving rooms. Since it wasn't often that I traveled to Terraway, Carter made a big deal about it, calling in other super special dignitaries and whatnot. I mean, I'd seen them all at the last council meeting but apparently this was a big to-do that needed to happen. It was sweet of Carter to throw us a party before the big nationwide hurrah in the morning, but the formality of it all made me nervous.

I shrugged at Judge's gruff nature, my smile still in place. "I just never get to do stuff like this with you. Feels like our own equivalent of a family photo. Interrogating someone together. Who would've thought?"

Judge snorted at my humor. "I guess life's just funny

like that sometimes. Is Mason back yet? This won't work if he doesn't have what we need."

"He'll be here. He had to port to the mansion, then back to Hayop and run all the way from the porting spot to the castle carrying a bag with breakables. Give him time."

"I want Darius home. He should know his brother died."

I nodded, my smile fading. Terence was dead and our brothers were missing. Though I didn't reach for Judge often, I sifted my fingers through his while we walked. The urge to scrub my hands clean of germs was strong, but the need to keep my Judge close to me when life shifted uncertainly was stronger.

"Alright, baby girl," he said of my palpable nerves. "We'll find them."

Ana reached for me from her perch in Von's arms. "Mama, up!" she demanded with all the sweetness of a cherub.

I dropped Judge's hand and held Ana on my hip while we walked. "What do you think, little treasure? Are you ready to see King Carter?"

Ana reached over and felt Judge's face, pinching his nose and chin to investigate without preamble or permission. Kids are cute like that. Then she held out her hands to him. "Up?"

Judge scowled at Ana, who was used to her biological father's surly demeanor. She held her own pretty well against Judge's curled upper lip. "No. Manipulate these two all you want, but I've got a brother to find."

"Up?" she insisted, just as stubborn to get her way.

"No." Then he shook his head at me. "You've completely spoiled her. You were never so demanding when you were little."

I stopped in my tracks, my blood running cold as I turned to snarl at Judge. "Von, take Ana to Danny. I'll meet up with you."

Von obliged in arresting Ana from me but didn't move down the hallway. "Can't leave you without a Reaper, Peach. Have at it, though. I won't stop you."

I didn't want Ana to see my angry face, but it couldn't be helped as I scowled at Judge. "Listen to me, Judge. I wasn't demanding when I was little because a big, fat nothing would be offered to me if I did. If Bev would've held me, I would've done anything to get that to happen. Ana's mama can't hold her, so that's our job. If she needs something, she gets it. If she wants something as simple as a hug, we don't hold back. I turned out the messed-up way I did in part because I didn't have a mama to pick me up when I was too little to understand how to do that for myself. That girl's had a harder life from day one than either you or I have ever known. We had our mamas for years, for better or worse. She didn't get half an hour with Mariang. Your tough love crap is no good to her. I won't let you pull your garbage on Ana. Not when she's sweet enough to call me her mama. I won't stand for it."

Judge held up his hands. "Fine. I get it. You feel responsible for her. I'll be nice."

"Not good enough. You'll make up stories about dragons and princesses, the way you did for me when I was too young to understand that my life would never have the right kind of magic to it. You'll teach her how to tie her shoes and anything else you taught me without a single disparaging comment. If all of us try our best, it might be one-tenth the goodness Mariang would've poured into Anastasia. I won't settle for a half-effort from you. Not on my watch."

Judge stood taller, reminding me just who the adult was in the equation. "I think you need to check your tone. I know you're not ordering me around."

I held my ground, trying (and failing) to keep the emotion out of my eyes. I missed Mariang badly. The unfairness of her entire life and death squeezed me tight around my chest. I was failing. I'd lost my brother, lifelong friends were getting killed, and on top of that, there were little girls in the world who needed things I couldn't give them. Anastasia needed her birth mama, and I knew I was a poor substitute for the real thing.

The lie my mean brain often spouted in moments of weakness surfaced with a cool, *"Nature knew you'd be a crap mother, so your baby was taken away before you could mess her up the same way Bev messed you up."*

I ran my tongue across my teeth as I scraped at the scabs on the back of my hand, pushing the falsity down as best I could. "I'll do whatever it takes to make sure Anastasia believes in rainbows and hugs. She will live a good life, Judge, so help me. One of us is getting out of this with their childhood intact. If it can't be you and it can't be me, it'll be Ana."

Judge's shoulders deflated not in defeat, but in sadness, as if my melancholy had leapt off of me and infiltrated his defenses. "Okay, okay. I get it. You're trying to do right by Mariang, taking care of her kid as best you know how. I can play along, if that's what you need."

When Judge pulled me into his arms, a wave of sadness roiled inside of me, putting too much pressure behind my eyes. I knew if I blinked, tears would fall all over him, which was something I wasn't willing to permit. "Every little girl needs her Judge. I don't know what I would've done without you to make me feel like I was worth reading stories to and playing games with. When you kicked us out?" I shook my head into his chest. "Don't do that to Ana."

He shushed me, cupping the back of my head. His kiss to my forehead set loose a single tear, for which he earned a solid "knock it off" from me. He chuckled at my surliness whenever I was pushed over the edge. "It's okay. I'm here now. Anastasia can have her Judge, if that's what you want. Fat lot of good that ever did you." He held me for a solid minute, and with every second that ticked by, I could feel his angst building. His chest tightened and his arms tensed around me until his anxiety bubbled out. "Darius is in trouble. I can feel it."

I knew it would take both of us pushing hard against the world if we were to get our brothers back. No one else seemed to understand the urgency with which the situation should be treated. "Ollie should've been back too. He would never leave for so long like this."

"I know. Darius, neither. We'll get them back, baby girl."

We walked the rest of the way to the receiving room, my smile working its way onto my face as we strolled into the grand space. The hearth took center stage as the focal point for the huge area that could seat eighty comfortably. Everyone was milling about, but upon our arrival, they all bowed. Of course, that was after I jumped at the sound of my name being shouted into the room. "All bow to Lady October, the Omen who redeemed Hayop and all of Terraway!"

The sound of everyone taking a knee made my stomach drop. I never knew what to do in these situations. Mariang would've given a gracious bow of acknowledgment. For some reason, I decided giving everyone a two-fingered casual wave would suffice. Hopefully that was at least better than a thumbs-up. I suddenly wished I was wearing something more sophisticated than old jeans and my purple Peewee Herman t-shirt.

I was handling it alright until I saw that there wasn't a single person standing. I began to scratch the backs of my hands, my breath quickening when Ezra and Levi took a knee, Danny, Lavinia and even Judge. Worst of all was Mason and Von. I didn't want my husband and my boyfriend bowing to me. It was gross and weird and they deserved the accolade just as much. The look I shot them both had a plea to it, begging them to forgive me for... I wasn't sure, but I needed not to be separate from them on a status level. I didn't want them to think I assumed I was above them. Without them, I would be useless, stuck indoors and unable to touch a single person, for fear of accidentally reaping them and sending myself into a state of hypothermia.

Mason saw my distress and nodded once with a reassuring smile, letting me know that he understood that this scene wasn't me. Though I was acting the part of the important person, it wouldn't change who we were to each other. He touched his heart to let me know where my home was, and I was given the certain reminder that I loved everything about him.

I scraped at the backs of my hands, anxious at the eyes on me. Von rose, pulling Mason up so the two of them could flank me after Von handed Ana off to Ezra.

Danny followed the guys; the unspoken need for my Reapers triggering him to step forward as well. He stood behind me, running his curled finger down my spine to brush off a layer of nervousness. His scowl and broad shoulders reminded everyone that Ezra's daughter was well-protected.

The simple touch reminded me that I was loved.

Von took one of my hands and Mason clung to the other, the two of them silently warning me that they wouldn't permit any harm to come my way—even if it was self-inflicted. I longed to scratch open the backs of my hands but they remained stubborn in their love for me. I adored them for the sweetness.

It was a statement the four of us were making—perhaps several declarations to our family and to the heads of Terraway as we presented ourselves as a united front.

17

SHAKING HANDS AND SCARRED ARMS

The whole shaking hands part of the job was my least favorite, but the councilmembers had brought their VIP officials to meet me (still blew my mind), so I played nice. Actually, I played normal. It was normal to shake people's hands and not wash your own three times between each encounter. It was normal not to screech when someone swiped at their nose and then shook your hand. I whimpered to Von, whose palm remained on my spine throughout. To everyone else, I'm sure he looked like the supportive husband. Only Mason and I knew he was pulling so I didn't get worked up so much that I had a meltdown. It was a fine line between my medication actually working and my Reapers filling in the gaps.

But I had to appear normal. If I didn't, it would spread far and wide that the Omen was sickly, disturbed, or otherwise compromised. It had been expected that Mariang always looked like she was on death's door. She'd been the only Omen for years before I was awakened. Gone were the days of a high weekly requirement for reaping souls. This was the Age of Prosperity, so they expected a healthy and thriving Omen. Ezra had made this fact very clear, and I was determined not to give the nations cause to worry.

So I smiled. I smiled through my panic and shook hands with strangers. Strangers with germs. Strangers with dirt under their fingernails. Strangers with clammy, unwashed palms. I tried to keep the shadows out of my eyes that came from the many nights spent screaming in pain after too much reaping. My body wasn't nearly as strong as it had been a mere handful of years ago. In your twenties, you weren't supposed to grow weaker, more frail.

But I could feel it.

Von cleared his throat, letting Mason know he needed blood, and my favorite Matruculan/Duwende would need to take over the pulling for a while. Von and I were so much better at not pushing the limits of his self-control than we had been while we were dating. He wasn't so riddled with self-loathing that he felt the need to cover over his baser instincts.

Von stepped away while Mason's hand replaced Von's on my back. Mason's calloused mitts were bigger, and capable of crushing a boulder without much effort. But he was only ever gentle with me these days. I think he'd seen me through too much to assume I'd come out the other end unscathed. Though my workload was lighter than it had ever been, he was careful with my body, as if I was still recovering from too many of life's grave injuries.

The way Mason touched me was as if I needed protecting, but it had also the flavor of being cradled to it. His whole body curved toward mine. It wasn't more than half a minute before I gravitated closer to his warmth, swallowing the mere inches of space between us because we both knew they didn't belong. My shoulder rested on his chest while I shook hand after hand. He was spoiling me with safety, and I adored him for not being stingy with the simple gift I craved. I remember back when I was hung up on public displays of affection, needing breathing room as often as I could grab at it. We'd all been through too much to deny each other affection, even if we looked odd to people when we indulged.

"Now, now. She was my fiancée before she was ever your girlfriend," came the voice that made me grin. "Have you missed your king, Lady October?"

I beamed up at the freshly-scrubbed Langgam, casting aside my fear of germs as I threw my arms around his neck. "Only every single minute of every single day. Hey, Ruiz. Klark." I winked at the two men who'd faithfully served the only upstanding member of Sakuna's royal family. "It's not often I get to see you all dressed up. Tell me the fanciness and the hair-combing are all for me." I stepped back and fanned myself, making a big deal of the man I usually saw tracking mud through Ezra's mansion during the monthly council meetings.

Lang kissed my cheek and brought Mason in for a muscle-laden man hug. Man hugs in Terraway are vastly different than dude hugs Topside. Dude hugs are usually one-armed pats on the back with no eye contact. If your stomachs accidentally touch? Forget about it. Man hugs from heroes who've been through whole countries and monarchies changing involve two arms, stomachs touching and deep inhales of contentment.

After being present through the solace of so many man hugs, dude hugs seemed kind of pathetic by comparison.

Ruiz and Klark bowed before joining Kabayo, who kept watching me furtively from across the room, though he'd kept his distance. When I raised my shoulders at him to silently ask what his deal was, he held up his wrist, showing off the scarred X mark on the light brown skin of his forearm. His pure black horse's head was menacing on its own, but his hard stare made him look that much more the part of the no-nonsense King of Silo who wasn't to be trifled with.

I shrank, shoving my matching X-shaped pink scar behind my back as if that might make us less linked. I was embarrassed that he'd no doubt felt my baser emotions I'd tried to keep quiet during Terence's death and Judge's suicidal tendencies thereafter. I wanted to feel those things privately because my grief was my own. The fact that Kabayo and I were linked so much that the giant reverse centaur could feel my more harrowing swings definitely had its downsides. Luckily, once he saw plainly that my distress was emotional and not physical, he kept to the other side of the room. He was probably afraid I'd spontaneously burst into tears on his giant shoulder or something.

Buhay shoots were passed around, along with *baga* roots for Judge and me. Mason went so far as to feed me the nasty root that ensured I had enough oxygen for a twenty-four-hour period, though I'd already had two. I returned the favor by feeding him a *buhay* shoot. I loved the way his gray eyes drank me in with equal amounts of intoxication, trust and gratitude.

"I love you," I admitted, taking a break from greeting people so I could gaze up at my Viking king. I thumbed a crumb off his lip, wondering if he could possibly be more handsome with his superhero body, hair to die for, and kindness glittering in eyes that always had a low current of lusty mischief to them.

He motioned around to the officials who spoke animatedly to each other. "I love that you're here. I know we're not in Hayop for just fun, but seeing you in my homeland, looking up at me like that?" He leaned in, his lips brushing my ear. "Let them all see you as my queen."

My girlish blush couldn't be helped. When he pulled out a bottle of hand sanitizer for me, I loved my Viking impossibly more.

18

OCTOBER GRACE, THE STUPID WAIF

That evening, King Carter organized a nationwide celebration in a huge amphitheater in the center of the capital of Hayop, complete with dancing, singing, and a dramatic reenactment of Sama's fateful end.

The cast was just large enough to tell the story of my Terraway life to the nation of Hayop, who watched with rapt fascination and delight at history being retold in such an entertaining fashion. The man who played Mason was burly, and everything he did was met with applause. He lifted heavy things often. Like, in every scene, whether it made sense to the story or not, some prop was hoisted up to demonstrate the insurmountable strength of the Matruculan people. I glanced to my right to watch real Mason's blush on his cheeks at being portrayed so heroically. If you've never had the pleasure of watching a burly man blush, it's just about the most endearing thing on the planet.

My portrayal was not quite as awe-inspiring. There I was—auburn curls and weak as a daisy. The actress fanned her face and screamed in distress each time Sama came upon her in a dream. The two even acted out a few of my psychically-hijacked dreams. They kissed with passion so real, I couldn't stop clawing at my arms. I hadn't known he was Sama. I didn't know he was real. He'd been the romantic hottie Philip to me back then. How stupid I must seem to the whole of Terraway, hoodwinked by the obvious villain who promised he was a prince.

After a few cursory kisses, they skipped over my all-too-willingness to hop into the sack with Philip in the reenactment. My frown tightened when I watched Philip forcing himself on me to get me pregnant, which I'm guessing was more palatable to them than me begging for another wild trip to D-town from the bad guy.

If you've never seen a dramatic interpretation of sexual assault being played out on your body, I do not recom-mend it. My stomach roiled with disgust and chagrin as I prayed for the scene to end quickly.

I was the waif in all of it, weak and stupid, though they never laughed at me. It was all played like I was naïve and a victim in all of it. I was someone to be pitied, which left a foul taste in my mouth. Didn't they understand that I was a hard worker? Didn't they know it was because of me reaping between bouts of puking my guts out that they had food at all? In their depictions, I was a confused teenager with no grand ambitions. I was Sama's plaything, and nothing more. Maybe I had been naïve, but watching the actress throw the back of her hand over her forehead in distress when she found out she was pregnant made me feel like the colossal joke, and very, very small.

The actor who played Von was handsome and charming, as to be expected. When the point in the story came about that I didn't know who the baby's father was, there was a gasp-inducing scene where actor-Von tugged on one arm while actor-Sama clawed at the other, with actress-me shrieking in utter woe in the middle.

So beside himself with disgust was actual Von that only the smell of my fresh blood ripped him from the play and back to the present. His nostrils flared as he glanced down in our VIP box seats and saw that I'd scraped too many lines across the backs of my hands. Crimson dotted the skin so much that it gathered and dripped onto the floor. It was probably inconsiderate of me to scratch myself to such extremes in front of my vampire husband, but as the play unfolded before us, I found I couldn't stop myself.

He made to hold my hand but stopped himself, pulling back with caution. "Darling, you have to stop. I only brought half a bag of blood with me." He cleared his throat again, and Mason turned his head to us, his eyes widening at our conundrum.

Ezra was on it, discreetly passing his satchel down to us, so Mason could dig through it and bandage my cuts.

Maybe I had grown weak. Shouldn't I be totally well-adjusted and all adult by now? Yet here I was, hurting my skin when the screaming in my soul grew too loud to silence.

The climate of Terraway had once been swelteringly hot, but now it was temperate—a mild spring evening with a cooling breeze to tease the auburn curls away from my face. All I felt was cold inside, watching the next act of Sama's final moments. I was horrified when Finn's death played out as if it was all entertainment to be clapped at.

It was a widely known story now—that Captain Finn had given his life to save Terraway. He'd been memorialized over and over again for it, but each time, my stomach turned. He didn't want the accolade. He would have wanted to still be alive, planning out the course of Dagat and... and...

And reading mermaid novels to me while I lounged in his arms, wearing nothing but his shirt.

Teasing my toes with a lust he'd never been able to mask.

Taking me into his bed where we pushed the boundaries of all that we had, and everything we both wanted.

I swallowed my grief, tucking it away to be dealt with never. My polite smile couldn't find its way to my lips, so disturbed was I at watching some of the worst moments of my life play out on the stage, one after the other. Not many knew of Finn's love for me, which I guess was good. At least that little tidbit hadn't made it into the script. No, in the play, Finn's love was for Terraway, and he died the hero who saved the stupid waif.

I didn't think I was the kind of person who needed credit or praise for a job well done, but in that moment, I felt jilted. It had been *my* idea to go see Sama in the first place. It had been me with the dagger I could feel now in my pocket, and my plan to murder Sama. Finn had just beaten me to it.

And it got him killed. *I* got him killed. My love was deadly, and I knew that as long as I lived, I would not be able to breathe with that weight.

My love kept Von near his greatest temptation. If he ingested too much human blood, he would turn rabid, unable to know who I was or who he was.

My love had gotten Mason's strength temporarily taken away from him.

My love made it so Ollie felt he had to sneak away in the dead of night on a mission he still hadn't returned from.

My love for my baby had killed Mariang. Perhaps if she hadn't seen me being pregnant, she wouldn't have been so eager to carry her own child.

My love for September had done nothing. In the end, my love hadn't saved her. My love hadn't mattered to the universe at all.

"If you can't stop, I'll have to pull a lot harder, *hani*. I don't think you want that," Mason warned in a low voice.

I wanted to run far, far away and live in the sea of

that's-not-my-life. Denial felt like a warm bubble bath that always managed to soothe the disquiet inside of me. As Mason finished bandaging my hands and arms, I turned my eyes from the play to take in the worry creasing his forehead. For all the work I did to appear normal, part of me was still crazy, and crazy people ended up alone.

"Ollie," I whispered like a prayer. Ollie would understand how awful this whole thing was. He never made me talk about Finn, but when he sensed I was going somewhere bad in my mind, he sat with me, waiting out the menace that toyed with me far too often.

Mason nodded once, the promise firm in his eyes. "We'll find him. He's probably just taking a little vacation with Darius. He'll be back before you know it."

Judge was watching the whole thing with rapt fascination, soaking in the details I hadn't been able to articulate, and whole chapters of my journey Ezra had glossed over. I didn't want Judge to see the horrible look on Finn's face when he breathed his last.

Finn and I had a deal: if you live, then I breathe. I was still alive, but he had stopped breathing. Now every time I thought about Finn, I felt like I was suffocating.

I clawed at my thighs, unsatisfied when my jeans kept me from ripping into more of my skin.

Mason threaded his fingers through mine. "Deep breaths. It's just a play. They're doing what they can to make sense of their world. That's all this is. This is a gift for you, not a punishment."

I turned my chin up toward him, hoping the show would be over in the next ten seconds. "I would never make you sit through a reenactment of Kara's death. I would never expect you to be calm while everyone clapped because her death made for good entertainment. I also wouldn't let you sit through a play that highlighted your sexual assault. My body isn't a plot device. Those moments haunt me, and now everyone knows something that's none of their business." I slid my fingers from his so I could claw at the tender flesh on my throat. "They clapped, Mason."

Mason's eyes widened and then closed with revelation. "I didn't think of it that way. Here." He waved me to snuggle into his side. "Come on in and close your eyes."

Perhaps I was the waif who couldn't handle the darkness of life, but in that moment, I didn't care. I needed to escape, to hide from the reality I couldn't change.

Mason's burly chest was the perfect haven, strong and toasty with affection. He smelled like patchouli and man, distracting me from my grief, which wasn't a thing I wanted to feel in public. Granted, I didn't much care for grief in private, either.

"I fought against the zombie army, you know," I murmured. I didn't know why I needed him to take me seriously, but I worried that the guys might see the actress and assume that had been me—woefully scared of everything and waiting for the big, strong man to show up and save the day. "I ran out onto the field even after everyone retreated because one of Finn's men was down and couldn't get back in time."

Mason clutched my curls, and I could feel his distress as his knuckles tightened. "You did what?"

I'd never gone into great detail because I knew the lectures that would come about. But I would take the disapproval over being pitied any day. "And I cut the head off an Ekek when it tried to eat Von. I'm not useless."

Though I could tell he wanted to come down hard on me for leaving myself open for attack, he peered past his own agenda so he could see me clearly. "No one who has ever met you assumes you're useless. I know you're strong. I know Terraway is healed because you fought through everything to get us here." His words were timed perfectly against the actress' shriek for help as she fanned herself. Then she flat-out fainted at the sight of Sama. Give me a freaking break. I'd conjured up a dinosaur to eat the jaggoff once I knew who he was. I didn't like that me occasionally being a team player and leaning on the guys as much as they leaned on me was seen as me being a damsel without a brain.

Mason held me through the rest of the play, bearing my pain as your boyfriend is supposed to when you can't stem the gaping wounds of your heart. I'd comforted him last month when he'd woken up in a cold sweat from a nightmare that his hair had been shaved off again. The three of us had no secrets anymore. Von had gripped Mason's shoulder while I'd held him to my breast through his tears, sobbing for the trauma that still left marks on us all. To the world, we appeared unscathed by the battles everyone would just as soon forget in favor of celebrating prosperity. But the wounds on our family sliced deep, and still needed time to heal.

If anyone assumed that warriors never broke down and cried themselves to sleep, then they'd never met any who'd fought as hard as my Viking king. Now it was my turn to bury my melancholy in his chest, entrusting him with my exposed wounds. I had full faith that he would be gentle with all the things that haunted me, while the world cheered for the entertainment my life now was.

The plan for the evening after the grand ceremony of it all ended was for Judge and me to get Carter stinking drunk so we could weed out his lies. When the curtain closed and the amphitheater broke into applause, all I could think about was the promise of alcohol.

19

BROTHERS AND RULE-BREAKERS

King Carter was a charmer when he was sober but get some rum in the man, and he didn't hold back. "Tell me, Lady October, how is it you turned down a strapping Matruculan for a Duwende half-Vamp?"

I leaned back in my chair, clutching my drink to remind myself not to spill it. "Have you seen my husband's ass? I rest my case. And I didn't turn down Mason." To which Carter hooted at the scandal most people (including him) already knew. I mean, Mason introduced me to everyone as his girlfriend. You'd think the shock of it all would've worn off by now.

I'm sure I could've been more eloquent, but rum didn't mix well with my medication. Add that to the fact that I usually didn't drink much, and one shot should've been my limit. Plus, I was still a little on the small side, since I did all the reaping.

Oh, Allie offered to help shoulder the burden, but I wouldn't hear of it beyond the first few months she'd reaped just to learn the trade. She'd been through too much and her body needed time to heal. It worried me when she stared off vacantly for minutes at a time, then came back to the conversation at-hand with a confused look on her face. No, no. I would do the reaping, and she would finally have a life where people took care of her. Plus, she was pregnant, for which Ezra had established a hard and fast rule that Omens wouldn't be permitted to reap a single day while pregnant. We would be careful this time, since that was an option. I made sure to keep the count well above what was needed, hoping to sack away so many extra years of stability for Terraway that Allie wouldn't have to work ever again. She'd given up her childhood and adolescence for me. Now it was my turn to take care of her. She would have a good life, so help me.

I sipped my drink, knowing I wasn't being nearly as helpful in our casual interrogation as Judge probably hoped I would be. Images of Sama raping the actress who played me punched my brain over and over, so I drank, hoping to dull the pain. Judge kept shooting me worried looks as his paternal instinct kicked in. Yes, his baby girl was drinking more than half a glass.

I knew what I was doing. Mostly.

"I can't imagine why you never settled down, Carter."

The king of Hayop ate it up that I didn't use his full title away from the public eye. Like we had some sort of secret worth shrouding. I shot Carter a smirk that he returned, now that his brother's attention was occupied by the harp music coming from the far corner of the expansive private room. The ornate instrument was taller than me, and introduced a delicate calm into the air that I hoped would saturate my bones and stay with me forever.

Von was giving me a bit of space. Actually, he was off with Levi, Langgam, Ruiz, Klark and Ezra, giving my open cuts a bit of space.

Judge leaned forward in his seat next to mine, his elbows on his knees. "Oh, I think you know why there's no queen. Carter's a man like me. I never was one for settling."

Carter grinned, his eyes lidded as his filter began to lift with a hearty laugh. "Ah, that's very good. I'll have to remember that one. No, settling's not for me. Besides, I've got a country to run. Can't go dividing my focus like that." Though, as his gaze wasn't totally focused to begin with, I didn't really think that was the reason. His gaze flitted to a buxom woman standing near the door who wore no hesitation in her Cheshire grin.

I sniggered, probably a little too obnoxiously. "I love the noble spin you're putting on things. You almost fooled me into believing you're not a playboy." I scoffed so loud, it startled both Judge and Carter. "You don't want the responsibility of keeping it in your pants for only one woman."

Carter narrowed one eye at me. "Not like you're one to talk. Mason tells me all sorts of things."

"Does he tell you how good of a kisser he is? Because if he's keeping that part to himself, it's a G-rated story not worth a listen."

Carter barked out a laugh. "I admit, my big brother's not a braggart. He's truly that good?"

"Good enough that after all the double-jointed sexcapades Von and I get up to, Mason's lips are so incredible, he makes a kiss seem like a scandal."

Carter hooted his amusement at my liquor-infused candor, and then he and Judge started trading stories about their best make-outs. My mind drifted toward Mason, who looked ever the hero with his broad chest and knowledgeable eyes.

I sipped my drink, my eyes flitting to the harp again, the nimble fingers of the musician stroking and plucking so deftly, it looked as if she was combing her fingers through sand. Rest. That's what I wanted, but had a hard time asking for. That awful play thoroughly messed with my head, and the harp had come like an angel of mercy to soothe my nerves. The music, coupled with the rum, took the edge off my drive and siphoned the stiffness from my spine. Of course, I wasn't paying total attention to Judge and Carter at the moment, but it seemed like a decent tradeoff—work for rest.

Get your head in the game, Reese.

Judge pretended to take a drink, which was what I was supposed to be doing—not drinking so I could remain in control while Carter unraveled. I kept my tone airy as I followed Carter's gaze to the woman near the door. "The women of Hayop are stunning, for sure. That must be why my brother came down here."

Carter turned his chin, his lips pursed and slick with rum. "I told you, I haven't seen Oliver."

I faked a laugh that was lighter than the rage in my soul over being lied to. "Oh, I'm sure you're right. Ollie's no good at sitting around, drinking and doing nothing. He likes adventure and excitement. I can only guess that's because he found someone else who better understood all that Hayop has to offer." I drained my second glass, frowning that there wasn't much rum left. I needed to be smart and save the rest for Carter, who loved the foreign stuff. So I poured myself a third glass, selecting the liquor brewed in Terraway this time. Alcohol from Terraway was far more bitter than the good stuff we had Topside. Still, it did the trick. I could almost forget the sting of Sama's hands on me, trying to get me pregnant while I screamed for him to stop.

Finn died in my arms.

Finn's dead.

Finn's dead.

Judge pretended to scold me, thumbing the rim of his glass. I could tell he was choosing his next words carefully.

"That was out of line, baby girl. I'm sure King Carter knows how to show his guests a good time. He wouldn't send us to a stuffy old play and call it good entertainment. He's going to take us where he took Ollie and Darius. He's just keeping up appearances to play the good boy in front of Ezra." Then he shot Carter a conspiratorial look, as if I was being a child and only the two of them understood the way life truly worked.

I shrugged in lieu of an apology for my mouthiness. I didn't mind playing the dummy if it got me closer to finding my brother. Every hour that ticked by warned me that Ollie was still out there, wondering why I hadn't found Waldo yet.

Carter chuckled good-naturedly with Judge, as if they were old friends. Rum was good at making instant allies out of strangers. He pointed at Mason, who was still at the other end of the room, sitting in front of the harp so he could be closer to the music. "You know I can't very well say anything in front of my brother. He wouldn't approve of me taking you into the Baluki forest. There are laws against stepping foot inside. Mason doesn't approve of lawbreaking. He's been an old man for as long as I can remember."

My spine straightened but I tried not to give away my excitement. Carter's love for rum was my new favorite thing about him. He had the look of a responsible man wanting to be coaxed into playing the role of the bad boy. Judge kept his body language relaxed, encouraging me to calm down until we had all the necessary information. "The Baluki forest, eh? Are you sure you can handle another trip there, old man?"

Carter blew a loud raspberry. "You don't know what I can handle." He held up his glass, throwing me a wink. "One more of these, and she's about to see how much I can handle. You haven't lived until you've done it on a throne. Heightens everything."

Judge's smile tightened ever so slightly. His brotherly protectiveness flared at the blatant proposition. Still, he kept his cool.

I took another sip, playing the game as it shifted. "Pass. If you couldn't keep up with Ollie on a little nature hike, I doubt you can handle me."

Carter snorted. "Your brother and his friend are foolish, not brave. I can see you don't know the difference. Traipsing through the Baluki forest to find the *sigla* flowers is a thing not even our bravest soldiers would risk." He drained his glass, smacking his lips. "Plus, it's illegal. Are you a very bad girl, Lady Omen?"

"What are *sigla* flowers?" Judge asked, though the recesses of my brain pinged at the label I'd heard somewhere before.

"They have extraordinary healing properties. I wouldn't have granted Ollie access to the forest at all, but he said he needed them for his sister. I assumed he meant you," he nodded toward me, "but as you're sharing a drink with me, perhaps he was referring to the pregnant Omen.

I'm not sure I have the balls to deny Ezra's daughters or sons anything, even if it flies in the face of one of Hayop's oldest laws."

My mouth went dry, despite the rum that flavored my lips. "How long has Ollie been in the forest?"

Carter shrugged, not taking notice of my spiking anxiety. "A week. Maybe longer. I thought he would've come back to the castle to ask to be ported Topside by now, but I'm sure he's off sightseeing, enjoying Hayop."

My fingers gripped the arm of my wooden chair as the world tilted slightly, my teeth grinding as I worked out my indignation through my encroaching haze of too much liquor. "You took Ollie and Darius to the Baluki forest and just left them there?"

Carter snapped his fingers. "Darius. I couldn't remember the other fellow's name. Yes, well, they were insistent they be allowed access to the forest, but it's far too dangerous for my people to walk through. I escorted them to the edge and let them do as they pleased. But I never stepped foot inside. I'm not insane." At my gaping horror, Carter shrugged off his culpability. "Surely you don't think I'd order my soldiers to break the law of the land. I would never subject my men to the torments that lie in the thick of those trees."

Judge didn't look nearly as upset as me. "I don't understand. So they went walking through a forest. What's the big deal? We'll just go in and find them if they're lost."

Carter shook his head, his gray eyes darkening with

secrets of a land we knew very little about. "Foolishness and bravery are too sides of the same coin, and not one I would bet on. If you're not disturbed to the point of insanity before you step foot into the forest, you will be if you ever come out."

20

I'M FINE

I didn't want a discussion about it, but I also knew that running away from Von and Mason wasn't an option, either. As Mason and Ezra went back and forth on the subject, I began to regret my choice in being a team player and letting them all in on the plan (which would happen with or without their consent).

I'd been granted the largest guest bedroom in the palace, which was lavish and beautiful with notes of rustic charm. It felt like our back-and-forths were out of place in such a cozy room. I leaned against the roughly hewn wood wall, silently trying to convince the room not to tilt while I tried to reason with the rum in my system.

"I don't understand. October's fine. Why would Ollie need to go into the forest for the *sigla* flowers?" Mason looked wounded, as if Ollie thinking I might be faltering was a personal attack on his guarding abilities.

"It's for Allie," Judge replied. "Ollie must be worried that Allie's not doing well. Probably why Darius involved himself."

Mason's face pulled. "You truly think Allie's under half as much strain as October is? We're the ones reaping. We're the ones taking on the entirety of the Omen duties." He ran his fingers through his hair while he puzzled aloud. When no one replied, Mason directed his question at me, since I was the resident authority on all things Oliver Reese. "Do you think it's because Allie's pregnant he's more worried?"

I shrugged, not wanting to voice my concerns out loud. But I knew Ollie, and his worries were mine. I didn't want the guys to know I was on the verge of drunk, so I kept my words measured, hoping they came out cool and clear. "Sama lived in her head for a long time. Allie was in a coma for who knows how many years." I shook my head. "Three. We know how many. She was out for three years. I remember things."

I ignored Ezra's raised eyebrows, followed by the paternal look of concern when he no doubt surmised why I sounded like an idiot.

I breezed past it. "And even if all those years—three years—hadn't happened, she survived everything Bev put her through. I don't think Ollie's worried about her carrying the baby; he's scared of the same thing I am—that her mind might still be a little broken." I scratched at my throat, hating the fact that I was ratting out my sister, bringing her issues to public light. I missed my neck on the first two passes, but finally made contact, exhaling with relief when the pain, numbed though it was, did its best to center me.

Levi remained stationed at the window, his arms crossed over his chest—there, but not. His eyes flicked to my throat but he said nothing.

I didn't want to bring it up. None of us did. We all wanted to pretend we didn't notice her blank stares. My voice lowered as I delivered the blow. "She's going to be a mama soon. You can't do that if you're spacing out for minutes on end. You've all seen her do it." I tapped my temple. "Her brain. Something's wrong. Sama broke something important."

Ezra frowned at me. "Sure, but that's to be expected, considering all she's been through."

Von's arm coiled around my hips, offering me stability when my body swayed slightly. "Easy, Peach," he whispered, and then grimaced. "How much did you drink?"

"Less than more but more than less." I leaned into him, savoring the man who wanted to spare me the humiliation of appearing stinking drunk in front of my fathers.

Levi took in my lidded state and fielded the question for Ezra. "Allie's illness is to be expected for a time, yes, but eventually Ollie wants her to get better. He wants his sister not to be so haunted. Allie should have a shot at a good life." He ran his hand over his face and shook his head at himself. "The *sigla* flower has amazing healing properties.

Now that this is all in motion, it makes perfect sense. I can't believe I didn't predict him stealing away in the dead of night to unearth it." His eyes darted to my hand that scraped clumsily down my throat over and over again. "Frankly, I can't believe I didn't think to sneak off and do it sooner. I admit, I'm a little ashamed of myself that my son is smarter than I am, putting together the problem with a possible solution, dangerous though it may be."

Judge shook his head. "But why did he take Darius? Why not take Mason, since he's Matruculan and knows the lay of the land better?"

Mason shoved his hands in his pockets and stared at his shoes. "Oh, man. Ollie asked me about Hayop a couple weeks ago. Not about the forest specifically but the country I grew up in. We ended up talking about the Baluki forest, but I certainly never recommended taking him there. Back when Allie was in her coma and we were grasping at anything to wake her up, I made a trip to Hayop to see if I could go into the Baluki forest and find the *sigla* flowers, but there's a law against stepping foot inside that Carter wouldn't bend for me back then." He shrugged. "I can't believe Ollie went there." He shut his eyes tight. "This is all my fault. I shouldn't have entertained it as an option back then. It's no doubt me who planted that seed of possibility in him."

Von didn't look at me as he spoke but kept his arm around my hips. "But why Darius?"

A giggle slipped from my lips, though nothing was

funny. I cleared my throat and tried to sound coherent. "Darius is the perfect one to go with Ollie for something like this. He has limited knowledge of the danger, and he has been or is still in love with Allie."

Judge swore. It was an angry sound, directed at Darius, I'm sure. "That makes sense."

Von shook his head at the whole thing. "What I don't understand is what the *sigla* flowers can do that the healing waters can't."

Levi pointed to my scraped-up throat with a closed expression. "That's the difference, right there. October's been in the healing waters three times but she still claws up her body when she's distressed. There are some things the healing waters can't cure. To be honest, I'm not sure the *sigla* flowers can fix everything either. But if I was Ollie, and my concern escalated to panic, that's the route I would take. The healing waters cure the body, but the *sigla* works to cure the mind." He rubbed his palm over his five o'clock shadow. "Most think the *sigla* is a myth to be grasped at when things are dire. But it's very much real. Allie's mind could be cured by them, I'm almost certain." He held my gaze with a note of warning. "So could October's, if the flower was fresh enough."

"Knock it off, Levi," I groused. "There's nothing wrong with me. I'm still standing on my own, aren't I?"

My dad narrowed his eyes at me. "Given how drunk you are, that's very much debatable."

Von and Mason both straightened, taking a step toward

Levi with matching looks of anticipation. Von's voice dripped with hope that broke my heart. "Do you mean to tell me that a *sigla* flower could cure November? If we find the flowers, she might stop hurting herself?"

My eyebrows furrowed at the left turn the conversation took. "Hey, I'm fine. This isn't about me. This is about Allie. She's the one who was in a coma. She's the one who loses herself."

Von whirled on me. "Do you think it's easy for us to watch you mark yourself up to the point of drawing blood? Do you think any man would sit back and twiddle his thumbs while his bride is sliced up day after day before his very eyes?"

Emotion caught in my throat, stunning me that this was his reaction. After everything we survived, this was the thing that haunted him. I glanced around the room guiltily. "We don't need to talk about that now. It's private."

Mason pointed his finger at the floor. "No, we'll talk about it now. Dad, you really think this could help October?"

Ezra covered his face with his hand when Levi answered. "I think it's the only thing we haven't tried that might help. At the very least, it would do the trick for Allie. It might not fix all that's broken in my daughters, but it would do something."

Mason stalked to the door, his boots heavy with purpose. "Let's move, then. Danny can stay with October while we go find the flowers. I'll get him now. Lavinia can watch Anastasia in the palace while we're gone."

I balked at him, tripping over my own two feet when I stepped forward. "I'd like to know who you think you're edging out of the picture. This was *my* idea. I'm the one who got the info out of Carter with Judge. You're not taking me out of play right when it's time to score a touchdown. And the flower's for Allie, not me. I'm fine."

Levi's jaw was stern, so I expected a fight when he spoke. "Alright. If you stay by my side, I can lead you to the *sigla* flowers." My posture swelled with hope and a giant "ha!" directed at Mason and Von until Levi finished his statement. "But only if you promise to eat the flower once we find it—root and all."

The room went still, all eyes on the both of us. My throat went dry and I'm fairly certain everyone could see my heartbeat in my cheeks. "I don't need to because I'm not sick. I'm fine. Allie's the one spacing out. Allie was in a coma, not me."

At this, Von shouted at me, startling a squeak from my lips. "You were in a coma for a week after Sama died! A week! Or did you forget that?"

I rolled my eyes. "One measly week, Von. That's nothing compared to what Allie went through. I'm fine."

Von glowered at me with a seethe that stilled my bravado. "So help me, if you say 'I'm fine' one more time, I'm going to lose my temper."

Levi crossed the room, holding my gaze with a

command in his eyes not to deny him the proof he needed. "Show me your arms."

I held up my hands, my cheeks hot. "See? Totally fi... Totally cool."

My dad could've used force but he kept his hands slow and steady, unwrapping the bandages that found their way to my arms at least once a week, despite the constant pulling Mason and Von kept up. "Look at your arms, October."

My lips pursed with defiance. "I'm fine."

I winced when Von's anger filled the room. "Look at your arms!"

Levi was calm but firm. "No, you're not. But you will be." He raised my hand to examine my fingertips, and then pressed his palm flat to mine. His hand was so big, it swallowed my own, making me feel like a little girl in the presence of a king. "Do I have your word that you'll stay by my side in the forest? That you'll eat the flower once we find it?"

Ezra rubbed his forehead. "Why exactly can't we bring the flower back to October here? Why does she need to come on this journey?"

Levi was resolute. "The fresher the flower, the better the results. I would suggest Allie make the trek too, but with her being pregnant and this being a land of Matruculans, that would be suicide."

My pride warred inside of me, banging around in my chest to warn my very makeup that it didn't want to change, and this might be something big. "This will help Allie?"

Levi nodded once. "Yes."

"Okay, Dad. I'll eat the flower. If that's what I have to do to get help to Allie, I can get onboard." I'm sure I should've been offended at the collective sigh of relief that echoed across the room, but something in Levi's eyes looked like pain, distracting me from everything else. "What's wrong?"

"Ollie's love is... He's a better father than I've been. I didn't suggest getting the *sigla* flowers myself because there are many sins of my past buried in the forest. Unearthing them might..." Levi's hazel eyes flickered with traces of insecurity and a warning of impending heartbreak. "You might not want me in your life if you knew all I'd done when I was young and foolish, thinking the world wasn't capable of breaking." He stared into my eyes, letting me catch a glimpse of just how much it mattered how I viewed him. "But I see now I was being vain. My children's health should come before anything else, even if you can't look me in the eye after you see what sort of villain I once was. Now that Ollie's lost in there, I don't have much choice. I have to go get him out."

Our palms remained fused as the certainty of our family changing in undeniable ways hung between us. I wanted to tell him that I was scared—not of the danger in the forest, but of the flower getting into my brain and seeing the mess it had to clean up. Denial had gotten me so very far in life. A cure felt like a threat to all my hard work. My coping mechanisms had proved a sturdy enough structure to get me through life. If they were suddenly gone? I didn't know what that would look like.

"Forgive me." Levi's whisper came out strained. For all my dad's superhuman strength, he sounded genuinely afraid.

I blinked up at him, confused at the implications that he might turn out to be a bad guy in my mind after all was said and done.

CONGA LINE

Ezra and Lavinia stayed with Ana after I put my foot down that my sweet dad wouldn't be exposed to anything that might warp his mind. Ezra put up the same argument for me, but Levi came down with the judgment that my mind was sufficiently damaged, and in need of healing. The fresher the flower, the better my chance of "getting well." As if I was damaged. As if I needed an intervention. Give me a freaking break.

Danny cracked his neck as we stood on the edge of the forest, looking at the thick knotted trees that seemed too close together for the root systems not to be choking each other out. The leaves had spiky edges on them that looked like gnarled fingers aching to grab at intruders. If any forest was cursed, I'd put my money on this being the obvious choice.

This did not deter Danny, who was psyched to do something more harrowing than diaper duty. "Do we have enough *baga* root for a few days? I don't want to get in there and have to turn around because this one can't breathe." Danny jerked his thumb at me, as if I was a wuss for having limits like, you know, needing usable oxygen. *Jag.*

Mason, Von and Levi all nodded, patting their packs. "I've got enough for three days for her and Judge," Von volunteered.

"Two days," Mason offered.

"I packed enough to last a week for October, Judge, Ollie and Darius," Levi said gravely.

Judge wasn't fond of that little restriction when traveling to Terraway, so he bumped his fist to Mason's and Von's. "Thanks, guys. Appreciate it." He inclined his chin to Levi. "Dad."

"Of course, Son."

There was a gold haze that hung in the air of the forest I noticed when I peered through the branches. It seemed to hold itself up to just an inch or two above my height, never venturing lower. Levi addressed the oddity before we stepped inside. "Whatever you do, keep low. You won't like what happens if you breathe in too much of that stuff," he warned, pointing to the gilded fog. "Best keep your head from touching the golden air altogether."

Danny moved to stand beside Levi. It was clear he was chomping at the bit to rejoin guard duty. "Keep behind us," he instructed me. "Mason, stay behind October. Von, Judge, you're at her sides."

I rolled my eyes. "Guys, I've fought against a zombie army. I can handle a hike through the woods. I'm not fragile." I worried they'd already latched onto the actress' wilted flower impersonation of me, and now assumed I was useless.

Danny turned, taking out the machete he'd borrowed in preparation for the journey. "Fragile has nothing to do with it. We're good at our jobs, is all. If Levi wants you to have a flower straight from the ground, we can make that happen."

Von held my hand while Judge drew his gun. Of course he had a gun on him. "Where did you get that? I thought I took your gun away."

Judge cast me a withering look. "I love your dream life, where I own only one gun, and you have complete control over my actions."

I glowered at him but didn't press the issue further. Judge had a goal in mind, which meant he was pursuing that instead of sinking further into hopelessness. It was a big leap, but I decided to trust that Judge wouldn't turn the weapon on himself. I very much hoped I wasn't wrong.

The guys crouched as Levi and Danny took the lead, slicing at branches and vines that hung low enough to block our unmarked path.

The first step into the Baluki forest sent a chill down my spine. It was like dipping yourself into some bizarre version of Wonderland that had yet to reveal its true dysfunctions, but you knew they were coming, lurking in the shadows and waiting for their peak opportunity to pounce. The air was dense—a mist that clung to my skin and made me cold enough to shiver. Given the temperate climate of Hayop, it was a big enough shift to make me hesitate. Though nothing actually bad had happened, I could tell why the people of the land stayed away from the forest, legalities aside. Though no one but us was around, I felt eyes on me. I turned to see if it was Mason staring, but he was busy hacking at a low-hanging vine. Still, I felt the eyes boring into me with every step I ventured.

We moved further in, the guys crouching to keep under the mist. I only had to duck my head a little to keep the golden hue from touching my hair. We were quiet for the most part, too tense with purpose to alert the menace of the forest that we were there to take something precious.

When Levi stopped and held up his fist, we all froze. Though Von and Judge flanked me, Danny took a step back and reached behind him to hook his arm around my hip. I could feel his heart stuttering through his back, so I leaned my cheek against his spine to calm him. It's hard to explain the connection only I had with Danny. The best way I could describe it is that whenever he let me be kind to him, I felt his ribs expanding in a way that made me wonder just how restrained his breathing had been before-hand. It probably looked like he stepped back to shield me in case anything shady came for us, but I knew it was because he was scared, and couldn't admit aloud that he needed me to calm him down. I ran my fingers slowly down his side, and he responded by using the hand that was coiled around my waist to thumb at the back of my hip.

"This is the part where everyone has to do exactly as I say without deviation. Can you handle that?" Levi asked, but really it was a command. When we all consented, he nodded. "Good. Then everyone needs to close your eyes. Sama and I did many spells in here. We created greatness and true wickedness, which still roam through these trees. You'll feel eyes watching you but pay them no mind. You'll hear bodies moving through the forest, but if you don't look on them, they won't harm you. If you look, there is a very good chance you will be lost to us."

Von spoke up. "How are we to move through the forest with our eyes closed?"

"Form a line and hold onto each other. I'll lead the way. I helped create the darkness that moves in this forest, so it won't come for me. Though I admit, I don't look forward to being confronted with the sight of my wickedness."

I wanted to look up at Levi to see if the regret in his voice matched his countenance. Instead I closed my eyes, keeping my word to obey his instructions to the letter. "Dad?"

"It's alright, October. If you all listen carefully, we won't come to any harm. Keep low with your eyes closed. We'll get through this to the *sigla* flowers, which are closer to the center of the forest. We'll most likely find Ollie and Darius along the way. I can't imagine they made it all that far without my guidance."

We fell in line, gripping the hips of the person in front of us. Levi led the way with Danny behind him, then Von, me, Judge, and Mason at the rear. I'm sure we looked like we were readying to do a very grim conga.

It wasn't a full minute of us moving slowly through the forest that we heard a rustle in the branches to our right, and then our left. I heard quick-moving feet, like they were running straight at us. "Dad?"

Levi was firm. "The wickedness can't touch you if you keep your eyes from it. Close your eyes and keep low. It will pass around us if we let it. You cannot stab it with your weapons, so let it be. It will not touch you if you pay it no mind."

We did as we were told, though it was counterintuitive to every instinct we had. I was most proud of Judge, who relinquished the Alpha role to my father. His arms coiled tighter around my waist, though, and I could tell he was frightened.

"October?" Danny called out with mildly-controlled panic creeping at the edges of his tone.

"I'm here, Danny."

"Von, make sure you can feel her at all times. There's too much being left to chance here. I don't like it." His voice tried to reclaim its command, but it was clear he was scared.

"Stop for a second," Von requested. "Here, Danny. Will this help?" So deftly, it was almost like a dance, Von switched spots with me, moving my body so I was sandwiched between himself and Danny.

My arms wrapped around Danny's waist, and I felt relief wash through him in a sigh of contentment. "You alright?"

Danny collected himself enough to sound gruff. "Of course I'm alright. I'm not the Omen. If something happens to you, Terraway's in a very tight spot. Anastasia will have to be awakened far younger than she should be, and Allie will be put to work the second she gives birth. Think, October."

I dug my nails into his abdomen to shut him up. "Stop being a butthead. If you're worried, you don't have to be a jag about it. It won't kill you to say something nice."

"Bloody hell, woman," Danny breathed in exasperation. Though his lashes were shut, his words had the tone of rolling one's eyes.

Von's thumb traced my hipbone, soothing my nerves as the beings on either side of us rustled in the bushes. We stepped carefully, trying not to trip over complicated root systems we couldn't see. I felt a whoosh that was akin to someone running past me. That was disturbing enough. But what chilled my spine was a flap of fabric brushing my face. "Dad, are the ghosty things allowed to touch us? Can I stab it if I promise to keep my eyes closed?" My fingers itched to retrieve my balisong blade from my pocket.

Levi stopped, and we all bumped into each other. "What did you feel?" After I explained, Levi seemed far more worried than I hoped. I was kind of expecting him to be like, "It's totally cool to stab, just keep your eyes closed. No big deal." Instead, he said, "Stay where you are. I need to mark you."

"Mark me?"

"With my blood. They can sense things, the Magtakas."

"Magtakas? What are they?"

"Keep your eyes closed, October." I heard the slice of steel across Levi's arm, and bit my lip through a whimper when he slid a swath of blood across my forehead under my hairline.

Mason spoke up from the rear. "I thought Magtakas were a myth. Are you saying they're real, Dad?"

"Very real, Son." Levi paused the trek to deliver the crux of his guilt over his apprenticeship with Sama. "I created them."

22

CREATED WICKEDNESS

The limits of Levi's abilities weren't often discussed. Despite his ardent desire to be around Ollie, Allie and me, much of him remained a mystery to us. Ollie had interrogated him many times, back when he used to refer to Levi as "that dad guy." Now he and Ezra were "dad" without hesitation. But though Levi wanted to know every detail about us, he kept himself a closed book, especially concerning his time with Sama.

I'd chalked it up to Dad not wanting to talk about time spent with the bestie who'd ended up boning his daughter.

"What are you talking about? What even are they?" I felt silly having a conversation with my eyes closed, but I was too scared to go off-book now.

Levi moved back to the front of the line and led us slowly forward, his voice raised to reach all the way back while he chopped at the branches that impeded our path. "You all work for Ezra, whose only fault is an abundance of kindness. Sama and I worked for the Last Kapre—a giant who spoke in riddles and demanded only greatness of us. Once we achieved said greatness, there was only another task, and another. There was no job well done, no looking back, no time granted to perfect all we'd accomplished. He was a hard master, and though we respected his intellect, we hated him."

I was afraid to breathe too loudly, for fear of Levi closing up. I'd wanted to learn more about him for so very long. The beings rustling in the branches on either side of us didn't touch me now, but I could feel their eyes on me all the same. No one spoke, all of us wanting to know more as we stumbled along on unsteady footing. Von held me tight, and I could feel his anxiety over not being able to see his surroundings.

When Levi continued, I could hear a firmness in his voice, as if he was scolding himself for a job poorly done. "My project wasn't finished. I was close, but not quite completed. I hadn't tested them, but the master was firm that deadlines were to be respected. 'If we don't respect time, there's no use pretending we respect ourselves.' He was full of sayings like that—things that made you feel like a terrible idiot, but had enough wisdom tucked in so you tried harder. It's a good system, though not one I'd exercise on anyone I loved." I could tell Levi's pause was to brace himself for the next raw bit. I wondered if anyone knew the stories of his life. I'd helped murder the only person who truly knew him, and while I didn't regret that one bit, I wished my father didn't feel so very alone. "So I presented my work to my master. They were mostly finished but untested. I hoped my Kapre master would take a passing glance and assign me the next job, so I could go back quietly and work out any kinks. I should have known better than to present subpar work. His punishments were most severe. He tormented our minds so we thought we were in excruciating pain without leaving a mark on us."

For all the stellar qualities Levi possessed, he sucked at telling stories about himself. His next bout of silence lasted several minutes, leaving us all hanging with too many questions left unanswered. When he finally spoke, my heart rate picked up.

"My assignment had been to create a few apparatuses that could take a person's magic away and hold it, like holding one's breath. The issue I had was with releasing it. I couldn't get the magic to come back out and flow into the person from which it was stolen. Sometimes the magic didn't want to unstick itself, as if it was grateful to have escaped, reticent to return to the dank shell from which it was born."

Another long silence filled my ears, giving me the chance to hear whispers from the Magtakas. They were saying something but I couldn't decipher what. The whispers toyed with me, engulfing me with a lure to listen closer. Had they been talking, perhaps I wouldn't have cared to know what they were saying; it was the secrecy that drew me in. Lots of "H" sounds with "ahksa" sprinkled in. I guessed they were talking in a different language, murmuring magical spells that were far beyond my non-expertise.

Levi made an "oof" sound, and I fought with the temptation to open my eyes. "Dad?" Von called. "Are you alright?"

Levi's pause was deafening as we all came to a stop. "I'm fine, Son. Nothing to trouble yourself with. Keep your eyes closed and hold tight to October."

Von complied but I could feel his angst, as it matched my own. "Tell me about the Magtakas. Are they the vessels that keep stolen magic?"

"Yes. I should have accepted my punishment for not completing the task in the allotted time, but I was afraid. I presented my master the collection of vessels for him to test. He sent some of his psychic energy into them, and they did their job well enough. But when he made to retrieve his magic, the Magtakas would not release it. My creation paid me a grand favor and took away his bit of magic that allowed him to torture us without leaving marks. He was expecting that bit of psychic control to be returned to him after examining my vessels, but it remained stuck inside the Magtakas. Not even I could get it out. Sama bore the brunt of the abuse meant for me, since our Kapre master knew watching Sama in agony would cause me greater harm than any torment he could inflict on me directly. I released the Magtakas into the forest, which is where we stored many of our inventions that didn't pan out."

Mason had an unstable edge in his tone, but he kept his question academic. "Okay, then how do they work?"

"If you look them in the eye, they use the last Kapre's psychic magic that's trapped inside of them as a weapon. They cannot be destroyed; believe me, Sama and I tried. So here they remain, floating through the woods like spirits."

Von held tight to me. "Can they steal our magic, like they stole the Kapre's?"

"No. Not unless they release the Kapre's magic, which they're not capable of doing. They can only hold one person's power at a time."

Judge sounded pissed. "So basically they're mobile weapons that make you think you're undergoing intense physical torture. All we have to do is not look them in the eye, right? How many are there?"

Levi grunted as he chopped down something that blocked our path. "Six, if memory serves. It's not unwise that the kings in your bloodline banned citizens from stepping foot in the forest, Mason."

"How long do they torture you? What happens when they get tired and move on?" Danny asked.

Levi's tone was grave. "They don't tire, and they don't move on. They'll keep you alive for months if it'll give them more sport. They inherited the Last Kapre's tenacity, that's for certain. He used to smoke fat cigars while he watched Sama scream for days, like he was watching an entertaining television show."

My heart broke for my dad. I wanted nothing more in that moment than to throw my arms around his neck and reassure him that I wouldn't let anyone hurt him ever again.

"Do Darius and Ollie know not to look the Magtakas in the eye?" Mason's question resounded through us like a gong of doom.

Levi's voice was grim with regret. "I'm the only one who knows that fact, and I never told them."

I felt sick to my stomach at the thought of Ollie being tortured. "Dad, we have to find them!"

"My sense of smell is far sharper when I'm a wolf," Mason offered.

Levi sighed with a heaviness that made me feel weighted. "Mine, as well. I just didn't want to shift because you all need protection, and that's best done while I'm upright."

"You stay with them. I'll shift and sniff around for Ollie."

"Only if you keep your eyes closed and don't go farther than you can hear us."

There was a rustling, and I guessed Mason was now a wolf, and nudging his clothes into his backpack to hand off to Judge. He brushed my leg with his tail as he moved by me. I wanted to tell him to stay with us. It didn't feel wise to split up. In fact, none of this felt wise.

We were silent as we moved forward but the noise from the Magtakas was all-encompassing. Their whispers, though still indecipherable, grew louder and more insistent. I tried to distract myself with anything, but my mind betrayed me and went straight to Sama. I didn't like thinking about the charming Philip, but picturing him as the victim of torment over mistakes on the job my father made pushed me full-throttle into the visual I didn't want to see. Philip's white-blond hair and welcoming smile had been twisted into the molesting villain that made my skin crawl. Adding the image of him contorting on the floor while a sadistic giant smoked a cigar without concern for his plight introduced feelings I didn't want in muddying my stalwart opinion of him. I didn't want to feel sorry for Sama, who'd taken Allie away from me.

Von was saying something, but I couldn't hear him over all the whispering. "What?"

Von repeated himself but again it escaped me. The whispers grew so much that I felt disoriented, especially walking along uneven terrain with my eyes closed. A few minutes later, Von was gripping my hips tight, shouting something that was still crowded out by the whispers of the Magtakas.

The line stopped and I tripped into Danny. My voice came out at a shout, but I could scarcely hear myself. "Dad? I can't hear anything! The Magtakas are whispering like, super loud. Is that normal? Are you guys all having the same problem?"

I couldn't hear Levi but I felt him when he came near and pressed my forehead to his shoulder, crouched from the gold mist as he was. He murmured something, but it only made the whispers sound angry. They hissed with indignation over Levi trying to protect me. He cupped the back of my head, holding me firm to his form, which vibrated when he began shouting.

Finally a few sentences broke through when Levi pressed his mouth right near my ear and yelled. "It's because I marked you with my blood. I thought that would help, but it's only made things worse. They're driven by my master's urge to punish me by torturing someone I love. But they cannot harm you if you don't look into their eyes. No matter what, keep your eyes shut!"

It was then that one of the ghosty hands touched my ear. The finger was icy and almost seemed to pass through me, but could still thumb my earlobe back and forth. It was there but not, substance and vapor at the same time. "Ah! Get off of me, creeper!"

"It shouldn't be able to touch you!"

But the Magtakas didn't care that he wasn't allowed to

touch me; he just friggin' did it anyway. The cold smoothed over my neck and slid down my spine, making me shudder at the unwelcome sensation. I felt cold in my bones now, scared of the touch I couldn't see. My body twitched and contorted to get away, but the hand followed my movements, almost as if the whole thing was funny.

When the creature squeezed my butt, I let out a pathetic bleat. That's when all hell broke loose.

23

YELLOW-EYED AGONY

I heard indecipherable shouting and felt Von's body jerking while his arm flailed out in a stabbing motion. The shrieks of the vessels were the only thing I heard now. Soon my body was being bumped between Danny and Judge like a pinball machine, my teeth grinding as Levi and Von grunted with effort I didn't understand.

In the back of it all, I heard Von shouting—for help? From pain? In warning? I couldn't tell, but the sound of his distress fueled my rage that anything might separate me from the people I loved.

I'm not sure when I became the person who played it so very safe, but as I stood like a dummy in the middle of the woods, I knew this just wasn't me. No matter what danger was going down, there was no way I was going to let Von go off into the unknown without me.

I slid the balisong blade from my pocket, readying to slice as I gripped the jade handle. Each time I touched it, I felt the promise of Finn's protection echo through my body. It's the main reason I rarely took the thing out. His protection was my agony, because in the end, I hadn't been able to save him. I was his undoing, yet here he was, guarding me even after his death with the blade he'd given to me.

When the warning sound mutated into Von's clear howl of distress, I summoned my inner Bruce Campbell and launched myself out with my eyes peeking at the ground. I saw translucent swaths of a brown cloak swooshing around where legs should have been, but weren't. I used my limited sight and jump-tackled the thing around the middle, closing my eyes as I stabbed into it. My head brushed the golden mist, but I knew I couldn't worry about the fallout of that just yet.

I'm not sure what I was expecting when my knife sliced into the Magtakas, but a shot of electricity through my arms wasn't even in the top ten. My elbows were frozen, unable to let me pull the knife back out.

Electricity coursed through me, arching my spine and pushing a scream from my lips. I could feel the agony ringing in my teeth and all through my bones. Too much pain engulfed me, and I could do nothing but endure. The ghosty being rolled me onto my back, not caring at all that my knife was still embedded between two of his ribs. The shock forced my eyes open, refusing to let me remain in the dark.

I'd thought it couldn't get any worse, but when a second Magtakas came into view, I knew I was wrong. His slippery fingers caressed the hollows of my cheeks, warning me with a chuckle that whatever pain I'd known before would soon be a pleasant memory. His burlap hood slipped from his head, revealing a gray skull with brown and black patches of fur accenting his face. It made him seem a mix of almost human, almost animal, and entirely undead. The eye cavities appeared to be empty, but as I had no choice but to peer inside, frozen mid-electrocution as I was, yellow irises illuminated to let me know it had me exactly where it wanted me.

My body endured agony that radiated up my arms from the first Magtakas my balisong blade was still stuck inside. The second Magtakas kept his cavernous yellow eyes locked in on mine, and shot torment from my head downward. Within seconds, my entire being was awash in endless stabbing sensations I couldn't escape.

The Magtakas was gentle with my cheeks. He pinched my face, testing the elasticity of my skin while his buddy took the time to torture me with electrocution so very calmly. A third one stroked my legs, each pass tearing into my flesh over and over, as if filleting skin from bone.

Then another joined in, stroking my throat with skinless, fur-lined bony fingers so it could feel the vibration of my screams. Their touch was intrusive, to be sure, but their demeanors seemed curious and almost affectionate. They leaned in to savor my screams, their yellow eyes slanted as if they were smiling at one of my stupid jokes.

The one stroking my throat pressed his bony thumb into my windpipe, playing my screams like a flute. I couldn't struggle or get away; the electricity held me firmly in place. I'd set out to fight my way to Von, but now I was their plaything, just as helpless as the damsel Hayop's theatre troupe had made me out to be.

Levi cracked a branch down on the Magtakas atop me, severing the current enough for me to rip out my knife. Danny dragged me a few feet away, but the two other Magtakas certainly weren't finished with play time. One of them reached out and cuffed my ankle, breaking all the bones in one go. I gripped Danny's bicep so hard, I'm fairly certain I drew blood.

Danny shouted... something, but I was beyond help, beyond reason, just... beyond. I didn't think I could take any more pain, but then the other one coiled his cold fingers around my knee, shattering the cap to the point of utter uselessness.

Bishop. Serena's people had kneecapped Boston's twin brother. I hadn't been able to save him. He'd died in my arms, his last moments filled with the sound of my sobs. I should've found a way to save him. I should've done something to get him out. It was fitting that the Magtakas went for my knees. It was poetic repayment after all Bishop had endured.

Maybe I didn't deserve the pain they'd put me through before this, but I knew I deserved to suffer as Bishop had. I hadn't been able to save him.

Though I had plenty of agony to scream about, my lungs couldn't bring themselves to commit to the effort as I struggled for breath. I was sweating from head to toe—cold and hot all at once. Each shiver rattled my broken bones while I begged without the coherency to form words.

My pain maximum wasn't enough for them. They leaned in to pry open my mouth and poke at my teeth. Every touch felt like a drill from a sadistic dentist who didn't believe in anesthesia. When a deafening shot rang out, that seemed to be the only thing that spooked them, impervious as they were to Levi and Von, who were doing... something.

I'd told Judge not to bring his gun, but in that moment, I forgave him for ignoring my requests.

One of them jerked and fell with a thump loud enough to be from that of a whole person, not a ghost. The Magtakas breaking my legs panicked, his yellow eyes going wide. Wanting to get away from the thing that killed his buddy, he dove skull-first into my opened mouth, his body shrinking to slide down my throat, burning and scraping as he slithered inside of me.

That's when the real pain started.

Having grown a human inside of me before, I can say with confidence that it's often a struggle to house two beings in one body. There were times when September twitched or rolled inside of my uterus so violently that it made me double over. This was far different. The Magtakas inside of me bumped into my vital organs, twisting and burning everything he touched. He was a pinball in my ribcage, banging into parts that were meant to go unmolested. I jerked on the floor of the forest, my broken bones rattling in my useless legs while I screamed.

Von was suddenly in my eyeline, shouting something I was too overcome with agony to decipher. He was kneeling at my side, his eyes wide with fright as he felt my stomach for the alien element. My body spasmed as sweat poured off of me. My spine twisted like the most experienced contortionist.

I didn't understand what was happening when Levi pushed Von out of the way.

Confusion swirled in my brain when Danny restrained my panicked husband, using a chokehold to keep us apart.

Why would Danny do something so cruel?

The entire scene played without sound, so muted was everything else to the pain that felt all-encompassing. Judge and Danny each grabbed one of Von's arms while he shouted with panic, as if Levi might hurt me. As if Danny and Judge would be totally cool with letting my own dad cause me pain. The entire thing made no sense. None of them would ever harm me, yet Von was reacting as if my own dad was about to chop my head off with a rusty blade.

Levi's face was grim as he hovered over me. He tilted

my chin and shoved a light-brown root into my mouth, and then closed my lips so I would swallow. Everything felt raw as it went down, scraping the sides of my esophagus. It tasted like mulch but I trusted Levi, despite Von's thrashing that I be allowed to escape the evil clutches of... my dad?

Suddenly I felt something wash through me, and just like that, all my pain was gone. The Magtakas inside of me suddenly evaporated, my spine going limp as my stomach deflated.

My fist released the balisong blade, and not for the first time, I felt Finn slip through my fingers.

The world felt incredibly still as the pain went from beyond excruciating to complete and utter nothing. A puff of brown air escaped my lips, and that was that. My mouth remained lolled open, my eyes unfocused as all the fight went out of me in a gust of lifelessness.

I lost consciousness to the confusing tune of Von cussing out my father.

24

MARRIED AND CARRIED

I came to under the light of the moon, which was barely visible through the thick knotting of trees. It wasn't the shouting that woke me, but the drops of condensation on my face. My lashes fluttered open to the sight of Von, utterly distraught. I couldn't lift my hand to brush his tears aside. I couldn't turn my neck, either.

I wanted to ask him what was wrong, but my body was weak and entirely useless.

"Good. She's awake. We have to keep moving. We won't get so lucky next time," Levi urged in a quiet voice at Von's side. He seemed reticent to break the hushed atmosphere, but duty-bound to lead effectively nonetheless.

"You call this lucky? You fed your daughter the very thing that murdered your grandchild! What if she'd been pregnant? What then?"

Levi didn't respond but Danny surprised us all by

being level-headed. "She's not pregnant, Von. Maybe there was another way to get the Magtakas out of her, but I bloody well don't know it. Levi wasn't trying to harm his own daughter; he was trying to save her."

The creeping venom in Von's voice scared me as he spoke through gritted teeth. "Does she look saved to you?"

"The Magtakas only made her *feel* as if her legs were broken and her body electrocuted. Those things didn't actually happen, though. She will recover from the pain, Von."

Good to know my kneecaps weren't actually shattered, though my legs were completely useless now.

My balisong blade. I needed to find it but I couldn't access my body. Panic welled up in me as I fought against the entire world. I needed my knife. I needed Finn, even if his weapon was all I had left of him.

Levi stood. His tone was still humble but his stature and barreled chest asserted his dominance over the pushback. "She looks like she's just been through the ravaging of a Magtakas. The *patayin* root kills anything inside of you, so while I regret what happened to her with losing her daughter, this was the most pragmatic way to save her from the Magtakas." He ran his hand over his face. "I'm guessing this is what Ollie and Darius are still going through. They didn't know not to look into the eyes of the vessels. It's very possible they've lost their minds to the pain by now. We have to find them. October is your wife and my daughter, but Ollie is also my child and your brother. We cannot linger. Give her to me; I'll carry her."

"I can carry my own wife."

Danny spoke reason into the bickering. "Von, she's bleeding. You can't carry her."

"Fine, but I'll not hand her over to Levi. I can't even stand to look at him right now, let alone trust him with her."

Patayin root, I realized, probably a little too slowly. That was what the Manas shoved down my throat to murder September. It was what King Geon used to taint the water so the women of Sakuna all lost their babies.

Danny's voice was rough but certain. "Judge, take my knife and be ready. I can't fight with a person in my arms."

"On it."

My body was handed over to Danny, who was careful with me. Every step taken as we moved through the woods was an effort not to jostle me too much. Danny had to duck to keep his head from the golden mist hanging in the air above us, so carrying me while crouching was a feat I wished I had the strength to spare him. Though honestly, it was a pretty safe bet that during the scuffle with the Magtakas, we'd all endured a brush with the forbidden haze. I tried not to worry about what that might mean.

Danny's chest was firm but snuggly. Not many people would guess that Danny was good for cuddling, but as my side was cradled against his torso, I confirmed what I'd always known—Danny had real warmth to him.

I wanted to walk with them so I didn't have to be carried. I knew it couldn't be easy to lug a grown person around the woods when you couldn't even stand up straight. I needed to get my blade. Finn's knife was abandoned, as if no one cared about him at all. I cared. I cared very much.

I strained my neck but couldn't even get my head to lift an inch. *Pathetic*, I chided myself. Instantly the image of the damsel actress flooded my mind, her hand across her forehead mid-swoon. I closed my eyes, wishing so many things about my life could be different.

"Stop it," Danny scolded in a firm, quiet voice as he trekked along while the night darkened around us. "I know you're getting frustrated that you can't walk yet, but it is what it is. Those Magtakas barely cared about the rest of us. The whole team of them went for you alone. It's going to take some time before you're back to your old self." He paused for a few beats, and then more quietly he added, "I found Finn's blade on the forest floor. It's in my pocket. You've nothing to worry about."

All the fight went out of me in an exhale of sadness and relief. Then curiosity settled in on me. I hadn't been paying all that much attention to the others while I was being tortured, so I hadn't noticed I was the only one in pain. Why had the Magtakas all gunned for me?

Levi spoke up from his place in the lead. "You can all keep your eyes open now until I tell you otherwise. The remaining Magtakas have moved on from this area." His fist clenched and loosened. "I thought my blood on her forehead would have marked her as off-limits. I'm not sure where I went wrong there."

Judge spoke up, adding a surprising amount of clarity to a faction of the world he knew very little about. "They went for her *because* you marked her with your blood. The vessel things trapped the part of your master's magic that can inflict psychic torture, which it sounds like he mostly used not directly on you, Levi, but on Sama, because you two were tight. He used Sama's pain to hurt you, so the vessels probably are wired to do the same thing. Go after not you, but the one you love." Judge paused his conjecture to slice a vine that was about to smack Danny in the face. "I use that trick all the time. No better way to manipulate someone with a heart than to slice it open and make them stand there while it bleeds."

Von groaned at Judge's cruelty. "Do not say things like that in front of my wife. She can't tell you how horrible that is, so I will. The methods you use to get results are what twisted, evil menaces do. I hope you see that connection."

Judge was quiet, though I could tell it wasn't in a "wow, thanks for pointing that out. My life is totally changed now" kind of way. When he finally spoke, his tone was resolute. "Then maybe I'm twisted and evil."

I wanted to scream at Judge that life was a series of choices, that he had responsibilities to Darius to be a good man. I wanted to shake Judge and shout in his face that he had a child on the way, and there was no amount of justification for carrying on how he'd been doing so far in life.

I wanted more for my Judge, but after all our years of back-and-forth, I understood now that he had to want those good things, too. Giving up the business was a start, not the entire brunt of the journey.

Danny didn't grunt or complain as the minutes ticked by and he was stuck hefting me through the woods. On the contrary, he seemed energized by the promise of hard work only he could do. His sole request was that Levi turn on his finger lights so he could better see the way as we moved slowly through the forest in the night.

When my neck could finally support my head, an ache resounded throughout my entire being. It was the illusion of being electrocuted, followed by all of my muscles tensing and contorting for far too long. All of that was coupled with an adrenaline spike and crash. I was weak but I would heal. Danny assured me as much, even going so far as to give me a slight pull to take away some of my aching. "Easy," he whispered when my muscles started cramping up as they came back to life. Then he stopped walking. "Hold up, Levi. She's sweating so badly, I'm going to drop her."

Danny didn't lower me to the ground but sat cross-legged and draped me across his lap. My head was cradled in the crook of his arm, giving me a whiff of his cologne-scented deodorant. I tried to focus on the smell to distract myself from the muscle spasms that were ricocheting through my legs and stomach. It was like hoping to be gently woken with a sweet song, but getting a blast of AC/DC so intrusive it made your teeth rattle.

"Easy," Danny cautioned again, smoothing my stray pieces of hair away from my sweaty face. Judge and Levi took the opportunity to grab a few apples from our packs and pass them around, but Danny refused. His eyes were locked in on mine, as if we were the only two people in the forest.

When Von moved away from the group to drink from his blood bag in private, Danny shifted us so his back was to the others. He thumbed my cheek so sweetly, no one would believe it if I told them. I expected him to bark at me to quit whining about the pain, but he didn't. Instead he was kind. I barely recognized him.

"When Mariang overreaped and was in too much pain to move, I would hold her just like this." He glanced down and lifted up my wrist. "And her hand would be just here." He pressed my fingers to his chest so I could grip his shirt. My knuckles were feeble, but it helped to have something to hold onto while the echoes of pain rippled through my muscles. "She liked me to pull right here when her legs were hurting. A direct shot of something to numb it all. Does that help?" He tucked his thumb under my knee, tracing a line slowly back and forth along the underside of my thigh to send a concentrated pulse of pain relief through my legs.

"Oh," I breathed. My legs relaxed like slow-melting

chocolate at his tender touch. My words came out mumbled but my chin could finally move enough to form words. "That's so much better."

A small smile of pride shone on Danny's face. He needed to be useful. He had years of on-the-job experience that were invaluable in situations like these. When Mariang had died, he'd lost his wife and his purpose. It's impossible to lose your spouse and function normally right afterwards, but people who have a purpose are generally better at finding their way eventually. Missions like these gave Danny back a little piece of himself. Despite the excruciating road to get us here, I was grateful for the sweetness all the same.

He cuddled me closer and rubbed his cheek against mine, his scruff prickling my skin in a way that was surprisingly pleasant. "I can fix this," Danny promised. "If I'm around, there's nothing to worry about at all. We'll find Ollie and Darius. We'll cure Allie's brain. You'll be running headfirst into trouble in no time." He was in his element, looking after an Omen who could barely raise her head.

But I didn't want to be that girl. I lifted weights with Mason three times a week when he was Topside so I didn't wither away. "Danny," I whispered, my lips slick with sweat.

He leaned in so my lips were pressed to his ear. "Yeah?"

Maybe I shouldn't have said the next words, but pain does strange things to a person if left unchecked. "Please don't let me die."

Danny's entire body stiffened. He pulled back to study my fear, showing me that he was capable of worry. "Why would you say something like that?" Then he turned his chin over his shoulder and barked, "Give us a minute. Would you want a bunch of gawkers when you can't take care of yourself? She's not hungry, I'm not hungry. Eat your bloody apples and leave us be." Then he turned back to me, his voice hushed. "Look at me, October. You're going to be just fine, today and for always. We'll find Ollie and Darius and go home, where I'll make sure extra charms are put in place to keep out intruders. You're going to live to be an old woman with white hair." He thumbed my curls. "You'll complain about wrinkles. When your arthritis aches you, I'll be there to take your pain away." He stroked the underside of my knee again in a manner so loving, I nearly cried. "I will always make things better for you."

My heart stuttered in my chest at the beautiful pledge that crackled between us, shifting in the nighttime air. When Danny leaned in to kiss my lips, I decided to let myself believe in the beauty of his promise.

GOLDEN MIST

Levi kept watch that night when the trees proved too thick to move through any longer without the help of daylight. He covered our bodies with a blanket from his sack in hopes of keeping the remaining Magtakas away from me as they roamed through the forest.

I ended up sandwiched between Von and Danny, who did a double pull to keep my body from seizing up while I slept. Judge wasn't a snuggler, so he kept to the furthest edge of the blanket on Von's other side.

"I was scared for you, Peach," Von admitted. "I don't do well when you suffer and I have to stay away. I should've brought more blood."

I kissed Von's lips, my stomach fluttering as Danny thumbed my hip while he slept. He did that often—little comforting gestures he couldn't own up to during the daylight. Danny spooned me, my head on his no doubt aching bicep, while Von threaded his legs through mine. I was so used to being squashed between Mason and Von during the nights that this was just more of the same, minus the cozy mattress to cushion us.

Von looked tired, the demons of our past wars haunting the outlines of his eyes. "Levi shouldn't have done that, forcing the *patayin* root on you. I tried to stop him. I'm so sorry, November."

The sadness that swept over me wasn't nearly as bad as Von's grief, which seemed like a freshly-sliced wound tonight. "Honestly, I'm okay with it. Let's not go there in our minds. It's a bad place, and we're already stuck in one of those. I want to go somewhere beautiful with you."

A shadow of Von's smile slowly bloomed. "Do you think we can get away with going to our makeout place?"

Levi's voice was firm. "No. As quiet as you think you're being, my senses are sharper than the average father. Go to sleep, kids."

Despite the gravity of the day, Von's eyebrows danced playfully in the night, his hand ghosting over my cheek to relax my clenched jaw. "Goodnight, Peach. Don't have too many filthy dreams about me."

"Only a few, then," I consented, my eyes closing to take advantage of what little rest we were granted.

I'd been hoping for a solid few hours of sleep but when

my eyes opened again, the sky was still dark. Mason was sliding his pants back on, having shifted from his Matruculan form back into a man. I sat up with much effort, proud of what felt like Superman strength that was returning to my body after a little rest and a whole lot of pulling. I was finally able to prop myself up on my elbows like a boss so I could peer up at him.

Mason shot me a devious smirk as he zipped up his pants. "Ready to love me forever?"

"Only forever? I was already set to love you for all of eternity. Guess I'll have to dial back my affection a little bit."

"I found Ollie and Darius, but we've got to move." He shoved his bare foot in front of Danny's face to wake him, tickling his nose with the big toe. "Rise and shine, campers. Home stretch, here."

Von sat up and stretched while Levi gathered our things. My husband was quiet, pensive, and I could tell by his lack of humming any sort of Rat Pack song that he was somewhere else in his mind entirely. I moved in to hug him while the others were packing up and taking sips of water, grateful that my body seemed ready to cooperate and face the day. When his hand migrated to my abdomen, I knew he was thinking of our daughter, and wishing the results from the fertility specialist we'd gone to privately over the summer hadn't been what they were.

We contented ourselves raising Anastasia Grace and

doting on Penny, but I knew the devastation might always be there underneath the surface of our smiles. If the healing waters couldn't cure whatever had gone funky with my bruised uterus, then in my mind, there wasn't much hope. Von still carried a small glimmer of optimism that one day it might happen for us. Perhaps that's why he was so devastated month after month when it didn't. The doctor gave us a five-percent chance of ever conceiving. After I'd lost September, I'd been assured that I could still carry a baby, no problem. Maybe that was true, but the getting pregnant part seemed to be the hurdle we couldn't overcome, no matter how masterfully we wrecked our bedsheets.

My fingers laced through Von's and Mason's as we tromped through the woods with our heads down to avoid making eye contact with any Magtakas that might not have gotten the word that we weren't easy targets. But as we hacked our way through the underbrush, they were nowhere in sight.

"Over the felled tree there. Not much farther after that. Maybe another mile or so," Mason announced, squeezing my hand. We were so attuned, the three of us, that my Reapers knew to keep up a slow dose of pulling to ease any difficulties I would have with the whole sleeping on the ground and not washing my hands thing. Von had even packed hand sanitizer for me, the romantic.

We all walked in silence, which was only broken up by Levi's occasional remembrances of a life gone horribly wrong. "Over there is where Sama murdered a man who called him insane. He told me he'd killed him in self-defense, but I found out later that hadn't been the case. I trusted him so blindly back then."

Every bit Levi revealed of himself was treasured and tucked in my heart as part of a grand secret that had helped create this great man in my life.

When Levi stopped to sniff the air, his spine stiffened with the crack of something new. His chin jerked to the right. "Mason? Come with me. Danny, Judge and Von, don't move from this spot. Keep my daughter safe until we return."

My lips pursed at being sequestered to damsel status once again, but I knew part of the job was staying safe, even when it injured my pride. My body wasn't in pain anymore and I was fully functional, still I had to stay back. "Fine, but next time you, Ollie and Mason go to Sombi on a hunting expedition, I'm coming too."

Levi's head whipped toward me, his eyes narrowing. "Over my dead immortal body. Do as I say, October. You don't know this forest as I do, and you certainly don't know Sama as well as I did. I can sense... Just stay here."

I wanted to spout back that I knew a fair bit about Sama, down to the length of his manhood, but I held myself back for the sake of not sounding like a brat, or sounding like, well, a girl who'd slept with her father's best friend. I winced at the ickiness of it all.

"Come on, Peach. Ezra wants us all back in one piece."

Von ran his thumb across my knuckles and then brought my hand up to kiss the back of it. "We've spent our fair share of time in the thick of the action. Best not throw ourselves in front of every single train that zips by."

"Oh, fine," I harrumphed.

As Mason and Levi went off to do something cool and dangerous, Von turned and brought my arms to fasten around his waist from behind. Without needing to be asked, Danny pressed his back to mine, drawing his knife while Judge kept close to us, his gun at the ready. The guys remained crouched a few inches, making sure the gold mist didn't touch the tops of their heads.

"Guys, do we know what happens when the golden air touches us? Because I'm thinking in the fight back there with the Magtakas, we probably all got a brush with it at least once."

Von's hand moved to my wrist to secure me to him, and Danny's hand migrated around my hip. "No," Von replied with a grave note to his voice. "I mentioned that possibility to Levi when you were passed out, and he said 'what's done is done,' and left it at that. I've been too worried to press him about it further. If we can get to Ollie and Darius, then grab those flowers, Mason and Levi can port us all home. We'll deal with any other fallout then."

The woods were quiet, with no whispers of the Magtakas to send a chill down my spine. Part of me hoped we'd killed the only ones in the area, but I knew better than to assume we were in the clear. There were no animals, no birds—nothing to make us feel like the trees weren't about to swallow us whole. My eyes darted around, cataloging every rustle of a branch that might prove to be a menace.

It was Judge who broke the silence, though when his words tumbled out, I almost wished he hadn't. "It sounded bad, what those hooded ghost guys did to you. If Darius is going through that..." He shook his head, rubbing the back of his neck. "I need to find him now. Stay with Von and Danny, okay baby girl?"

My snarl couldn't be helped. "If you think I won't tackle you to the ground if you split off from us, you don't know me. We're staying together."

Judge shook his head. "The gold air touched me. Like, my whole face. I don't feel any different now, but it's probably still coming. I can't lose myself when we're this close. I have to find him. My brother needs me. Ollie needs me, too."

Von was calm when I was ready to fly off the handle. "Both brothers need you to stay alive right now. If you go wandering off, you will get lost, and then we'll have to waste time we could have spent rescuing Darius because we'll have to save you. Levi and Mason will be back in no time. For Darius' sake, stay with us."

Judge consented, which meant I didn't have to lay him out. When twenty minutes passed, Von relaxed against me, sheathing his knife. Danny was the gargoyle who didn't relent. Even when Judge suggested we all sit down while we waited, Danny paced, knife drawn and a "come and freaking get it" sneer on his face. He lasted two hours before he sat down with us.

Judge and I each munched on a *baga* root in silence. All four of us were unwilling to put volume to the worry that Mason and Levi should have been back by now. When night fell, Danny offered to keep the first watch while Judge and Von made a sandwich out of me on the forest floor.

Judge kissed my forehead, his whisper not quiet enough to go unheard by the Vandershot boys. I thought he might tell me goodnight, but his lips froze on my skin. I could feel his fear in his suddenly tensed body. "Baby girl! Tell me you see him!"

I glanced around to the spot past my head where he was staring as if he'd seen a ghost. His eyes were wide with fright, and his fingers gripped my arm to steady himself. "Who? I don't see anyone, Judge."

He sat up, standing as a sob broke loose from his composure, which was rapidly crumbling. He moved to a nearby tree and caressed the air in front of the bark as if it was his long-lost friend. "Terence? Are you really alive?"

My heart stuttered as I watched Judge embrace something utterly not there, hugging an invisible shape. "Judge, honey, there's nothing there," I warned as I scrambled to my feet.

Judge wasn't interested in any logic that took his brother away a second time. His voice was dripping with emotion and worry. "Terence? T, come on! Don't play me like that, man!" Judge was seeing Terence, whose ashes were currently in a jar at Sherita's place.

It wasn't until then that I understood the sadistic nature of the golden mist.

ALL THE LOVES WE'VE LOST

e watched with mouths agape as Judge fell to his knees and covered his head, howling his distress at the nothing before him. "T, I never should've pulled you back in. You wanted to get a job at the grocery store stocking the shelves, but I made you feel like it was a stupid choice. I didn't know you were gonna up and get shot! I didn't know! I'm sorry, T. I'm so sorry!"

I knelt behind Judge to wrap my arms around his torso, but at his gasp of horror as his head whipped to the right, I stayed back. "Mama? Mama, I'm so sorry. You told me to look after Darius and Terence but I let you down, Mama!" Actual tears dripped down his cheeks, shocking me to my very core. "I wanted to make you proud and give you nice things like you deserved, but you didn't live long enough to see any of it. Now T's gone, and you're..." He paused, as if listening to her speak. Then he covered his face, bowed his chin and wept as a man does only when he's being spoken to gently by the woman who sees through all his bullshit.

Mama McCray had loved her boys, flawed as they were. When she'd been buried, the entire world kept turning without her smile and without her kindness that took in starving and filthy children who'd been cast aside.

I sat behind Judge, wrapping my arms around him through his dip into his deepest regrets. I wanted to tell him it would all be okay, but I wasn't sure if that was a lie. Mama McCray was still dead, and so was Terence. There was nothing okay about that. I held my Judge so at least he wouldn't be completely alone, even if that's what he felt.

The effect of the glittery mist was a slow-moving wave through our collective, starting with the tallest and working its way through the group. Danny and Von both hissed at the same time, and even though they were behind me, I could feel their hackles raising. "What is that? It's not..." The horror in Danny's voice scared me. If something was haunting enough to rattle Danny's cage, I knew things were about to go south real quick.

"Bishop?" Von whispered, his tremulous voice filled with wonder. He took a step forward, extending his arm to a pointed spot. Though there was nothing there, his hand didn't close around the void but gripped it as if the hand clutching his were invisible. When Von brought his deceased brother in for a hug, the hairs on the back of my neck stood up. Von's shirt twisted a bit, as it would if he was holding an actual person. My hand covered over a scream when his hair ruffled as if Bishop was truly there, actually running his fingers across the top of Von's head.

"Von, it's not a ghost. It's not a vision. He's really there! Bishop is touching your hair!" I didn't know if we should be excited or very, very afraid.

Judge stood and clung to his brother and mother, weeping openly on their invisible shoulders.

I sat on the forest floor, utterly perplexed at all that was going on around me.

"Danny, come here," Von urged, waving his hand toward his brother.

Danny shook his head in rapid jerks, taking a step back as he opted for fear in lieu of a bizarre family reunion.

It wasn't often Von turned sharp on his acerbic brother, but at his bark, both Danny and I stiffened. "You'll come here right now and hug your brother. If you couldn't be bothered to while Bishop was alive, you'll hold him now. This is your only chance to be with him again, so stop being a coward and get over here!"

Danny's feet moved like lead blocks as he stumbled forward. It was hard to be sure but it looked like Von was released, and Danny was being hugged. It took several beats for his arms to gather up the courage to wrap around his baby brother, but my heart swelled when Danny finally held onto Bishop. "I didn't do this hardly at all when you were alive. I should've... I don't know why I thought it was better to keep myself away from you all. I'm sorry, Bish. I didn't save you. I did all I could but I still failed."

Von took a step back, keeled over and let his tears fall to the forest floor, utterly beside himself with grief. "You all were mine to look after. I should've sent you home the moment I came back. You were only brought into the mess because I wasn't looking after November as I should've done. I was rubbish at guarding her back then, so my responsibilities fell to you. That's not how it should've gone!" I wanted to correct Von but it seemed Bishop was on it. Von shook his head. "Logic doesn't matter when you're dead, and we're all broken because of it. Forgive me, Bishop."

A chill washed through me as I watched the trio of Vandershot boys hold each other together while they all fell apart. Slowly, in swaths of color and finally shape, Mama McCray, Terence and Bishop became visible to me. They were themselves, not zombified versions of the undead. They weren't laden with bullets, stumbling or bleeding. They were composed and ready to welcome their family with open arms and no condemnation.

No condemnation. Man, I wasn't expecting that.

I nearly screamed when an elbow nudged my side. Mariang's sweet voice sounded like a bell in my ear. "How long do you think it'll take for Danny to notice I'm here?" She said it like a joke, but when I turned my head, there was nothing funny about the woman sitting by my side on the moss.

My last encounters with Mariang were when she had been resurrected by Danny to be a Woman in White. She'd been bloody, translucent and terrifying. But now she was my ballerina incarnate, whole and healthy with the tiniest bit of pink in her cheeks.

I wanted to talk to her, beg her to forgive me for not being able to save her in the hospital, and then for stabbing her phantom form, but when I opened my mouth, I couldn't find my voice.

Mariang looped her arm through mine, and I could feel the silk of her skin, the give of my arm against hers. She wasn't a mirage, but a warm body holding tight to mine. I was on the verge of crying, screaming, running, and never leaving this spot again so I didn't have to be parted from this miracle. She leaned in, as if it was totally normal for us to share secrets these days. As if she wasn't dead at all. "I'm not sure I ever told you this, but Danny clenches his buttocks when he's holding himself back from things he doesn't want to feel. Watch." She pointed, giggling at Danny's butt that, sure enough, danced a little as he hugged Bishop.

Of all the things I wanted to think about, Danny's butt was not on the top of that list. "I don't think you're supposed to know new things you haven't told me back when you were alive. You're a memory, right? A hallucination? I'm... This is... What are you?"

She blinked at me. Her black hair was pulled up in a bun, and a smile teased the corners of her mouth. "I'm your sister."

"But you're dead," I said bluntly, unsure if I was being rude.

"Then enjoy me while I'm here."

My vision blurred, and it was only then I realized that I was crying. "Does it hurt, being where you are?"

Mariang shook her head. "I feel better than I did while I was alive, that's for sure. Tell me you pilfered my closet. It's an absolute waste for all my dresses not to be worn."

I shook my head, holding in a scream while Mariang brushed away my tears. They actually moved around, the moisture smearing into my cheeks, adding evidence to the conjecture that Mariang was real, and not some hallucinogenic byproduct of my medication. "I could never wear your clothes. They make me think of you."

"What a lousy fib that was," she teased, the apples of her cheeks lifting. "You prefer your jeans, no matter what gorgeous gowns are at your fingertips. Please tell Allie to wear them, then. She'll appreciate the fine materials."

"You know about Allie?"

Mariang nodded. "I get to watch all of you on occasion. I can't believe how spectacular my daughter turned out. She was worth it. Every part of it."

I shook my head, unable to wrap my mind around it all. "Anastasia Grace is the best little girl in both worlds, for sure. But she needs you. I have no idea what I'm doing!" Panic seized me around the throat that I was face-to-face with the mother of the little girl I was helping to raise. What if she didn't like the kind of formula I'd bought? What if I didn't spend enough time snuggling Ana for Mariang's liking? What if Mariang was also opposed to Anastasia sucking her thumb? "How do you want Ana to be raised? Tell me what to do, and I'll make it happen. I'm sorry. I know I'm blowing it all over the place."

Mariang tsked my tears, continually swiping them off my cheeks. "Now, now, you can't keep carrying on like this. You'll have no tears left for when I have to leave. I want a sobbing mess of a goodbye, understood?"

I nodded. "Tell me how to raise her."

Mariang kissed my wet nose. "You're doing a beautiful job. If you could keep reminding her that her mothers love her, I would be most grateful."

"I do, and I will. Every day. I promise."

"Thank you." Then her nose crinkled. "I know this request is petty, but if you could ask Danny not to dress her in that green jumper that has a stain on the belly, I would appreciate it."

I nodded so quickly, her laugh drew Danny's attention. His head turned like the crap of a whip, astonishment flying out from his lips in a cry of disbelief. He sank to his knees, holding his chest as if his heart might explode out of his chest. The way I could see the entire whites of his eyes, I wondered if it just might.

Mariang released me, her eyes on her husband. "I love you, October. Tell Dad he's the best parent in the entire universe, and I want him to marry Lavinia. I want him to be happy. I know he feels miserable with guilt every time he smiles, but it's enough. Life is for the living, and Lavinia makes him come alive. I want that for him."

"I'll tell him."

"Thank you. I think I'd like a few moments with my husband now, if that's alright. It's time for you to go to her."

"Ana's back with Ezra."

Mariang shook her head, jerking her thumb behind her. "Not Ana. Our mother. Go to her."

I froze as dread coiled itself in my stomach. If Mariang could touch my arm and wipe my tears away, I didn't want to get beaten over the head with the business end of a hairbrush. I turned slowly, vomit rising in my throat as I was confronted with the one woman who'd formed me the most.

At the sound of my name on her lips, I scrambled away. I'd gladly face a zombie army, but I was a terrified child when too many guesses flashed in my mind as to what Bev might do to me in her afterlife.

ENOUGH

"October Grace, wait!"

I couldn't even glimpse Danny and Mariang's tearful reunion as I scurried to my feet and darted away into the woods. Judge's family embraced him. Von's brother held him. Danny's wife checked out his butt. I really didn't want Bev to beat on me. I didn't like defending myself against her. It tore me up more than I liked to let on. Madness is my specialty, and she's the one who drove me to it most often.

The branches scraped at my face but I didn't care. I needed to get away from the wreckage that my childhood had been with her as the center.

"October Grace, stop! Honey pie, I'm sorry!"

That was probably the only thing that could've slowed my race through the trees. I turned, completely confused by the thing she never ever did when I'd lived with her. "Did you just apologize?"

"Yes! I'm sorry, October Grace." Bev caught up to me, her entire demeanor different to match her more subdued look. She didn't have high bangs and platinum blonde hair pulled back with a pearl clip she'd fished out of a pile of garbage. She didn't have flashy clothes on that shoved her boobs in everyone's face. She wore a pressed rose-hued blouse and khaki slacks. Her hair was pulled back in a ponytail, of all things. She didn't have a stitch of makeup on, and I've got to say, I've only seen her without makeup when she was fresh out of her sagrado stone haze and coming back to her true self—whoever that was.

I backed up when she stepped too near, my butt bumping against a tree as my mouth opened in a silent protest.

Bev studied my fear and left a healthy three feet of space between us. Though I could see she wanted to reach for me, she dropped her hands and clasped them in front, her mouth pulling to the side as she thought through what the crap she could possibly say to make things cool. "I guess this is probably pretty frightening for you. I know I should stay away but this is my one chance to talk with you. Not that you have to say anything. Just being near you is enough. Maybe if you don't want to talk, you can hear me out?" She held up her hands, grimacing when I flinched at what I assumed would be an assault.

I don't know how I found the wherewithal to nod, but

my chin moved up and down as my words remained tucked inside of me.

Bev's shoulders relaxed that I wasn't still running, and I was willing to listen. I guess being stunned into motionlessness would make anyone a stellar listener. She twiddled her thumbs, her Southern lilt more pronounced when she was nervous. "Ezra's told you to forgive me because I wasn't in control of myself, what with the sagrado stone and all. Ollie's said the same thing, but I don't want you to brush it all under the rug. Just because I wasn't in my right mind doesn't mean all of that didn't happen. I was awful to you, October Grace." She touched her lips and then her head. "I want you to live a better life without me. Find a way to move on from me. If that means forgiveness, have at it. If that means turning away from it all because it hurts too much to sort through, that makes sense too. I rest easier knowing that you're nothing like the mama I was."

Still stunned, I couldn't do anything to even pretend I absorbed the depths of all she said.

Bev seemed to understand my flabbergast. Even that was strange, since she'd never made an effort to understand anything about me. She kept her voice quiet, laced with tears that were just barely held back, but choked her words all the same. "Can I... Would it be okay if I looked at your arms?"

It took a few beats, but my chin acted on its own, bobbing up and down, giving Bev permission to step closer. My heart was erratic inside my chest, unsure which way was up anymore.

Her touch was gentle when her unpolished fingernails brushed over my forearms. I didn't have the brainpower to deny her, but her hands caressing me felt utterly foreign. When Mariang had snuggled up to my side, it was freaky, don't get me wrong, but it also felt like déjà vu. It was an extension of something totally natural because we'd done some variation of the snuggle too many times to count. But Bev had never held me like she loved me. She'd never touched the marks on my arms as if they mattered or bothered her in any way. Yet here she was, wet tears dripping down her cheeks and splashing on my wrists. I could feel them touching my ugly parts. I felt her pain. Her remorse. Her devastation.

"These scars are... You're breaking my heart with this, honey pie. I wish you would let me help."

It was here that I found my croaky cadence. "No one can help me. This is just how I am."

Bev shook her head, sniffing as she thumbed away a few of her tears. "After all the damage I've done, if you would let me, I just want to do one thing right now. Then I promise I'll leave you alone forever."

My chin answered for me once again, my eyes widening when Bev pulled out a marker from her pocket.

"This might sting a little. I've never done this before. If you give me this next minute, I won't take any more minutes from you for the rest of your life. Deal?"

I swallowed hard, unsure if I had it in me to deny a simple request from someone who had such a humble demeanor. It was a strange color on Bev, to be sure, but she was so earnest with her big, pleading eyes. I kept my arms outstretched as she pulled off the cap and started scratching out a single word on my forearms.

Though it looked like a regular fine-tipped permanent marker, the tip was almost like a knife. It didn't draw blood as it scraped along my forearms, but it was painful enough that I could've sworn it was slicing through veins. The urge to resist the pain occurred to me, but my psyche leaned in with a sigh of relief the more it burned.

I kept my eyes on her, not on whatever it was she wrote. Her nose was wet and pink, her eyes focused as if she meant to pour her very being into that one word on my forearm. When she finished, she picked up the other arm and wrote once more with her pen that pierced my protesting skin.

When she finished, she nodded with a glow of triumph. "There. That's all I wanted." She picked up my right forearm, turning the tender inner flesh upward so I could examine the one word she had inscribed into my skin in the blackest ink.

"'Enough'?" I questioned.

Bev let more tears fall on my forearm, as if she expected something inside of them might have the power to heal me. "You are enough, honey pie. No matter what you think about yourself, I hope you hold this one truth in your heart. You are enough for whatever lies ahead."

I bit down on my lower lip to keep from arguing. I wasn't enough. I couldn't reap enough to keep Allie from inevitably going back to work, and one day, Anastasia. I couldn't heal Danny enough, or Ezra. I was a part-time mother to Anastasia. I would never be enough to fill the gap Mariang's absence imprinted on that precious baby. I was a crap daughter to Levi, I was certain, never knowing if I was being too much or not enough. But as Bev rubbed her finger along the word on my right forearm, she looked so very certain in her verdict that I wasn't falling short on all the roles I'd found myself cast in. "How can you be sure?" I whispered.

Bev looked into my eyes, her hand reaching out to touch my cheek. "I'm your mama. I just know." Then she turned over my left arm, displaying the same word scratched there in black, wreathed in red.

I quirked my eyebrow at her. "In case I forget, you wrote it twice?"

Bev curled the fingers of my left hand in hers, closing her eyes in earnest. "This one is to tell you that it's been enough. All that you've put yourself through, whatever punishment you think you have to endure to feel worthy of getting out of bed in the morning, it's enough."

Whatever dam I'd constructed to wall off my heart suddenly began to splinter, allowing a small but significant trickle of life to push through. I shook my head, wondering if she was right, and if that even mattered at this point. "I think it's too late for me," I admitted in a whisper.

I didn't shirk away when Bev wrapped her arm around me and pulled my body in for a hug. It was the maternal touch I tried never to need. I only ever soaked it in via Allie. Somehow Bev had found a way to crack through my defenses, breaking down a barrier I never thought I'd be able to function without.

There in the woods, my mama held me while I sobbed on her shoulder for all the things I wasn't, and the horrible things I sometimes still was. She didn't judge me or shush me, but let my self-loathing breathe in the fresh air, in hopes some of it would float away, never to return to the tight hold I usually had on myself.

She kissed my cheek in the way I'd seen mamas do on TV, and the way I hoped Anastasia felt my love for her. For that brief slice of time, we were the Brady Bunch. Then Bev whispered in my ear, "Levi doesn't remember where the *sigla* flowers are; he's been leading you in circles. Take a few minutes while I tell Von where they are. Eat the flower, honey pie. Take some to everyone back home, too. There's no easy fix for a life you barely survive, but they'll help." She held up my right arm, looking me in the eye to tell me that I was enough. Then Bev held up my left arm, reminding me that I had been through enough, and it was time to stop punishing myself. It was time to start choosing things that were good for me, whether or not I felt I deserved them. Whether or not I had any faith in the power of goodness anymore.

I didn't know if I believed her, but of all the things she'd branded on my soul, I wanted this one promise to be true. "Thank you," I whispered.

Bev looked over my shoulder and then winked at me. "Maybe take more than a couple minutes coming back. I'll cover for you."

I turned to see what she was looking at, certain we were alone.

Nothing could have prepared me for the sight that filled my watery vision. Strong and handsome, barrel-chested and in-control, the man whose very presence had strengthened me far beyond his shortened lifespan stood against the thick knots of trees. My mouth felt dry as my lower lip quivered.

When Finn said, "Did you miss me, Lissima?" my legs went out from under me and I lost my grip on consciousness.

RICARDO AND LISSIMA

I awoke to Finn and Bev fanning me and slapping my cheeks, but when my eyes focused on the face I adored, my heart nearly gave out. "Finn? What are you... How are you..."

"I'm here, *sinta*. I'm sorry it took me so long. I was trying to sneak September through to see you, but you have to walk through on your own, and she's stuck as a newborn, so she couldn't." Then to Bev, he said, "Go on. I need some time with her. Keep the others busy as long as you can."

Bev nodded and then trotted through the woods toward the camp where the others still were.

"But you're dead!" I protested. Though truly, I should have stuck with this logic the moment Mariang had come to me. Somehow seeing Finn in the flesh was one leap too many. His sand-colored hair was still military short, and the gills on his neck still beckoned my fingers to poke at them to test their pliability. He wore a black no-nonsense t-shirt, matching pants and sturdy boots, looking exactly as he had back when he was… when we were… "How, Finn?"

"Don't you know by now?" He shook his head to scold me. "'If you live, then I breathe.'" He made a show of his chest expanding and contracting, as if my very existence powered his own.

My breath came in hard gusts, and I errantly wondered if I might hyperventilate. "That's not possible. None of this is." I needed facts. I needed verification. I reached up and touched his face, ran my fingers through his soft hair, and brushed my thumb over one of his light-colored eyebrows. I reasoned it would be hard to fake real eyebrows.

Finn rocked back on his butt and pulled me to sit on his lap as only he could. I'd never been much of a lap-sitter, but Finn had always been one to push my boundaries. He touched my curls as if they were precious and not at all ragged in their haphazard ponytail. "But here I am. I might only get you for a little while, but I'm not about to complain. You're just as stunning as you've always been." Then his voice took a darker turn that gave me the chills. His thumb and forefinger spread out, gripping my chin in that controlling way that did deviously bad things to me. "Tell me you ache for me."

I bit down hard on my lower lip, unsure if I was

allowed to be honest, or if that would be a slam on Von, Mason and Danny.

Finn narrowed his eyes at my silence. The answer was written in the blush on my cheeks. "Of course you would tease me. In my first life and now this one, you're still keeping me waiting."

I didn't want to say the wrong thing. I didn't want to speak at all. I wanted to see. I wanted proof that what we had wasn't small or fleeting. It was real. And even in this magic-addled forest, I wanted us to be real, if only for a few minutes.

I didn't ask permission, only took what I wanted, which was what he had always offered to be for me. My lips met his, spooking him with a jolt of surprise that I wasn't holding back this time, as I had always done right up until the end. It had taken a sea monster to get me to admit that I was in love with him in our first life, but this was our second, brief though it may be. I wasn't about to waste our precious few minutes talking about the weather.

I wanted green. I wanted silver.

I wanted our hut on the beach with the palm trees, coconuts and the ocean.

The introduction of the psychotropic nature of our kiss was jarring for us both. I was so used to kissing Von, Mason and Danny. But this was different. This was a vision I'd held in my heart for two years now, praying in earnest that I wouldn't forget the details of a life too spectacular to be buried.

It was simple, our world—the one where he wasn't a fish, and I could swim.

My tongue touched his without regret, tasting the man I'd been so afraid to love. When I smelled the salty air of the ocean, I sobbed into his mouth, holding onto him for dear life.

"*Sinta*, look around you. We're not in the forest anymore." There was a note of claiming me to his voice. "I knew you still loved me. Even when you belong to them, you're still mine. Always mine."

Though part of me wanted to protest, the evidence around us was pretty damning. The palm trees were brushed with a blush of purple as the green and silver sparkled in the air around us. The blue ocean that lapped at the sand was clearer than any body of water I'd seen since.

"I'm not supposed to love you," I said lamely, as if that would somehow erase what I knew had been engraved on my heart.

Finn kissed me again, his hand migrating down to squeeze the underside of my thigh, as if I belonged to him. Perhaps part of me did. Perhaps it always would. His lips were firm yet soft, his quiet moans of longing utterly delicious as I devoured one after the other. When he lowered me to the sand, my hands roamed where they wished, feeling the firm planes of his torso. Each ripple had been born of torpedoing through the water, the hardness of his body and soul forged from fighting to save a country that had wrecked his childhood.

He knew I wanted a better view, so he sat up and tore his shirt over his head, casting it onto the sand as if the whole world was our bedroom. Sand, not grass. We weren't in the forest anymore, but in our makeout place that only appeared because of our love.

Finn hitched my legs up around his hips and leaned back down to press his body atop mine. I wanted nothing more in that moment than to make Finn a part of my very being so that nothing could separate us ever again.

"How long do I have you?" I asked between kisses, pawing at his body like a horny teenager.

"Forever," he pledged, jerking me around with promises that could never be.

I tugged on his hair, pulling his head back an inch to scold him for the lie. "Actually how long?"

A tender agony softened the lust in his eyes. "Not long enough. Never long enough. Promise me you have a good life. Tell me it wasn't all a waste."

I nodded, swallowing hard as he hovered over me. "It is. Allie's alive. Von and I are good. Mason's happy. The kingdom's settled." I ran my thumb across his sun-kissed cheekbone, marveling at the feel of his skin. Every caress ached my insides, bringing back a flood of memories I wasn't sure I ever wanted to live without. "I had a statue of you erected in Dagat. It's on the palace grounds."

Finn's lips curved into a slight smile. "That's sweet."

Tears glistened in my eyes as the green and silver glittered around us in our own personal haven. "I lay flowers on it a few times a year."

At this, Finn's mouth tightened. "I don't want you going into Dagat without me there. How about instead of flowers on my statue, you leaf through one of my books? That's more us than anything else."

My chin trembled at mention of the language we shared. "I haven't been able to pick them back up. Without you here, it's not... There's just no point in finishing the romance without you."

"Lissima," he breathed like a prayer that was filled with reverence. How I loved the way Finn could take the mess that was me and turn it into a true moment. Somehow he was able to force whatever sweetness life hadn't stamped out of me to the surface. He leaned in to brush his nose across mine. "Finish the series. It's got a satisfying ending. Finish it and think of me."

I shook my head, my voice tremulous with the vulnerability I tried to keep buried down deep. "That's exactly why I can't finish it. I was halfway through the last book, and I haven't been able to pick it back up." I looked into his eyes, admitting things I'd been denying to everyone else. "I don't want it to end."

Finn studied my tears for the fresh heartbreak they were, and leaned in to kiss me just once. Then he rocked backwards, standing in a fluid motion that bespoke his agility I'd always found impressive. When he extended his hand to me, I reached for him, knowing a portion of me wouldn't, couldn't be parted from him.

We walked in silence toward the yellow cottage with white shutters framing open windows that welcomed the ocean's breeze. The wooden porch was connected to a long dock that ended in the ocean, beckoning for us to come inside. Because we lived here. Because this place, this life, was ours alone. I could see the hammock hanging in front of the picture window. "I forgot how perfect this place was."

Finn kept his eyes glued on the cottage as we moved up the porch. "I didn't. I remember every detail." He stopped me before we could go inside, surprising a squeak out of me when he hefted my body up in his arms like a bride. "That's right. I know Topsider customs. I'm to carry you over the threshold."

I opened my mouth to protest that he wasn't my husband, but closed it before the words could break our beautiful moment. If all we had was this dream, this flash of fulfillment, I wouldn't sully it with reality.

Finn didn't bother with the lantern on the wall as he carried me past the kitchen and living area toward the back of the cottage. The lavender and brown rug was littered with sand, but I didn't care about the mess. Oh, how far I'd grown.

The red sheets of our bed beckoned us to unmake

them from the militaristically tight arrangement. This time, I was ready for the challenge. I knew exactly how fleeting life could be. Finn had taught me that, among so many other things.

But I also knew my body might have a certain weakness for psychic sperm, so after my shirt was tugged over my head and cast onto the wooden floor of our haven, I put my hand over his to stop him from popping open the button on my jeans. "I can't get pregnant," I admitted between kisses.

Finn's lips slid down my sternum, making my back arch as he played my body like a fiddle. "That's what you think. I want to try."

A thrill of my mind being blown rocketed through me as Finn familiarized himself with my curves. That he could say such incredible things to me nearly broke me all over again. "I love you for saying that. But we shouldn't. Getting knocked up—possibly psychically—the first time was an accident. Twice would be overkill."

Finn moved his hands from my jeans and made himself at home playing with the parts of me I made available to him. Everything was heightened. Each touch was electric, sending jolts of desire through me that brought me higher and higher far faster than was my usual proclivity. It seemed each nerve ending was on the same page—make the most out of the fleeting moment.

Finn's body was a thing to be admired, so my hands made quick work of tracing every ripple and each muscle that pulsed with need for me. It was incredible to think that someone so strong, certain and smart could be taken with me. Though Graham had put his foot down that Ollie's friends would no longer call me "kid" or "Bait," they still slipped from time to time, reinforcing that no matter how grown I got or how much my position in Terraway was respected, I might always be awkward and on the outside of my own life. But here, tangled in the sheets that existed only because of my love for Finn, I felt like everything I was might somehow be enough to find myself in a bed with the great Captain Finn Fredo.

Finn's kiss made me feel like my entire being was constructed from pure magic, my skin sparkling with an effervescence I felt rippling over my flesh. His kiss was everywhere, consuming my worries and replacing them with a certainty that nothing else in the world existed aside from this kiss, this cottage, this life that was mine, if only for a short time.

"I love you, Finn," I admitted, unsure if I'd said it enough or in the right way so that he truly heard me. I'd held myself back from him too many times in our first life, denying the thing that was obvious to anyone who'd spent more than five minutes with us. "I love you. I'm so sorry I... Oh..." I moaned, my body writhing as he proved he knew exactly what to do with me if he was granted the chance.

"I don't want you to be sorry. I want you to be happy. Remember us this way. Remember this place."

"How do I find you? If I come back to the forest, will you be here again?"

Finn caught my earlobe between his teeth, then let it slide out so he could drag his lips downward. "We only have today. You can't come back here, *sinta*. Promise me."

"No!" My body went rigid as I sat up. "No, I can't promise that. I want this! I want more of exactly this."

When Finn realized that sexy times were being paused for conversation, he sat back on his haunches and picked up my foot. For all my indignation, my entire being melted into the sheets with a groan of indulgence. He knew exactly how to calm down my angst so he could wedge some logic into the mix. He massaged my arch and dug his hand into my heel, chuckling at my lidded eyes. "How easy it is for you to seduce me. To see you so pliant and willing like this? Mm... Tell me you think very dirty thoughts about me still."

Though I was shirtless and completely exposed, that brought out a blush to my cheeks. "We were talking about me visiting you more often here."

Finn's smile vanished as he rubbed a tricky spot around my ankle. "You can't come back to me; I'm not the only thing in the forest."

"Right. The Magtakas. Those things suck. Oh! Right there. Did I mention that I love you?"

"You might've, but I keep forgetting, so never stop telling me."

"I love you, Finn. I can handle the Magtakas." I wanted

to promise him all the things to make up for the fact that I'd given him nothing in his first life.

He pinched the underside of my thigh to center my bravado. "No, you can't, and I don't want you to. It's too dangerous."

I motioned around the peaceful cottage, gazing up at the man who loved me enough to rub my feet. "Where's the danger? I'll just venture into the forest far enough to stick my head into the golden mist, and blammo, sexy times in our love shack." I grimaced at my words. "I'll come up with a better name for our cottage than that."

Finn chuckled, and the sound was deep and velvety. "I can't wait to hear it. This is all we'll have, *sinta*, so enjoy me now."

I was about to protest but his lips turned my words into mush when he sucked on the spot behind my ankle. A rush of unfettered desire raged through my body and lit my nerve endings on fire. My legs opened wider, inviting him to come closer, always closer. "Finn, you're making me crazy!"

When his tongue laved between my toes, my brain melted in a string of nonsensical mutterings. I was a puddle of malleable lust on the mattress, shifting where he turned my body, and giving him access to parts I'd been embarrassed to show him before.

It wasn't until a voice interrupted us from the doorway that my eyes shot open.

"That's not how she liked it with me," the uninvited

guest commented, making me wonder just how long we'd had an audience.

The teasing tone set my teeth on edge. I sucked in a breath, hoping with everything in me I wouldn't come face-to-face with the man I both hated and feared.

When I turned my head, there he was, my secret voyeur and psychic lover.

29

MY DARLING DALITA

"Philip? You're dead!" I shot up from the mattress and pulled the sheet up around me, yanking my foot from Finn's mouth as I backed up to the furthest edge of the bed.

"Indeed. So is your fishy lover. I'd no idea you had a foot fetish, my sweet. Oh, the fun we could've had."

His square jaw with the dimple in the center was clean-shaven. Philip stood with his arms crossed over his chest. He was the picture of ease, leaning against the doorjamb as if it was all very humorous for him to be watching me in bed with another man.

Finn sighed heavily, tossing my discarded shirt to me and pulling his own over his head. "I told you I wouldn't let you near her. Go on, get a good look. You're not going to lay a hand on October, Sama."

My head whipped from Philip to Finn in confusion.

"You two know each other?" I mean, obviously Finn knew of Sama. He'd gotten close enough to deliver the final blow that ended Sama's life, which effectively brought his own days to a close as well. But the way they were talking sounded as if Finn was bored of a rowdy employee's antics.

Philip smirked at Finn, crossing his arms over his beige shirt, looking like a thirty-something with all the answers. Paired with black pants, his bright white-blond hair stood out all the more—an oddity no matter the setting. "Finn is my *dalita*. I'm very fortunate to have someone so tenacious in this life. Most *dalitas* get bored after the first month or so, but Finn here never tires. Every day is a new adventure for me. Quite the difference from my first life, which was spent largely in solitude."

I'd gone from blazing hot to feeling like I'd been doused by a bucket of ice water. I shivered from the cold that Philip's words pressed into me. I straightened my shirt around my ribs and backed up off the bed, keeping the mattress between myself and Philip. "What's a *dalita*?" It sounded like a term of endearment, but I knew that couldn't be accurate.

Philip smiled at me as if we were old friends, which maybe we were. We'd confided in each other and grown decently close before he'd revealed his true nature and tried to force himself on me. "Finn ended my life at the same time I ended his. Both our deaths involved a fair bit of magic as well, so here we are. Fate chose him to be the *dalita* of the two of us. Can you believe that?"

I huffed, my hand on my hip. "In English, Philip. Honestly. It's like you're purposefully trying to piss me off." I wondered if I should be fighting him with bare fists already, or if being aggravated when you saw the man who'd haunted your nights was an appropriate response. "How are you even here? This whole place only exists because of Finn and me. Our love created this. You were not on the guest list."

Finn made a contented "mm" sound at me proclaiming my feelings for him aloud, and in front of a witness, no less. "Magic lasts far longer in the Baluki forest. We're seeing the cabin; Sama's seeing the trees and whatnot."

Philip met my eyes with a steady command. "Come to me, little one. I'll explain everything."

Finn seemed to have a better grip on the situation than I did. He edged himself between us, tucking my body behind his so I was smooshed between his back and the wooden wall. He turned his chin over his shoulder toward me while keeping his eye on Philip, who hadn't budged from the doorway. "When two people murder each other at the same time, one of them becomes the *dalita*. Fate decides who is doomed to be chased and perpetually killed, and who will be the one doing the killing. Fate was not so kind to me in my first life, but in my second? It's the hunt of a lifetime every single day." He paused for my intake of breath and all the implications that played out in my imagination. "Most *dalitas* grow tired of the chase after a month or two, but not me. Sama put his hands on you, so in my second life, I'm allowed to punish him for as long as I wish." The corner of his mouth twitched upward as his eyes raked over Philip. "Look at him sweating through his bravery. I've killed him so many times, you would think the thrill of it would grow tiresome to me, but I guess not."

I chewed on my lower lip, unsure how I should feel about the mischievous glint in Finn's tone when he spoke of perpetually murdering someone. Then again, Philip had molested me and left Allie in a coma after raping her. The part of me that loved my sister bit my tongue to keep any scolding tucked away. "Does it hurt?" I asked quietly as I peered around Finn's side.

Philip's eyes darkened, and I saw the malice that had turned on me so many times. "Getting stabbed through the stomach always hurts. It's my least favorite way to die."

"He was hiding from me for a while, but I knew when you stumbled into the forest, he would turn up. How would you like me to kill him today, *sinta*?"

Philip hissed, his shoulders tightening as his body shifted from feigned relaxation to a live wire of tension. "Do not call the mother of my child that."

I rolled my eyes, as if Sama's anger was a joke. "Give me a break. You don't give a crap about me. You wanted a baby and I was your ticket. Don't act all protective now." I shoved my shoes and socks back on, and then resumed holding Finn from behind.

"You are wrong, *sinta*. Sama is obsessed with you." Finn shook his head at Philip's sneer as a shudder of disgust rolled down my spine. "You don't know September was your baby, Sama. She could just as easily have been Von's."

My chin jerked up to Finn's face, my heart racing afresh. "I don't want Philip near me."

"Sama," Finn corrected me. "His name is Sama. Never forget that."

Too many emotions roiled through me as Sama and Finn traded acerbic insults.

Philip's tease had a bite to it now. "She gave herself to me over and over, Finn. More than she ever gave herself to you."

I cringed at how those words made me sound.

Finn's voice was a deadly snarl. "Slowly today, I think. I'll kill you nice and slow. I might even ask her to watch so she knows that no matter which life you're in, you'll never get close to her again."

I pressed my cheek to Finn's spine, soaking up his warmth that served to center me when I felt like I might burst apart into a million pieces. Each particle of my being was on edge, wary of the next move, whatever that might be.

"Be careful," I warned, worried about the smallest scrape that might mark the beautiful man who loved me through whole planes of existence. I reached into my pocket, pulling out the balisong blade to defend what belonged to me.

"Put that away," Finn assured me, his directive delivered in a soothing voice. "No one can kill him except for me. It's my destiny, *sinta*. Though, I'm glad you keep that on you. Always keep me with you."

"I will," I promised, pocketing the blade.

It was a simple motion, me moving my hand to wrap around Finn's hip to rest on his navel. His palm covered my fingers, thumbing my knuckle in a way that not only make me feel safe but also cared for, as if I was special enough to protect when I had no idea what was going on.

"Do not touch him like that," Philip ordered, his tone going sharp.

My hand froze—the calm before the storm.

The next part happened so fast, I could scarcely make sense of it all. Finn lunged over the bed toward Philip, who scurried the long way around the room toward the spot where I stood. I raised my fists, which didn't slow him down one bit. I knocked Philip across the square edge of his jaw, but his hand gripped my bicep through the pain I could see playing out on his face. "Finn's had his time with you. Now it's my turn."

When I started the scream, I was in the cottage. When the scream ended, I was back in the Baluki forest, fighting against Sama with Finn nowhere in sight.

30

BURNING TOUCH

I wailed on Philip, punching him across the face and in the stomach with all my might. Maybe he thought that by not fighting back, I would lose my steam and he could sneak one in on me, but I wasn't about to test that theory. I wasn't sure if I could actually do lasting damage to him, but I was sure as Sunday willing to exhaust myself trying.

"Only Finn can kill me, you know," Philip said as he put his arms up to guard against me clawing at his eyes.

"Then it'll be an easy murder for him after I'm finished with you." Another hard punch across the face that snapped his chin to the left gave me a satisfied glow. I wasn't the damsel in the play. I wasn't the girl afraid to go to sleep because the monster would come to prey on me in my dreams. I was a force to be reckoned with, and this was Philip's judgment day.

It was when I landed a solid kick to his groin that Philip decided he'd had enough. After letting out a groan of distress, he whirled me around and pinned my arms down, securing my back to his front while my chest heaved. "Calm yourself. You were such a sweet girl to me before. Let's go back to those days. The ones where you adored every inch of me and didn't hold back your affections."

I did my best to elbow him but it barely made a dent. "I'm nothing to you, and you're nothing but a nightmare for me. Let me go, Philip."

"Listen to me," he whispered, jerking me against him so tightly, I couldn't wiggle away. "I know your mind better than most. You don't want to be an Omen. You want to see the world. Don't you recall our time together, staring at the many wonders that took our breath away?" I wanted to punch him for being insightful but I couldn't move my arm. His voice tried to be gentle, to lull me into doing something he wanted. "I can give you all those things. In this life, I've seen it all. We can go anywhere, experience everything."

"What are you talking about?"

"Come away with me. It'll be painless. We can make love in every country, sweet girl."

My stomach heaved with bile that threatened to explode out of me at his assumption that I would go anywhere with him. "Obviously that's a no. Let me go!"

"You wanted me! Before Ezra could poison your mind

against me, you wanted to spend all your nights by my side. You lit up at the sight of me. Don't you understand how powerful that was? I can make it just like it was before it all got wrecked."

"You hurt me! Don't you get that? You hurt me and you nearly killed Allie. I could never love you after that. The thought of how stupid I was about the whole thing makes me sick! Let go!" I squirmed but he was just plain stronger.

His lips touched my ear, and I knew he was confusing my disgusted shudder for a lusty shiver. "Easy, Gracie. Let's not waste our precious time fighting. I knew Finn would go to you at the first opportunity. He doesn't know that you belong to me. Your mind was mine long before your heart was his."

"Get off me! Von!" I screamed, unsure where exactly I was in the forest.

Philip cupped his hand over my mouth, trapping my cry of distress inside. "Do not say his name in my presence. He is nothing, do you understand? Nothing! He is an insect who knows little of what could be done with a mind like yours." His hand trailed down my shoulder, stretching my shirt to the side as I shivered with revulsion. "Finn won't stop until he finds me. He's relentless. We don't have much time."

I hated the shriek that erupted from me when he ripped my t-shirt from collar to hem in one go. The only silver lining was that his arms moved just enough to give me the space to break free. I popped my hip out, tipping his balance as I gripped the arm he'd banded around me and used it for leverage. I flipped that bastard clear over my body and landed him with a thud, splayed before me on his back.

That's right. I'm not helpless. I've fought inmates, rulers, Ekeks, Manas, and even the occasional zombie.

The breath knocked from him, he choked out a feeble, "Stop!"

I ran through the woods, my torn shirt flapping and snagging on branches. My hands worked to tie the edges of the fabric over my torso as I darted between trunks that were too close together for him to easily fit through. My horror rose in my throat as I did my best to outrun my tormentor.

"You will give me an heir, so help me!" he called, still on the chase.

"Von!" I shouted, ducking under branches and splashing through a stream.

"No, Gracie!" The fear in Philip's voice almost made me stop short, but I charged onward with soaked feet, unsure where the crap I was headed, only that it was away from him. "The river is cursed! Your legs... You shouldn't have done that!"

Not five seconds after he said that, my feet felt like they were on fire, the invisible flames stretching all the way up to my knees where the water soaked through my jeans. "Ah!" I cried out when my legs felt suddenly weighted as the fire devoured them, to the point that I couldn't run any further. I collapsed in a gust of agonizing defeat, slapping at the flames I couldn't see while my skin burned. "Help!"

Philip swore when he caught up with me, dropping to his knees in what looked like genuine concern. "No! Hold still, little one. I'll fix it." When he gripped my calves, a mixture of pain and fear lit me up on the inside and the outside, consuming me from all angles. I tried to fight him off, but my legs were too heavy to move. Plus, Philip actually looked like he might be trying to help me, which was totally confusing.

"Honey? October Grace, where are you?"

My heart soared at the sound of Levi's voice. A sob belted out of me, hitting the air with the smack of fresh desperation. "Dad! Help me!"

"Levi, hurry! I don't remember the incantation!" Philip sounded just as scared as I did.

When Levi burst into view, my heart soared with relief, momentarily trumping the perpetual pain. One thing I knew about dads from my education with Ezra was that if your dad showed up, everything was going to be okay.

Levi's wild eyes took in the scene with a shudder of shock, as if he'd seen a ghost. Of course, he was seeing his dead best friend, so that part was pretty spot on. "Sama? Brother, what are you doing here?"

"She ran through the stream we cursed to protect the *sigla* flowers! How do we make the burning stop before the fire penetrates her skin? I can't remember!"

"What?" I screeched, my head whipping between the two men as my legs screamed at me to make the pain stop.

Levi turned to face me, kneeling on my other side. He gripped my hand like we were gearing up for an arm wrestle. The skin on his fingers was rough, and his meaty hands looked as they always had—capable of true greatness. His eyes bored into mine with the purpose of invoking something far more powerful than a simple pep talk. "Do not let go of my hand, October Grace. No matter what, hold on tight."

"Dad, it's burning me!"

Levi closed his eyes and pressed his lips to my forehead, murmuring in a whisper a string of syllables that I hoped would make it all go away in a blink. The pain, sure, but also I wanted Philip gone. I didn't want him near me when I couldn't kick him in the groin.

My legs were immobile, though it felt like they should be spasming and twisting from the pain. Levi kept steady with his chant, scaring me when whole minutes started to tick by.

It wasn't until my head lolled back when the pain ramped up to a level that made me nearly delirious that Philip reached out and took hold of my other hand. He gripped me in the same way Levi was holding on tight, murmuring in the same rhythm.

"Don't touch me! Don't you friggin' touch me!" I shouted, trying to rip my hand from Philip's.

But Philip didn't listen. Instead he moved his free hand

under my head to keep it from flopping back, cradling my curls as if I meant anything to him. I didn't want his help. The feel of his touch made me sick inside. It wasn't just that he was a sadistic rapist, which would have been reason enough. It was that I fell for it all. Every time I looked at him, I felt like the kid in the group who was gullible enough to believe in Santa Claus when everyone else knew the truth.

I hadn't known his true nature. That was a crime for which I still hadn't forgiven myself.

"Do you remember now?" Levi asked his friend, and Philip nodded.

I wanted to throttle my dad when he pulled back, leaving Philip's lips to recite his incantation against my naked forehead. I wanted to vomit through my horror. I didn't want his lips touching me ever again, and yet, here they were.

Levi slid his knife from his belt and cast me an apologetic look. "These have to come off where they touched the water, sweetheart. Hold still, if you can."

I couldn't actually move my legs, so that part wasn't totally up to me. I wanted to kick at Levi for leaving me vulnerable to Philip. I wanted to shout at him for letting his creepy friend sneak in kisses to my forehead.

Levi slid off my shoes and socks and sliced a line all the way around on my jeans, just above the kneecap. The second the fabric was removed to change my pants into a pair of impromptu shorts, the searing agony lessened to only pretty bad. It was enough that I was able to draw in a full breath, leaving my body a limp noodle of relief.

Philip's hand on my cheek was gentle as he wiped away a line of my sweat. "I would have taken such good care of you. You had no cause to resist me. It was Ezra who poisoned you against me, making you think I was some sort of monster. I'm a pragmatist, just like you. People like you and me, we get the job done, no matter the cost."

I wanted to scream at him to get away but my breath was still coming out in uneven chunks as the ancient charm made its way through me at an agonizingly slow rate.

Philip ran his thumb over my lips, his eyes studying my fear with curiosity. There was a note of confusion in his eyes, as if he couldn't understand why I was on the verge of a panic attack when he got too near. He opened his mouth to say something, but I never heard what lunacy might come. It was at that precise moment that a branch clocked him clear across the back of his head, dropping me from his grip.

A female voice rang out through the woods, making my heart skip several very important beats. "Don't you touch my daughter ever again!"

31

PARENTAL PROTECTION

I'd never seen Bev with righteous anger before, only the self-righteous kind, which was a very different look on her. She used the branch like a baseball bat, walloping Sama across the ribs when he tried to pick himself back up. "I know you don't think you're sniffing around my baby girl!"

Levi blinked up at Bev in much the same way I did—with confusion and wonder. I'd only ever seen her turn violent on Ollie, Allie and me. To see her unleash on Sama for being a creeper distracted me just enough to forget about the pain in my legs as it slowly ebbed.

"Finn!" she called. "I found her!" Then she bashed Sama over the head with the branch, ensuring he wouldn't get back up anytime soon.

Levi dragged my useless body away from the fight, propping me up on a nearby tree trunk so I could watch the brawl from a safe distance. Then Levi moved to Bev's side as she wailed on Sama. My dad's wide eyes silently debated if he should try to protect Bev, or if he should just stand back and let her go to town.

She only paused her tirade when Finn joined us, his mere presence bringing me a bucket of relief. "He'll tell you. Tell Levi, Finn. Tell him about Sama's obsession." Then she bashed the branch down on Philip's ankles when he looked like he might try to stand. She was wild but controlled, feral and feminine in her strength. It was... It was incredible.

Finn glanced at me, worry flashing in his eyes at my obvious distress. He turned his focus to Levi as he drew his knife. "It's nothing you don't know. Sama wants to get October pregnant because he's convinced she's the only one who can give him an heir that can age. September's useless to him, because she'll remain an infant forever. He's done all he can to try and break through the barriers that keep us separate from the living." He postured, puffing out his chest to enforce his dominance. "But I won't let that happen. I'm his *dalita*, and I will never tire of watching his eyes close." Then to me he gave a sharp command. "October, I want you to watch me carefully."

Bev dropped the branch to the forest floor, surrendering her weapon now that Finn was there. The rhythm of it seemed natural to them, as if they'd done all of this before, perhaps many times over. "He's right, honey pie.

All you have to do is stay away from this forest, and we'll make sure Sama never bothers you again."

I let out a quiet bleat of worry. "Is that possible? Can he bring himself back to life?"

Finn managed a glimmer of a smile at me as he shook his head. "Not if I'm here to protect you. Every day, I hunt him. Every day, he'll die for what he's done. You can sleep without fear, *sinta*. No matter what, I'll keep you safe."

My heart pounded in my chest at the implications that scared and enchanted me. I didn't want Finn to never rest in his second life, but I really didn't want Philip anywhere near anyone with a pulse ever again.

Finn stood over Sama and yanked him up by his white-blond hair. With panic in his eyes, Philip reached out for me in a plea that scared me to my very core. "No! I was so close! I'll come back for you!" As if that was what I wanted.

Then Finn sliced a line clear across Philip's throat, letting the blood splatter all over the grass. He didn't stop at my bleat of terror, but stabbed Philip through the stomach as well, dragging his blade sideways to let my tormentor's innards spill out.

I covered my mouth at the sight. No matter how justified, violence is violence. I knew that image would remain burned in my brain for years to come.

Finn dropped Philip's body and stood, rolling his shoulders back as he let out a long groan of satisfaction. Then he reached out and bumped his fist to Bev's. "Your swing is getting more accurate. That was really fantastic.

You had him practically incapacitated before I even got here."

Bev beamed at Finn. "Just doing like you taught me, is all."

I balked at the two, unable to put to words what the crap I was watching. "Huh?" was all that tumbled out of my mouth, drawing all three sets of eyes to me.

As one body, they all pounced on me, fawning over my legs that I was just now realizing were dotted with angry red splotches. Fresh water from Finn's palm smoothed a coolness over my forehead to rinse away the sweat. Then he ran his palms down my shins, easing some of the ache that felt like freshly burned flesh.

"You... How?" Was all I could manage.

Finn shrugged with a modest smile. "When your mother isn't being warped by the sagrado stone, we actually get along pretty well. We have a common goal, so that makes us a tight team. We'll always make sure Sama never gets his hands on you." Bev and Levi took off my shoes and socks, fanning my legs while Finn leaned in to speak more privately to me. "I promise to look after your mother, *sinta*. No harm will come to her if I'm around. She has a much better life now; I made sure of it. Together we keep September safe, so you don't need to worry about her, either. Mariang watches September mostly, and sometimes Mama McCray helps. Bishop does his part, too."

My chest shook at the perfect thing I didn't realize I wanted him to say. Too many emotions bubbled up and crashed around inside of me, shaking up things I was usually too afraid to touch. "Mariang's raising my baby?"

Finn smirked at me. "Well, September doesn't actually age, but yes, Mariang's the one who mostly looks after her. I thought you'd appreciate that. Your daughter is treasured, *sinta*."

Tears spilled over my cheeks, soaking my resolve that I wouldn't waste our precious few minutes together by losing it in front of Finn. The broken bits of me that often felt chaotic and beyond repair began to settle in pitter-patters of potential peace. My daughter was with Mariang. "Thank you. I don't deserve you. After everything I put you through, I can't..." I clumsily swiped at my eyes. "I don't know how you can be so good to me when it's my fault you're dead in the first place! Now you're bound to hunt Sama for all of eternity? That sucks!"

Of all things, Finn sniggered, leaning back on his butt to draw me carefully onto his lap. My legs had stopped hurting unless they were shifted, but they were still pretty useless all the same. "It's the greatest reward for someone like me. I would be bored to tears, sitting around doing nothing. A hunt that's new every day? The woman I love safe because of me? Her family in my care?" His eyes met Bev's with something that looked like true appreciation. "A mother who isn't ashamed of me?"

My breath caught when I saw it plainly—a son who'd been given away by his mother, and a woman who desperately wanted a shot at motherhood redemption.

Bev raised her chin with the firmness of a promise. "I would never turn my back on you, Son."

I shook my head, touching his face just to feel the prickle of his cheek. I wanted to burn him into my memory for all of eternity. Finn was my family, however far removed. "But what do you get out of this?" Though he'd just told me, it didn't seem like enough.

Finn thumbed away one of my tears, staring into my eyes with such unfathomable love that it looked as though he was savoring the sight of me. His ribs expanded and contracted contentedly. "*Sinta*, don't you know? 'If you live, then I breathe.'"

PRECIOUS PETALS

inn hoisted me up as he stood fluidly. He was tall, making the ascent a bit jarring. I slung my arm around his neck to be sure I didn't fall, though really, I was hardly useful in that department. My legs were completely numb. He turned us to face my parents—*my parents*—and bobbed his head at Bev. "We'll give you two a moment. I'll take her to the *sigla* flowers, collect a few for Ollie, Darius, Allie and the others, and then head back."

"Sama won't come for her?" Levi inquired. I was a little relieved to know that I wasn't the only one who didn't have a behind-the-scenes knowledge of the second life that Bev and Finn were totally rocking.

Bev fielded that one. "No. It takes Sama a solid half a day to come back, and I want you gone before he does. You'll be out of the forest by then. You and Mason will need to port everyone home. Can you see to that?" Bev placed her hand on Levi's tricep. His whole demeanor softened, leaning in towards her. It was the cutest, most surreal thing. I had never seen my parents together before.

"Anything you need. Of course, Beverly." Levi met her eyes, and I began to see why Finn wanted to give them some space. There was sadness there, mingled with longing. It was a strange color on Levi, for sure. I'd never seen my dad interested in a woman before.

Finn turned us away and started the trek through the woods. He was quiet for a few beats, then said quietly, "Your mother's apologizing to Levi right now for her shortcomings when she failed to raise you three." I didn't know what to say to that, so Finn pressed on. "I told her that this wasn't on her. It was on Levi for giving her the sagrado stone to begin with, but even that wasn't his fault because he had no idea it would warp her as it did. I hope she doesn't waste the entire time apologizing."

"I cannot picture that. The whole thing is so far out there; I can't really wrap my mind around it all."

"Speaking of your mind," he said, lowering me to the forest floor near a patch of what looked like enormous white calla lilies with petals stretching the length of Finn's hand, "you need to eat one of these flowers. They'll help heal all that's gone sour in you. I'll pick a few to take to the others." It was the only spot I'd seen in a while where a large beam of natural light shone through the branches above, lighting up the Holy Grail of flowers.

I wanted to dig my heels in at the prospect of my

neurosis being brought to light, but instead I breathed through the grudge I had against just plain life, and plucked a flower from the clearing. I examined the petals with caution.

Finn didn't glance over at me as he picked a dozen flowers, but I knew he was tracking my movements all the same. "So help me, if you fight me on this, I'll shove that thing down your throat."

"There's nothing wrong with me, Finn. Allie's the one who needs them."

"And she'll get one. But make no mistake, you need one of these flowers. You have two Duwendes yet you still gouge up your arms. Do you think that doesn't break me?"

I winced, glancing down at both forearms. Bev's inscription hadn't smudged or washed away, reminding me that I'd been through enough. Resisting help now, however it came to me, would do no one a lick of good. If I was to reap enough to sustain all of Terraway on my own, I shouldn't let my pride get in the way of my sanity. Beneath Bev's writing, I could see the claw marks for what they were—an expression of agony. Part of me, however glossed over or disguised, was in palpable pain.

After everything I'd been through, maybe I didn't want to live in the pain of it all anymore. Maybe I wanted something better. Something brighter. Something that didn't break as soon as I touched it.

Finn's voice was strained. "I can only introduce you to

peace. You're the one who has to want it. You have to make the choice. I can't make it for you."

I could tell he very much wanted to make good on his offer to cram the flower down my throat, but this part of the process mattered to him. He wanted me to want to get better, which meant acknowledging I had problems. Panic clawed at my insides, and finally I saw the choice clearly. I was choosing fear. I was cuddling up to anxiety. A chance at a better life was presenting itself to me, and I was clinging to the darkness like a little girl afraid to let go of her blankie.

"So, October Grace Reese, what's it going to be? Survive or thrive?"

The second the white petal touched my tongue, I tasted something that can only be described as pure sunshine. As if life itself was breathing into me its own source of healing, my lungs expanded with the CPR that knocked me backward and slowly pumped my chest in a loving rhythm. I can't explain how I knew it held affection for me, but the thrum of a heartbeat can't be fabricated.

It wasn't like the healing waters, this presence that breathed newness into me. As I gazed up at the sunlight through the trees, I still couldn't use my legs, but the mess of Sama and all of that seemed... different now. Like I could view the whole experience through a lens, stepping away from the mess as needed instead of feeling engulfed in fear and question marks. My body didn't feel healed, exactly, but I could see beyond my limitations, noticing possibilities of hope that sparkled like glitter in my mind. My psyche had felt so very fractured, but now it felt whole, calm, and dare I say it, sane.

Madness had been my specialty for so very long. I barely recognized myself now, laying without overwhelming angst on the forest floor.

A tear rolled down the side of my face as I raked in the beauty all around me that I'd failed to notice before. The greens seemed lush now, the trunks twisting up toward the heavens not to wall me in, but to shout about their triumph over having burst forth from mere seedlings however long ago. They were still happy about their growth after all this time, and perhaps they were also cheering on my own, which was only beginning.

"I need to take one for each member of the council, Finn."

"The council?"

I nodded once. "I just know that if only they could see the world with clarity like this, Terraway could be a far more peaceful and perfect place. I want that."

Finn's gaze burned with adoration as he gathered up several more flowers. "I love you. Of course I'll do that for you."

Precious. That's what it was. I saw not that everything in nature was perfectly in order, but that it was precious. As Finn carried me through the woods toward the others, I realized that because I was part of that same heartbeat, I was precious, too.

33

PERHAPS A BETTER LIFE

Finn stopped as soon as we heard Von's voice just ahead. "I can't take you any farther. You can call for your husband and he'll come for you."

"Is it your time to go back to your other life?" I swallowed hard, trying to put on a brave face for him.

Finn sucked in his lower lip before answering. "Yes, but that's not why. Sure, the magic in the gold mist is starting to wear off on you, but honestly, I can't hand you over to Von. I just can't do it." Then, as if anticipating me chiding him, his neck shrank. "I know. He's your husband. He's good to you. Believe me, I've kept an eye on it all. Still, I can't do it. It's like my body won't let me."

I didn't know what to say to that, so I snuggled into his warmth as he sat down in a small clearing just spacious enough for the two of us. He set down the bundle of flowers and then laid me on the grass. He reclined beside my form, kissing me twice as he settled in.

I touched his chin and his lips just because I could. "Finn, can I tell you that I'm sorry it ended how it did?"

"No." He leaned in and kissed me again, nipping on my lip just long enough to bathe our clearing in green and silver. A low, sultry trumpet played its jazzy melody in the background, giving us something seductive to hold onto. "You can tell me that you love me with no regrets."

"I do love you." I traced my clumsy fingers down the side of his cheek, cherishing the feel of having him so very close.

"You can tell me that you'll have a good life, and that you'll stop being afraid."

"I'm not afraid," I protested.

"You're afraid of lots of things. You're afraid anything might hurt Allie, so you freak out if there's so much as a fly that bothers her. You're afraid for Mason every time he goes to Sombi."

"Well, those are all legitimate concerns, Finn."

He reached down and ran his knuckle over my naked abdomen. Man, even simple touches felt heightened, now that there wasn't a low thrum of agony undermining every move I made. "You're afraid if you get pregnant, it'll all end as it did the first time. It won't, *sinta*. Stop reaping for a while. You know that's what's keeping you from conceiving. Your body needs time to calm itself, otherwise it'll never happen."

I closed my eyes. "You don't understand. If I stop reaping, then one day Anastasia might have to be awakened. I don't want this life for her." Because we were alone, and because it was Finn, I confessed my deepest, darkest worry. "If I have a baby, she might turn out exactly like me! I can't... That would be..."

Finn listened to my heartbreak without dismissing it. "She will learn, as you have. She will make the world better, because you will teach her how to love recklessly. That seems to be your way." He sniggered at me. "A husband, a boyfriend and a Danny. Reckless, indeed."

I shook my head. "My body's been through too much. It's too late, Finn."

"It's not. But you're right that you can't share your body with a baby if you're constantly donating it to the kingdom. Stop putting your dreams on hold for Terraway. Give yourself the space to rest, and it will happen." He brushed his nose across mine. "The world needs more of you, not less."

When my vision clouded over, I slammed my palm onto the grass between us. "Damnit, Finn! Stop saying the perfect thing! I'm trying to hold myself together over here."

So apparently the flower didn't erase my temper. I was still me.

He wasted no more time covering his body with mine, kissing me as if there would be no more tomorrows. For us, that was accurate. This would be our only chance to say goodbye properly—our second chance that life had been kind enough to grant us. We were two lost souls who'd found their way to each other in the dark in one life, and now in the next, as promised.

His thumb traced from my lips over my chin, down my breast and around my navel. "I love you, *sinta*. Promise me you'll never come to this forest again. Breaking my heart is the best thing you can do for us both. I couldn't handle it if Sama found a way to come back for you for real."

Goosebumps erupted on my skin, and for all the times I'd felt torn when indulging in the luxury of Finn's kiss, I felt no division now. Everything was simpler, clearer after ingesting the *sigla* flower. It was all so very easy to love Finn without reservation, now that my brain didn't hate me so very much. "But what if I want to see you again?"

He let out a bleat of distress into my breasts as he kissed his way down my body. "We have to stay strong, Lissima. Promise me that you'll remember me forever, exactly like this. When you cross over into the next life, we'll find each other, but not before then."

I pulled him up so I could study the torment in his eyes. The storm brewing in his soul was evident, but Finn was a soldier, so he knew the benefits of denying himself for the greater good. I drew him in so I could kiss his lips once more, imprinting the flavor of Finn in my memory to last me until I grew to be an old woman. "I promise."

"I don't have long." He shuddered against me, laying flat over my body as he trembled. "Beaches."

"What?"

His chest heaved unevenly, his eyebrows pulling together in frustration that nature was taking us away from each other. "Every time you go to the beach, will you think of us?"

"Every single time. Without a doubt. I might even take swimming lessons, so I go more often."

Finn climbed back up my body and buried his face in my neck. "Oh, you drive me crazy, woman. I begged you to let me teach you to swim but you always resisted."

I chuckled, the movement of my breasts reminding him that he hadn't kissed me in far too long. The green and silver danced around us while a sole trumpet played a sad, slow song. We held on to the love that didn't belong in this world any longer, no matter how badly we protested that it should and it must.

The weight of him atop me was a comfort but the moment his body vanished, a sense of void trickled down all around me. The urge to claw at my arms was still there, and might always be. But I thanked the new chance I'd been given and balled my hands into fists, keeping them at my sides. I stared up at the ceiling of the forest, wondering if my life would always feel so very filled with hope. Perhaps I wasn't doomed to pass my neurosis down to the next generation. Perhaps I would go back to Anastasia and present that precious girl with a mama she could look up to and run to when life threatened to shred her to bits from the inside out.

Perhaps I could step away from my job for a spell.

Perhaps I could take some time for myself. Some time for Von. Some time for rest.

Maybe I would travel to the places I've always wanted to go, but believed someone like me didn't belong. Maybe I belonged exactly where I put myself. I was finally beginning to understand that those choices were far more vast than I realized.

My brain danced all over, touching on things I'd buried and lighting them up for me to examine with new eyes.

Though, it wasn't all sunshine and lilies. Finn was gone. I took a few breaths to acquaint myself with that cold fact. I could hear the others in the distance but I remained on the forest floor, staring up at the thick overhang. The trees promised to keep my ocean of sadness a secret that I would leave here. I didn't want to hide it from anyone, but it was mine, this connection I had to my eternal warrior. It felt sacred somehow, so I took the time in the quiet of the woods to savor the silence, giving all that we'd shared a moment of respect.

34

TOGETHER, AND THEN TORN APART

I didn't mean to lay there for so long, but when night began to fall, I heard Levi tromping through the underbrush. "Dad?" I called to him.

"October? What the... What are you doing here, laying out in the open like this? Did Finn vanish before he could get you back to the others?"

"Something like that. The flowers," I reminded him, and he scooped them into my arms before hoisting me off the ground.

Levi moved through the woods carefully, as if I was too fragile to be jostled. "You need to eat more. When we get back, I want to sit down with Lynna and check your calorie intake." He bobbed my body in his arms. "This is too light."

I smirked at his hovering that I found absolutely adorable. To have a parent tell me I needed to eat more was a sharp contrast to being called fat while being starved. Ah, memories. "That's a good idea." The image of my parents locking gazes resurfaced in my mind. "Did you and Bev do it?" I asked with no lead-in.

Levi tripped and nearly dropped me. "Pardon me?"

"You heard me. We gave you plenty of time for at least a little something."

Levi's cheeks pinked but he didn't answer. At my chuckle, he changed the subject. "You haven't asked when you'll be able to walk again. Did Finn already tell you?"

I shrugged. "He didn't say. I figure it'll all work out eventually."

Levi turned his chin to raise an eyebrow at my newfound Zen. "Yes. I guess it will. Should be at least a week, if you're worried. Mason and I found Ollie and Darius, but they're in bad shape. When you see them, just be prepared. They're physically okay, but the Magtakas have been torturing them for weeks, feeding them scraps of food and *baga* root to keep them just alive enough to torment. Darius hasn't blinked yet, and Ollie was passed completely out when we found them. No doubt the *sigla* flowers will help."

"How about the healing waters?" I suggested.

Levi shook his head. "There weren't any cuts on them. It's all mental, which is what the *sigla* flowers can cure. They're in shock. I'm not sure either of them realize they've been rescued."

I thumbed one of my dad's dreadlocks that had fallen

from its nest at the base of his neck. "Where did the flowers even come from? Did your tool of a Kapre Master hocus-pocus them into being, or did you just happen to stumble across them one day?"

Levi let out a derisive snort. "That would involve him actively making the world a better place, which was something he had no interest in. I created them a very long time ago. They were a sort of insurance policy for Sama and me. But the tools I used to conjure them don't exist anymore, so these are literally the last petals in either of the worlds."

"Insurance policy? What do you mean? Like, you were going to make your fortune selling them?"

He walked a few more steps before answering. "Insurance for my own sanity. If the fearsome things we were tasked with creating ever took a toll on us that we couldn't come back from, I needed not to lose myself. I didn't like to admit it, but there were times I suspected Sama of..." He pursed his lips, his eyes going out of focus as if he was seeing his younger self alongside a more redeemable Sama. "I looked the other way on a lot of things with him. Knowing how our master could mess with our minds, I didn't fault him for his lesser villainies. Now I know that I should've intervened." He cleared his throat. "I created the flowers in case we lost our minds to madness. He was all I had." He took a few more steps before adding in a quiet voice, "I couldn't fix everything that's broken in the world, but I had to try."

"That's the big difference between you and Sama. He

set out to create chaos, but you planted peace. Literal and actual peace. Peace that you're passing onto your children."

His mouth drew to the side as he pondered my assessment. "I suppose I should like to be a man who can do that —plant peace when the world falls to ruin. I don't always choose it, but I want to."

I let his life lesson simmer in my heart for a few beats. I loved that I came from a lineage that had nobility like that threaded through it. Levi knew he couldn't change his master, his upbringing or even his closest friend. But the desire to make the world a better place burned so brightly in him that he couldn't be content turning a blind eye to the world's problems. I wanted to be like him. I wanted that unbreakable kindness that planned for long-term healing. How I wanted to be a person who put stock in redemption. "I think that's beautiful."

Levi shook his head. "Beautiful and broken, as seems to always be the way of things. I don't wish to discuss this anymore. Pick another topic. Literally anything else."

I was quiet while he maneuvered around a twisty tree trunk. "Do you think that Bev can get pregnant wherever she is? Like, did you two just make me a little brother or sister?"

Levi stopped short, his nostrils flaring. "No, I don't think it's possible. And we're not discussing this, either. It's grownup matters that don't concern you."

"Are you coming back to the forest?"

Levi's jaw was firm. "She told me not to. Said Sama

might find a way to hold me captive here to lure you into the forest. It was a pretty compelling argument."

I pursed my lips as a heavy sigh escaped me. "Then I'm glad you had some time with her. The way she touched your arm... It was sweet to watch."

Through gritted teeth, Levi muttered, "October Grace, I swear."

I sniggered at his chagrin, calling out to Von when I worried Levi might drop me on purpose. "Von, I'm here!"

Von bolted to us, trembling when Levi handed me over to him a few yards from the group. "Where did you find her? Are you alright, Peach? Oh, you're shivering!"

Was I? I didn't feel it. Or maybe I didn't care if I felt cold.

Von smelled like cinnamon and home. And also like he needed a shower. I gazed up at him, seeing him anew under the serenity the *sigla* flowers had washed over me. Von had always possessed a glow about him that generated from his natural charisma, but this was something entirely new to me. I loved the way he looked against the backdrop of nature, as if all of creation had shown up just to get a peek at the beauty that had been dreamt up when Von entered existence.

"My gosh, you're beautiful!" I whispered, loving the way he looked even more from this closer vantage point. Every chiseled angle was something to be studied and sculpted. I reached up with clumsy fingers to turn his chin left and then right, admiring him as if he was the first man that ever was. "Have you always been this stunning?"

Von gave me an incredulous look before belting out a laugh. "I must say, whatever happened to you in the woods, I rather like the color of it on you. Tell me again how much you adore me."

"I adore you, Von. Look at your dimple. I mean, has it always been that deep? I want to stick my finger in it."

Von's eyebrows rose as if he thought I'd gone crazy during our brief time apart. Really, I'd found my sanity, strange as that sounds. "Stick your finger in it? Save the sexy bedroom talk for when we're not in front of your brother, November."

At this, I perked up. "Ollie's here?"

"He is. That was my way of telling you."

I squirmed in Von's arms but my legs were still pretty useless. "Ollie? Ollie!"

I glanced around the camp but didn't see any sign of him or Darius. It was then that I took in the tone of the group, who didn't have the benefit of the *sigla* flowers to center them through the emotional upheaval. Mama McCray had disappeared. Judge was holding Terence, unwilling to let go of the brother who'd released his grip on life far too soon.

Danny was sitting with Bishop, his shoulders vibrating with grief. Looking around, I could see Mariang was gone now, and Danny was broken afresh. I could appreciate now just how beautiful Danny was when he let himself feel, his

Monster of Frankenstein features scrunching up as his ears turned pink. He was like a tea kettle trying to hold in his steam, always trying to keep himself together, no matter how great the pressure. As I watched him, I knew one thing for certain: I loved Danny dearly, no matter what state in which he came to me.

I wanted to hold him through his grief, but gave Danny his time with Bishop, who looked completely perplexed that his big brother was capable of breaking down. "There, there, Danny boy."

I wanted to scoop Bishop in my arms, but his moment with Danny was more important. It seemed similarly selfish to try and pry Terence away from Judge for a quick hug. Danny and Judge needed their brothers, and I needed mine.

"Where's Ollie?" I asked Von.

"Just behind those trees with Darius. We made them a bed of leaves to lie on, since everything seems to be hurting them. The light, sound, touch—anything. I'll take you." Von paused, looking down the scope of my body with worry wrinkling the space between his eyebrows. "Your shirt is torn. Tell me what happened to you."

"Sama," I breathed, trying not to let worry seep out in my tone. I didn't want to make Von afraid, but that's exactly what the truth did.

His volume climbed to a shout. "What?! How are you so calm about this? That should've been the first thing out of your mouth! Why would you go on about my dimple when you've just been face-to-face with the monster who..." His chest barreled, jostling my body. "Tell me all that happened."

"Who do you think tore my shirt?" I glanced down at my t-shirt that I'd tied back together across my torso as best I could. It covered the more scandalous parts, but not much else.

Von let out a bleat of distress. "I didn't realize it had been viciously torn! I thought maybe you snagged it on a branch, or you were trying something sexy to seduce me by showing off your midriff."

I sniggered, but he was in no mood for levity now.

Von's hands trembled as he lowered me to sit on the ground. I was grateful I had the wherewithal not to remain supine, but could prop myself up by leaning back on my elbows. He drew his knife, pointing it toward Levi. "Take me to Sama. He touched my wife, so he's about to die all over again."

Levi tilted his head to the side to study Von's flared nostrils and wild determination. "I appreciate the hustle, Son, but Sama's gone. Just as Judge's mother is gone, and soon his brother. Just as Mariang, and soon Bishop. Their time with us is brief. I brought my daughter back, we've gathered the others and the *sigla* flowers, so we'd best be on our way."

Von sheathed his blade with an angry, jerking motion. "Will he come for her again?"

Levi started gathering up the packs. "Not if we never

return to the Baluki forest. None of us, do you understand? The moment the golden mist touches anyone October loves, Sama will take them and hold them hostage to draw her into the woods." Then with an air of finality, he added. "We've plucked all of the *sigla* flowers, so there's no reason to return here."

I gaped at my dad. "All of them?"

"I gathered up the rest, so there's no temptation. I'll do my best to see if they can be transplanted, but that's the least of my worries right now. We need to get out of here."

Von cleared the gap between himself and Bishop, drawing up his baby brother and holding him tight.

Terence released Judge and looked down at his fingers. "I don't have much time. Make Mama proud, Judge." Then his eyes slid to me in the middle of the clearing. He tsked and shook his head, moving toward me so he could hoist me up. Being in Terence's arms was slightly frightening because he was so very tall. It wasn't the first time he'd scooped me to safety. Flashes of the many instances Terence had lifted me up throughout my life fluttered into my mind like butterflies with wings too delicate to be touched. Terence carried me to Judge, handing me over to the big brother who was completely beside himself with life-altering grief. "I want to see Darius one more time before I'm gone."

"Whatever you want, T." Judge carried me through a band of trees and over a smattering of stumps, just a few yards from our clearing. I saw Mason first, who was standing guard over the two with wet eyes that he kept from me.

My voice came out quiet and respectful of his pain that looked fresh. "Mason?"

"I saw Kara and my parents. It's fine, *hani*. I'm fine."

I didn't have to ask how things with his deceased family members had gone; I knew it would be a long road to healing for him. Perhaps for all of us.

At the sight of Ollie's bare toes, I wanted to demand someone give my poor brother some socks. But my wave of Zen flooded through me, as if on an IV drip that flooded into my veins whenever I felt a tsunami of anxiety. It was a sharp intake of breath and then a slow stream of release, letting the tension leak out of me as much as it was able. "Ollie? Are your toes cold?"

"October?" I think he meant to say, but it came out more like, "M-fo-ber?" Then a sorrowful cry erupted from my big brother, coating my heart in sadness that such an awful sound could come out of my Ollie. "You-affta go!"

"I will, big brother. And so will you. We'll get you out of here."

"It hurts!" he moaned, breaking my resolve.

I didn't have to ask Judge; he knew that I needed to be closer to Ollie. I had to make sure my brother wasn't still being tormented. Judge lowered me slowly onto the forest floor in between the two supine men. They cried out at the tiniest touch, so I kept my hands away, though I wanted to hold Ollie so very badly.

"Terence wants to say goodbye," Judge said to Darius.

Darius wasn't coherent. I'm not sure any of us expected him to be, what with too much torture, and then being rescued only to learn that your brother died while you were away. His usual goofy grin was nowhere in sight. I was grateful I had years of memories of the smile I adored to pull from. I wagered it might be a while before any levity graced Darius' lips again.

It was difficult for Terence to kneel, but he managed the feat as he bent down on the other side of his brother. "Darius, I have to go now, man. I love you, you know."

Darius didn't answer but his mouth opened and drool leaked out. His eyes saw Terence though, so that gave me some hope that he might be okay, given enough time and care.

Terence's gaze flicked to me with unconcealed worry. "I don't think that's normal. Gracie, can you give him a look?"

"Of course. I'll do it first thing when we get back. Now come here, before it's too late." Terence gave me a look that had a hint of bashfulness to it. He leaned over his brother to let me kiss his cheek, giving me a single memory of sweetness to hold onto. "I love you, Terence. Thanks for saving my life in the prison."

"Thanks for reading to me." His thick lips bloomed into a smile. Then he craned his neck to look at Judge, doling out a stern command. How I wished he'd stood up to Judge more often in his first life. "Be good to each other this time around. Gracie, make sure Judge doesn't die alone."

Judge scoffed through his tough guy tears, but I handed Terence a fist-bump of solidarity. "No problem."

The corners of Terence's mouth curved up. "That's my girl."

It was the last thing Terence said to me before he disappeared, taking part of my heart with him.

35

THE FIRST SUNSET OF THE REST OF OUR LIVES

We all watched Allie eat the *sigla* flower as tears rolled down her face. Within the first hour after the petal was in her system, she was a new person. Allie was on her feet, ignoring Judge as only she could get away with as she organized a memorial for Terence. She called everyone to invite them, made arrangements for Judge to be moved permanently into the mansion, and scheduled a lunch date for her and I to take Sherita to a nice restaurant. It was my Allie without the brain fog. It was my amazing sister who could make a dress out of men's old shirts. It was Allie as she was meant to be. The blank stares were gone, and in their place was a sharp mind and the clarity that gave her enough confidence to move through life far easier than the struggle she'd been mired in before.

Best of all was when she paused from her phone call

with Sherita to ask Graham if he could get her a glass of water.

Allie never asked for anything for herself. It was a miracle, and I got to see the wonder up close. I've never seen everyone move so fast in their lives. It was a stampede to secure a cup of water for our girl.

Boston trumped us all and thumped a pitcher before her on the table. "Beat that, Graham." Then Boston planted a kiss to the back of Allie's hand.

Allie angled her chin up, motioning for her brother-in-law to lean down. Her sweet peck on his cheek turned the tips of his ears pink, which was just about the cutest thing in the world. "Thank you, sweetheart."

Graham was careful with her body, as always, holding her hand and taking notations to do as she requested while they planned out the memorial. They were a seamless team, both quiet but politely direct in the way they conducted themselves now.

Each Vandershot boy had been given a petal to eat (though Danny had refused his), along with Ezra, Mason, Lynna, Lavinia, the McCray boys and Ollie. The council had each been given a petal that they ate with Levi at the mandatory meeting Ezra called the moment we returned, and Anastasia's was kept in a sealed jar for when Danny okayed it.

Terraway had a chance now. With the sagrado stones in place, several years of reaping under our belts and a unified council, I knew our roughest days were behind us.

Kabayo stuck around for an hour after the meeting, offering himself up as my personal chauffeur, since I still couldn't walk. His enormous horse head always shocked Judge a little, though he'd hung with Kabayo plenty of times before.

Kabayo kept his voice low as he carried me from the conference room in the mansion down the steps toward the living room. "I felt your pain in the forest. Then your happiness. Not to the degree you felt it, I'm sure, but my mark lit up on my arm. I ran to the edge of the Baluki forest, but King Carter wouldn't let me in."

I stroked Kabayo's mane as if he was my plaything. "Your coat is gorgeous. Has it always been this shiny?"

Kabayo chuckled at my delight in the little things that had for some reason escaped my awareness before my trip into the woods. "I couldn't tell you. Where would you like me to take you now?"

"Oo, the porch swing. Fresh air sounds amazing right now. Do you know what we should do?"

"I'm sure you'll tell me. I've never seen you this way. I didn't know the flowers could make such a difference. You look happy."

"You know what would make me happier?"

"I'm at the very edge of my seat."

"If we made a horn and stuck it right here on your forehead. Then you could be a unicorn. I could dye your hair pink. Oh, Kabayo, can't you just picture it?"

"Can you picture me dropping you right here on the

floor? Because you're one more terrible suggestion away from crawling your way outside."

He carried me out the front door and sat me down on the porch swing King Langgam had made for me with his own two hands, back when he was a prince. It was beautifully crafted but I hadn't taken the time to enjoy it as I wanted to. The call to work was always stronger than my need for respite. Life seemed so much clearer now, and time on the porch swing felt like the obvious choice when the sun was fending off the twilight as brightly as it was.

Ollie and Darius had been given a petal each to eat, and then a sedative to knock them out while their bodies came to grips with the fact that the torture was over. Rest seemed best for them, though I fought the urge to check on my brothers for the tenth time since we'd returned. Nine was enough.

Kabayo didn't sit with me on the porch swing but stood next to it, leaning against the mansion with his arms crossed over his chest as we studied the evening sun. I couldn't tell you how many sunsets I'd missed, but I loved this one. It felt like the mark of a new era.

I was ready for this new season of my life, finally not feeling as if I was being dragged into something I never agreed to. If given the option of working at the prison, knowing nothing of Terraway, I knew what my choice would be. I would choose my enormous family with all of its eccentricities. I would choose to carry the weight of a nation on my shoulders if it meant I felt loved and cherished by this select group. As the swing glided slowly forward and back, I let gratitude wash through me that I'd been given the chance to choose peace that surpassed all I'd been through to get to this place in life.

When the door opened, Kabayo bowed at the waist to me and went back inside, leaving me with Mason and Von. My husband's flirty demeanor hadn't vanished, but it had gone through a softening after all we'd endured in the forest. Learning that September was out there in the other realm being watched by his brother, Mariang and the rest was a lot to digest. Von kept a pleasant but pensive look about him as he sat next to me on the swing, chewing on his cinnamon stick while he figured out how the turmoil inside of him was going to land in his psyche. He didn't say much since we'd returned, but kept close, finding his way to my side if we were parted for more than a couple minutes. His arm slung along the back of the swing, his fingers curling in my hair. "How are you, Peach?"

I waved my hand toward the sunset. "I don't think I have much of a choice but to feel alright. There's pink in the sky. I think that kind of guarantees that life's going to be okay."

"A guarantee? I quite like the sound of that." He scooted me closer to his side. "Sit down, Mason. Apparently the pink sky has spoken to our November."

My Viking king had been quiet since we'd returned, which was no real surprise. When the swing shifted with his weight, I sighed contentedly as his fingers wound through mine. "You missed it. I was this close to getting Kabayo to wear a horn so he could be my unicorn. That's the one thing this place is missing."

Mason snorted, a small smile finding his features. "I'm sure you were just on the edge of convincing him." He ran his thumb over my knuckles. "How was your time in the woods? I feel like you only gave us the highlights."

I knew he was asking about my encounter with Sama. "I'm here now. I think that's what matters most."

Mason kept his eyes on the sunset. "I think it matters a great deal if Sama raped you. If there's a possibility you're pregnant, I need to know."

Von didn't stiffen, which told me they'd had a conversation about this on their own and came out to double-team me with a low-key interrogation.

I shook my head. "Nope. Didn't get that far. I'm fine."

At my unequivocal no, Von's chest vibrated. Though his tears of angst and relief didn't make a sound, they fell all the same. He turned his forehead and ground it into my temple, wetting my cheek with fears of all the evils no husband ever wants to imagine could happen to his wife.

Mason kept the swing gliding at a languid pace while I stroked Von's cheek. His voice was rougher, like he was holding back tears, afraid that if one fell, he'd add an ocean to those Von was shedding. "When I saw that your shirt was torn, I..." Mason bit down on his lower lip to keep all the horrors from hitting the air. His arm draped atop Von's around the back of the swing behind me. My heart swelled when he thumbed Von's back, offering up a solidarity the two of them had fine-tuned over the years. Then Mason moved his hand to thumb my shoulder, so I leaned into him, my hand finding its way to the inside of his knee. "I'm glad you're okay, *hani*. We were worried."

The three of us sat in silence a few beats before I spoke. "How's Kara?"

Mason looked down at his empty finger where his wedding ring had once been. "She's well. Wants me to be happy. Checks in on me from time to time." His lips quirked. "She thinks you're funny."

My eyebrows lifted in surprise. "Really? Because I was only half-joking about Kabayo being my unicorn. I'm thinking I just figured out what to get him for Christmas. They make headbands that have horns on them, you know." Von snorted against my cheek and finally gathered himself up enough to straighten and wipe his tears on his sleeve. My other hand fell to the inside of his knee, claiming the men I loved without apology to the color-brushed sky.

"Did you see anyone besides Sama and Bev while you were separated from us?"

I swallowed hard, knowing we would have to discuss this sooner or later. "I spent some time with Finn. He's dedicated his afterlife to keeping Sama away from both September and me." I studied the hints of orange and purple that mingled with the bright pink in the sky. "I won't be seeing him again."

Mason was quiet as he thumbed one of my curls.

Von took his cinnamon stick from between his teeth. "You have two Reapers, November. Mason and I are meant to be in your life exactly like this. The moment we stopped fighting it, everything got loads simpler. Our love doesn't look like everyone else's but it works. We don't even mind when you ease Danny's pain. We get it. But I'm glad Finn won't be reappearing any time soon. That feels like one too far for me."

I brushed my fingers up and down over his jeans. "Noted. How about you, Mason? You still okay with our arrangement? You're not thinking of cutting your losses and ditching us?" My tone was light, but there was always that fear lurking that Mason wouldn't want to share. That he'd wake up one day and decide this wasn't for him anymore.

Mason ran his hand over his face. "Did it ever occur to you that I've put myself exactly where I want to be? I like my life as it is. No wife is going to be thrilled I'm putting down Amalanhigs during half the month. One of the reasons we work is because you don't give me too much grief about it. You don't try and tame me, and I need someone who lets me be who I am."

"I mean, it's not my first career choice for you, but it makes you happy."

He shot me a faux glare. "*Hani*, you know it's more than that. You got the council to recognize my passion. You put a crown on my head, if you recall. I needed a purpose, but you made it my kingdom. Half the month, I get to be King of Sombi. The other half, I get to help sustain all of Terraway and take my girlfriend out around town. And frankly, I'm grateful you have Von and Danny. I wouldn't be able to step away and sort out my kingdom if they weren't around." The corner of his mouth tugged upward. "Plus, there's the whole minor detail that I'm in love with you, and can't fathom that changing any time ever."

My cheeks pinked just about every time he called me his girlfriend. "You don't feel shortchanged?"

"Does any of that sound like I'm unhappy? It's an ideal life for me. When I want someone to kiss me like I'm her hero, I have you. And I've never had a problem with you cuddling up to Danny. If you ever died, I can't imagine what it would take to get me out of bed. He's been through too much; he needs you."

Von tsked him. "Now, now. You have me, ripe and ready for a good snogging, Mason old boy. Not just November. You never take me up on it, which is a tragedy I can't believe you insist on suffering through." The two grinned at each other and then kissed my cheeks, drawing out a bashful delight I didn't bother concealing.

I'm not sure exactly how I could be expected not to kiss Mason after saying something so sweet as all that. My lips found his, as they often did. "I love you."

"I know," my Viking muttered between kisses. "You're very good at it."

Our kisses tapered off into love-drenched pecks of

appreciation. Then Von turned my chin so he could collect a few for himself. When he pulled back, I debated between indulging in a fresh swoon and frowning at the illogical nature of it all.

"Since we're talking about things we don't usually discuss, I've got something." Mason ran his tongue over his top row of teeth while he mulled over his next words. "Don't get upset, okay?"

I groaned. "Stellar beginning. Go on."

"We're years ahead on the count for how much we need to reap. I was thinking maybe you and Von might want to spend one night a month in Sombi with me. I've been building a fence around my property to keep out undead wanderers. It's safe enough to keep Ezra's blood pressure low." When my mouth popped open in excitement, he held up his hands. "Not to go hunting. Nothing like that. Ezra and Levi would have a heart attack. I just want you to be with me in my land for a little bit. A kingdom's not all that exciting if you have no one to share it with." Then before I could respond, he dug in deeper, as if he assumed we were on the verge of saying no. "When I'm away for half the month, I come back and it's like this whole life happened without me. I want more time with you than just work." I loved Mason for the squirm he got whenever he wanted something just for himself.

"You do?"

Mason turned his chin and blinked down at me. "*Hani*, you two are my family."

Von twisted his wrist behind me to grip Mason's shoulder. "I think that sounds bloody fantastic."

My head bobbed. "Actually, I was thinking of taking some time off of work. A day here and there in Sombi might be just fine. Clear it with Ezra, and I'm there."

Mason and Von froze. "Wait, what? Time off of work? Are you serious? How much time?"

I shrugged. "Enough to give my body a break." I debated how much I should confess to Mason. What he said was true. He was my family, and I'd been too ashamed to show him my imperfect parts. My fingers tangled through my husband's as I dove into the muck of life's stickiness. "Von and I went to the doctor and got some fertility testing done this summer while you were away."

When the next words felt stuck in my throat, Von finished them for me. "The results were less than ideal."

Mason closed his eyes and brushed his nose to my hair, inhaling with his mouth closed so he didn't say anything trite. "Talk to me. What are we dealing with?"

"It's bad enough that things have to change if we want a chance at that sort of thing. My body needs some downtime if Von and I are ever going to get pregnant." I laced my fingers through Mason's, so I was holding onto both of my men. I relished the feel of his skin on mine, rough as it was. There was no urge to wash my hands, no compulsion to scratch at my flesh. There was only the portion of peace that should be present when you're with your family. "I think I want that chance."

Mason was quiet a few beats while he studied our joined hands. "I think slowing down is a great idea. I believe I suggested it last month, and the month before, and several times before that."

"Yes, well, you're very smart. Every once in a blue moon, I listen to you."

Von shook his head in disbelief. "I'm not sure I believe it. You're truly capable of not working?"

"I'm capable of all sorts of things."

Von's smile was precious, so I took a mental snapshot and savored the curve of his lips, storing the image in my heart so it would never leave me. "I have no doubt. This one, though, I'll have to see to believe."

"Game on, Mr. Vandershot." I pressed a kiss to Mason's rough knuckle. I steeled myself to speak my true desires aloud. Philip had known my lust for all sorts of things—namely travel. I'd seen the world with him in my mind, but precious little of the actual globe. "Promise not to laugh?"

"I can't imagine making fun of you right now."

My voice was quiet but it was there—timid and worried I was asking too much of life. Finally I had enough solace in my mind to at least tell my boyfriend the things I wanted. "I think we should go traveling, the three of us. Maybe Danny and Anastasia, too. Instead of spending your two weeks Topside working, I was hoping we could pick a new destination and go there."

"Like, going camping?"

I swallowed the memory of my camping trip with Finn.

"I was thinking bigger than that. I've never been to Paris. I've never been lots of places. Neither have you. I've completely failed you as your Topside tour guide. I think we should go. No reaping, just fun."

That was the thing that floored them both. "No reaping?" they said in unison.

"Not a single soul. Just us, and just fun. My body's breaking down faster than the healing waters can rebuild me. It's no big secret why I'm having a hard time getting pregnant."

Von laughed, folding his arms over his chest. "Truly? You want to take time off of work and go traveling for... for fun? Who are you?"

Embarrassment hit me like a hard slap but I held my ground, though I'm not sure the guys could hear my voice that barely dared more than a whisper. "I'm the girl who's tired of putting my whole life on hold. We've seen too much of Terraway; it's time we did some fabulous nothings Topside for a while. I'll do my part to make sure Terraway survives, but maybe I want to make sure *I* survive, too. Maybe I'm finally realizing how much that matters. Does that sound okay?"

Mason's flabbergast was utterly adorable. "Um, yeah. That sounds amazing."

My eyes darted between the two of them. "Really? You're fine with taking a bit of a break?"

Von raised an eyebrow at me. "With you? Of course.

Forgive me for not believing it'll actually happen. I cannot picture you resting."

"Then I guess I'll just have to show you." I breathed deeper now, and didn't feel torn at all on my decision to live my life instead of merely endure it. "When we get back, we'll spend that one night a month in Sombi in your cabin before going back into parent-mode with Ana. That sounds nice. I love your cabin, Mason."

"I love you in my cabin." Mason tapped me under the chin, turning my face up so he could kiss me. The sunset painted the sky with streaks of glittering red and yellow when he sucked on my lower lip, which was just what nature needed to make it the most spectacular sunset yet.

We'd come so very far that he could ask for what he wanted, and I could confess my dreams aloud. I loved my Viking king, and told him as much when our lips parted.

The moment the kiss ended, Von enveloped me in his warmth. We didn't talk more about the glory or the horror of our woodland adventure. Instead we counted ourselves lucky that we could hold each other through the first sunset of the rest of our lives.

36

LOTUS

"So, where was the person on death's door?" Perhaps Von could've been more tactful, but honestly, after reaping as many people as we had over the years, you gain a certain amount of a shrug that just plain has to be there if you want to be able to keep on going in the morning.

Von kept tight to my side whenever Ollie's friends came over. Instead of the usual kegger, the ambiance was pleasantly subdued, with Jordan, Beto and Nick playing poker in the kitchen and the rest of us hanging in the living room of my home on Lenoy Avenue.

Von and I leaned against the wall, and though there was disorder aplenty happening all around us, I didn't have the same anxiety about it. The eighties rock didn't blare tonight, but sang at a reasonable volume in the background because I finally told Gabby that it was just plain too loud for me.

I sank into Von's side, where I belonged, and shrugged. "There wasn't anyone to reap. I just wanted to check out that museum. I told you and Mason last night on the porch swing that we were done working. Didn't you believe me?"

Von's eyes widened. "No. I guess I didn't. So then I don't understand. What was the trip to the postal stamp museum this afternoon for?"

My shoulders bobbed. "For fun. I've always been curious, and now I know: postal stamp museums are very boring."

"That was supposed to be entertaining? That's your idea of a jolly time?" He cast up to the ceiling, his head leaning back against the wall. "Bollocks. I played it all wrong. I was expecting to reap, so I didn't give the space much attention. What a waste. We didn't even make love in front of the stamps with pictures of your forefathers. I feel like I fell down on the job."

"Yes, that's the only reason we didn't have sex in public." I rolled my eyes at him.

Ollie made to reach for his glass of rum and coke on the coffee table but Gabby beat him to it. "You don't get your own drinks. You either, Darius. I can't believe you two were in a car accident. The fact that they couldn't identify your bodies for that long? I mean, what happened to your IDs?"

The story was barely believable, but it was either feed

Ollie's friends a lie or tell them nothing, which after his prolonged absence, wasn't an option. Ollie shrugged and reached for his usual response when anyone asked him details about the alleged car crash. "No idea."

When Darius shifted on the couch and let loose a quiet grunt, Rachel rubbed his arm. "Oh, Crayfish. You poor thing. How's the pain now? Can I get you anything?"

Darius wasn't into Rachel, but he also wasn't one to turn away fresh pheromones when they presented themselves in such a pretty package. He drank in Rachel's sweetness with a modest smile. "I wouldn't be opposed to having a drink with you after I get back on my feet."

"Why wait? Let me freshen that for you." Rachel shot him her best impression of a coy smile, though nothing about her was shy. I could see the two of them hooking up and having a grand old time for about two months before it imploded. Rachel wasn't one for monogamy, and Darius wasn't one for women who weren't Allie. Still, as she stood and gave him a nice, juicy shot of her tight miniskirt, I hoped Darius could find something comforting and fun to ease the transition to life without Terence.

Mason's tail curled protectively around my knee. He only wandered from my side when Katrina promised him a good belly rub. "Go on. You know you want it." I waved him off so he could enjoy the party in his own way.

My phone buzzed in my pocket, and though I probably should always take Judge's calls away from eavesdroppers, I didn't feel comfortable taking my eyes off of Ollie.

Though, Gabby was on anything he might need in a hot second. Gotta love the girl who hovers almost as badly as I do. Her black spindly curls swished and she darted to his side whenever Ollie shifted like he might be the least bit uncomfortable. I smiled at the two as I answered my phone. "Hey, Judge. How's Sherita?"

"Pissed at me. Thinking about forgiving me. Read me the riot act before we even got to dinner."

"Hm. Smart girl. Sounds like your groveling needs some work. Have you tried the whole apology in song form?"

"Do you know how many types of baby monitors there are to choose from? Screw it. I'm just going to use security cameras."

A small smile teased my lips as I cradled the phone with my shoulder. Von's hand on my hip was a permanent fixture lately, but he'd remained fused to my side since I mentioned I wanted to give having a baby a try. I wasn't anything like pregnant yet, but Von had a tenderness about his movements that bespoke his desire to be the best father in both worlds. For lunch, he'd insisted we not go out for sushi, since raw fish was on the naughty list for pregnant women. He even added extra vitamins to my regimen that he swore would guarantee we birthed the best baby in the world.

I thumbed Von's hand at my hip and turned my focus back to Judge. "You don't say. I almost don't want to tell you how many crib options you'll be looking at tomorrow. Can I please be far away when you research car seats?"

"Your gift worked, I think. She was tearing me a new one for walking away but when she saw I bought her a breast pump, she simmered down a bit so we could actually talk. Women are strange."

I could picture Sherita getting choked up over the one thing that meant more to her than it probably should've. "I'm glad it helped. She loves you a lot, Judge."

Von's thumb tucked inside the waist of my jeans, keeping up the slow tease he'd never learned how to turn off.

"You coming home soon, or are you staying with Sherita?"

"I'm still in the doghouse with her, but things are better than they were. We'll get there with enough time."

"Glad to hear it."

"You need me to pick up anything while I'm out?"

"I think we're out of almond milk. Can you grab some for me?"

Yes, we'd come a long way. Judge could now offer help, and I took him up on it. Two years ago, I never would've believed it possible.

"Of course, baby girl. I'm getting tired. I might just crash the second I get home. Can you make sure everyone's out of our room?"

I loved that he called my house his home. "Actually, you're bunking with Darius tonight in Allie's room, if that's alright. He's in more pain than he's willing to admit. Can you keep an eye on him?"

"Sure." He let loose a low chuckle. "I take it Von's tired of sharing his space with me?"

Von nodded, his fingers dipping lower so he could make it clear that he was keen on the idea of being alone for a night. Or several.

"Nah, Von loves you. I was thinking you probably wouldn't want to be around when he gets me good and pregnant tonight." Von froze at my flippancy. "But maybe I'm wrong about that. Did you want a front row seat to our Kama Sutra? I was thinking of trying this thing where he's doing the splits and I'm in the lotus position. You'll love it. Von always does this cartoonish cockney accent right before he comes. Totally sexy."

Judge started singing nonsensically to shut me up. At my snigger, his voice turned sharp. "I never want to picture anything like that again, understood? You want time with that guy, fine. Leave me out of it."

"Are you sure? Von's right here, and I think he's keen on the idea of having someone to prop him up for the finale. If we want to make a baby girl, there's a certain angle that's best."

Judge hung up on me, which was probably his smartest move. I laughed as I slid my phone into my pocket. A glimmer of pride hit me when I realized I didn't need to reach for my hand sanitizer. It truly was the dawning of a new era.

When I smiled up at Von, the corners of my mouth drooped when I took in his stunned expression. "What's wrong, babe?"

"You told him you wanted to try for a baby. It's official. You never go back on your word with Judge. Too stubborn to be wrong in front of him."

I sipped my water, keeping my eyes on Ollie. "Then I suppose we'll have to give it a real honest effort tonight."

Von leaned closer to inhale the fragrance of my neck. "How much time off work are we talking? I only half-believed you last night on the porch swing. Don't get my hopes up, November."

I shrugged. "I talked it over with Ezra, and he thinks twelve months off is more than fine. We've got enough supplies stored up for the next several years, so that's not a problem." "Supplies" sounded better than "souls" in mixed company.

Von dropped his grip on me and stepped back as if he barely recognized me. "Are you quite certain you haven't hit your head?"

My mouth drew to the side. "You're not happy? I thought this was what you wanted."

"I know it's what *I* want, but I didn't think you cared enough about it all to do something drastic like this." Then he stepped back into my body space and cupped my face in his hands. "We're truly taking a year off?" Then his voice dropped to a whisper. "You want to give this baby thing a serious go now?"

My simple nod gifted me with a smile so spectacular from the beautiful man, Von's whole demeanor lit up like the sexiest kind of Christmas tree. I don't know how he did that. It's like he could command light and energy and the butterflies in my belly to beam for him whenever he smiled.

He twined his fingers through mine and tugged me from my perch holding up the wall. "Let's go. They're fine without us."

"Let's go where?"

"The bedroom, obviously. I admit, I cannot do the splits, but whatever lotus position you have in mind, we can try that."

I laughed at the adamant jerk of his head toward our bedroom. "We've got company!"

He made a show of peeling off his socks, starting the striptease slow but public. "That'll always be true. What's the angle that makes a girl? I'll call Graham and make sure we do the opposite of whatever he did."

I grimaced through my laughter at the visual of Graham getting busy with Allie. "Do not give me a single detail of that."

He gripped his green t-shirt around the hem and peeled it over his head, drawing the eyes of everyone who'd been lost in pockets of their own conversations. Darius catcalled him, to which Von fondled his washboard abs to show off for the viewers. He didn't care that my cheeks were crimson. He didn't care that my brother was pale through a blanche. Von only cared about getting me pregnant, which apparently couldn't wait until we were alone.

"You'll all have to excuse us. You know where the fire extinguisher is? You know where the takeout menus are? Good. If you hear all sorts of sordid noises coming from the bedroom, pretend we're watching raucous wildlife mating shows. Carry on, children."

Mason sneezed, which meant that he'd watch the house while we defiled our corner of it.

I shouldn't have buried my head in my hands. I should've kept my eyes wide open so I could've fended off Von's bravado that drove him to hoist me over his shoulder and march me straight into the bedroom. He dumped me onto the mattress and locked the door behind us. I barely got out a sentence before he had my socks and jeans off. "Von, you're ridiculous! We have a whole year to..."

Von tipped me back with a kiss so passionate, my knees just plain knew they were supposed to fall open. "That's my peach. My delicious peach. Tell me again that you want to have my baby."

I laughed through our kiss as more clothes were shed. "You already know I do."

"Tell me about this lotus position. Tell me it involves your legs in the air for a good, long while."

I pressed my hands to his cheeks, slowing his manic state for a hot second of serious talk. "I love you, Von."

"I don't blame you."

Leave it to my vampire to say the perfect thing.

He pinned one arm out to the side, studying the tattoo Bev had given me, and then pinned the other so he could kiss the one word that fueled more of my steps forward than any other.

I had put myself through enough. Now it was time to truly live.

37

EAT IT

"*E*at it, or I'll march back into that forest, summon your late wife and bed Mariang so well, she won't remember the sound of your name."

Von and Danny had been going back and forth all morning, but in the end, all I had to do was run my fingers over Danny's knuckles that were white from being closed too long into angry fists. "Please, Danny? Look at me."

Danny was obstinate as we sat together at the dining room table. In true form, Danny wasn't willing to heed even the smallest request. "No."

"Don't I look better? I feel better."

"Good for you. I'm not sick in the head like you were. I don't need to eat any stupid flower."

I pursed my lips as I sifted through his sass to see the scared boy beneath. "If you want me to sleep in your bed tonight, you have to eat the flower." Yes, I was resorting to bribery, but to be fair, that was how I got Anastasia to eat her vegetables. Like father, like daughter, I guess.

Danny turned his chin to glower at me while Von rolled his eyes. "You're treating him like a child," my husband observed. Von's arms crossed as he leaned back in his chair on the other side of Ezra's dining room table. The gold-framed picture of a vineyard was behind his head, making me smile. This was the room where Von had first charmed me so many years ago. "What? Darling, you're looking at me as if I've forgotten to wear pants."

I shrugged, unable to tame my adoring expression. "My first time at the mansion, you two were bickering at this very table. It's nice to know that some things never change. You're adorable. Both of you."

Danny groaned. "Oh, shut it. If you're going to start up your mating ritual, there's a bedroom upstairs you can make good use of."

When Anastasia toddled into the dining room, I scooped her up in my arms and kissed both her cheeks. I swear, the girl might go to preschool one day and be totally shocked when she doesn't get hugged and kissed every five minutes. "Mama, finger hurt."

She held up the offending digit with a dramatic pout. I put on my nurse face and examined it from every angle. "How did you hurt it, Ana-Bear?"

By way of an explanation, she said, "Ducky is broked-d."

Von stood and held out his hands to her. "Let me see if

we can get some band-aids. One for your wonky finger and one for Ducky. That's right, darling. Daddy will fix it."

It had taken forever for that cutie to learn to walk. The guys were always swooping in and picking her up, afraid she might fall. I loved how careful they were with her, even if we were totally overdoing it. "Hold on. Let me fix your pigtail. This one's just about to fall out." Von gave her back to me so I could refashion the rubber band, since my legs still weren't working from mid-thigh downward.

I told Anastasia which curls were my favorite that day, and kissed her nose. Von and I were determined that neither of our childhoods would be repeated, so everywhere she turned, she saw a father figure. Every time she was near me, she felt loved and cherished by her mother figure.

"Oo! Pretty!" She pointed excitedly at the *sigla* flower on the table.

I kept my movements slow, so Danny would have the chance to stop me as I reached out and lifted it up for her to examine up close. "That's right. This is a very special kind of flower. It takes the things that are broken inside of you and helps make them better." I tickled her nose with the white petals, drinking in her precious little giggles as if they were the elixir of life. "Would you like to see how it works?"

"Yeah!" She clapped and sniffed the flower.

I tore off an inch of the petal and rolled it up, opening my mouth so she would follow suit. I could practically feel

Mariang cheering me on. "Swallow it, and your finger won't bother you so much."

Gotta love the girl who obeys you when you tell her to eat something that'll be good for her. I'd worn a fair amount of strained peas on my shirts to earn this level of compliance. I watched with relief as she munched on it and swallowed.

Von's eyes were closed in gratitude that life had thrown this precious baby a bone. "That's my girl," he whispered, leaning in and kissing her cheek. "Was it delicious?"

Ana glanced over at Von with the same wonder I often wore. "Daddy, so pretty!" She clapped her hands on his cheeks so she could touch the beauty that was Von. Like mother, like daughter, I guess.

Von chuckled. "Yes, Daddy is stunning, indeed. How about that daddy over there? So pretty?"

She turned toward Danny and gasped. "Daddy, so pretty!"

I handed Anastasia off to Danny, who had learned to be soft-ish for his daughter. He didn't have an ounce of Von's charm, but his eyebrows didn't do their Monster of Frankenstein thing when he was surrounded by his daughter's affection. "I'm pretty, eh?"

She poked at his cheeks, smooshing them upward to force a smile that just wasn't going to get there on its own. "Too sad," she commented when she dropped his cheeks and they went back to their familiar scowl.

I leaned in. "Do you think Daddy should try some of the flower? Was it yummy?"

"So yummy!" Her little exclamations came out with a British flair, winning my heart every single time. "Eat flower, Daddy!" She picked it up and opened her mouth as I always did when I was about to feed her.

"Daddy's not hungry," Danny insisted, casting me a glower at my subterfuge.

Her face fell, and I could see clearly her sadness. No matter how hard she tried, she couldn't draw Danny out of his hard-backed shell. But the *sigla* flower was already working its way into her system. What would have been sullen tears turned into a tired sigh. "Poor Daddy."

It was my turn to fix Danny with a sharp glare. "Your daughter asked you to eat the flower. You'll do anything for her, right?"

"October, honestly. This is beneath you."

I didn't back down; this was too important. I touched the cheek of my round-faced angel. She had Mariang's hair, Danny's ears, Mariang's eyes and Danny's lips. So help me, she would have my stubbornness. "There's nothing I wouldn't do to give her a better life. How about you? Are there limits on your love? Levi's trying to transplant these, harvest the seeds and plant new flowers, but it's a gamble. This might be your only shot at something better." I closed my eyes as desperate hope swelled up in me. "It's difficult to plant peace."

Danny's nostrils flared with indignation that he kept to

himself because there was a child in the room (my ulti-mate get-out-of-jail-free card). It took a few beats, but eventually Danny opened his mouth. A flash of fear lit up his eyes before he let Anastasia cure what ailed his aching soul.

Daughters are magical like that.

I tore off a petal for her, and she tickled his lips with the silk of it before he did as she wanted—as she needed.

Von and I exhaled in unison, knowing that now there was hope for the brother we loved. Von's fingers danced along my shoulder before he reached over to take Anastasia from Danny so his brother had a moment to process it all. "Come, little raspberry. Let's go for a walk outside. Papa Levi's sitting out back."

"Can you ask Levi not to shift into his dog form this time? Sometimes he lets Ana ride on his back, and it nearly gives me a heart attack," I asked on his way out.

"Anything you like, love. Only watch me walk away. That's all I ask. I need to know your lust for me is constantly at the ready."

I didn't hesitate on that one. I diligently studied his backside as he gave me a sexy little shimmy when he exited.

Gotta love the man who dances just to make you smile.

I watched Danny swallow several times before I was convinced he wouldn't try to barf the flower back up the moment I turned my back. "I hate that you made me do that." Then that same deep breath I'd found since ingesting the *sigla* petal moved his chest. "But I love you, even when you love me too much. Maybe I even need it."

I leaned over and pecked his cheek, but he turned so he could kiss my lips three times, as was our private routine. Browns and glittering bronze swirled in my vision, reminding me that not all I loved was lost. "I do love you, Danny."

When Ezra meandered in, I took a step back, knowing Danny didn't like people to see us together. My dad had Lavinia's hand in his and a look of boldness to him as if he was declaring something we didn't already know. "Kids, we have something to tell you. We're working our way through everyone. Though this might not be the best time, after taking the *sigla* flower, we realize we've been keeping quiet for far too long."

"You're getting married?" I asked with unconcealed glee.

Ezra turned pink as Lavinia paled. "No! We're... Did everyone truly know that we've been courting?"

I didn't hold back my look of incredulity. "Um, yeah. I walked in on you two doing your horizontal tango in your bedroom like, last year."

Danny pointed in the direction of the living room. "On the white couch two months ago."

Lavinia shrieked her regret. "Oh! That's dreadful. I'm so sorry, Danny! What you must think of me!"

Danny looked up at his mother with none of the wrinkles between his eyebrows displayed. He didn't look as much like the Monster of Frankenstein anymore. The transformation was so very jarring that everyone froze. "I think you look happy. Don't you know we all want that for you? To settle down with a bloke like Ezra isn't something you ever had to hide from any of us." Then he grimaced. "Except maybe Boston and Von. Their sex jokes are dreadful, so brace yourself."

Lavinia was stunned, her mouth hanging open before she could conjure up the right words. "I guess we were worried for nothing, then. Thank you, Danny."

"Love you, Mom." Then Danny stood, ignoring our collective flabbergast. "I'm going to go take Ana out for ice cream, if no one needs us."

I covered my mouth with my hand, my heart growing and expanding. Something as small as a flower had opened Danny up to seeking out his daughter to spoil her, instead of us constantly having to draw him in. "Do you even eat ice cream?" I asked through my astonishment.

Danny shrugged. "I think I did when I was younger." He frowned as he pushed his chair in. "I'm a bit behind the times, then. Maybe Ana and I should sample all the kinds they offer first." He didn't even notice my guffaw or Ezra's one-noted laugh at what our dad no doubt assumed was a joke. Danny didn't believe in stupid things like ice cream. He really didn't believe in indecisiveness.

"Danny, are you feeling alright?" I asked, pulling at the hem of his shirt so I could draw him down to check his temperature. I knew it was the *sigla* doing its thing, but the transformation was so very strange on Danny, I felt the need to check for influenza.

"Never better, sweetie." He kissed my lips in full view of our parents, ignoring the gasps and the red in my cheeks. Everyone in the mansion knew of our arrangement, but we'd been discreet about it all the same. Danny pulled back to scrunch his nose. "That didn't sound right. Everyone has their own nickname for you, so I should try a few out to see what I like best. Let's cross 'sweetie' off the list. I know you hate 'kid,' so I'll not call you that. I've been calling you 'honey' when it's just us, but that seems terribly generic." Then, as if he couldn't help but always kiss me in sets of three, he pressed his lips to mine twice more before standing taller to stretch out his back. "What kind of ice cream do you want, buttercup?" He grimaced again. "Ugh. That one's even worse."

My mouth was frozen in a mix of wonder and shock, which was exactly the expression painting Ezra and Lavinia. "You realize Ezra and your mother can see you kissing me, right?" I mean, I didn't mind, but he'd been so very private and finicky about it all, making sure to only be sweet to me in the dark.

To answer my perplexity, Danny leaned in and planted a deep kiss to my lips, cupping my face in a way that made me feel treasured. "You don't say," he teased as he pulled back. Then he touched my nose, casting me an affectionate grin. "Ice cream. I'll bring some back for you. Allie, too. Mom? What kind do you want? I should ask Lynna, too. You know what, just text me with the list." He pointed at me but locked eyes with Ezra. "Make sure she doesn't try walking while I'm out." Then he did something so shocking, I nearly fell out of my chair. Danny winked at me and said, "No dancing while I'm away, sugar lips." He blanched. "Oh, that one was dreadful. I'll keep thinking."

I was stunned that he'd cracked a joke, unable to ask him what the crap kind of alien had taken over his body and taught him manners.

Lavinia's tongue finally loosened with a crack. "Danny, are you alright, love?"

Danny paused in the entryway and turned his head over his shoulder. "You know, I think I just might be."

With that, ice cream came into our lives, promising us that no matter what life threw our way, we would never regret the path that had taken us to exactly where we were meant to be.

The End.

Love the book?
Leave a review.

UGLY GIRL

Enjoy a free preview of *Ugly Girl*,
book one in a 14-part fantasy romance series.

*J*udah's laugh was music to my ears as he high-fived me, our pool sticks clanking together. "That was an awesome shot. We should've bet more," he said, eyeing the pile of twenties on the ledge that were weighted by a cube of chalk.

The atmosphere in the noisy bar was just starting to hit its sweet spot, with the blaring music enticing the college crowd to remember everything that was good about being young and away from home. We frequently came here after I finished a soccer game, yet somehow there were always a couple guys drunk enough to challenge us, even though we were undefeated at pool.

"Is it mean to take their money like this?" I asked, tilting my head at my best friend's dark curly hair that was slightly sticking up in the back. Neither of us looked in the mirror all that often, but relied on each other to either comb out the quirks, or decide if they should be left to add to our slightly off-center personalities.

Judah guffawed. "Don't you dare start with that pesky conscience tonight, Rosie Avalon. They were sober-ish when we started playing." Judah scrutinized the pool table, and I could practically feel him bisecting right angles and saying nonsense words like "hypotenuse" in his head. Gotta love him. He took his shot and sank the ball, beaming that we were still on top of our game of round robin. We laughed as we did our obnoxious Cabbage Patch dance, the brown curls of my ponytail swishing in time with my pool stick. The guys on my soccer team chuckled at our usual antics, but a few people on the fringes gave us weird looks.

Me. They gave *me* weird looks. Not that I could blame them. I had scoliosis, which resulted in a pretty sizeable hump on my back. Pair that with my lazy left eye, and I was ripe for receiving at least one grimace a day. One of my stellar nicknames in high school had been Baby Got Too Much Back. The other one was Crater Face, due to the painful acne that never went away. Judah was my other half because he'd never once looked at me like I was the ugly girl, and I'd never teased him about being super into Star Trek, spending his entire life at the top of the curve, or being Jewish. (I mean, come on, people. It's the twenty-first century already. You'd think the anti-Semitic comments would've died out before we were born, but there were always a few jaggoffs whose mission in life was to derail the evolution of the species.) I'd learned to accept the girl in the mirror and not hold back my personality. Just because I wasn't a blonde cheerleader didn't mean I was about to sit on the sidelines and sulk my whole life.

I was the starting striker for the Blue Hornets. The cheerleaders could have the blondes, for all I cared. I'd found my people long ago, and they didn't need me to be prom queen. Their main concern was if I could score, which I had no trouble proving game after game.

"Don't feel like foreplay tonight?" I asked, taking in our opponents' frowns of frustration. Our competition was droopy-eyed from their newly minted legal drinking-aged licenses, and not amused at our dance.

Judah tapped his watch, which also served as his day planner. "You've got to study for finals still."

I felt eyes on me, but I tried to ignore it. I pretended I didn't mind being talked about. It was the pointing that did me in. I rolled my hunched shoulders back as best I could, but no matter how straight I stood, I was still a little stooped. I did my best to push out the world and focus on the game. "Double or nothing if I make this shot blind." Maybe I was showing off just a little. I was in a great mood after the shutout, flying high off the adrenaline that kissed my forehead on the soccer field.

One of our challengers who was four beers into his night leaned against the table. "Not a chance. I've seen you pull that trick before. I still don't know how you do it."

"Magic," I teased, wiggling my fingers as I lined up my shot. I paused to play with the locket on the thin gold chain around my neck. When my Aunt Lane had given it to me, she'd warned me to never take it off – it was my good luck charm. My luck tended to run freezing and scalding, but I placated her all the same.

Judah and I put them out of their misery quickly, since Judah was annoyingly right, and I did have to get home to cram for finals. It wasn't truly over until we finished off the chorus of Queen's "We are the Champions", which we nailed because we sang it at least once a week in this very bar after just such a victory. Our pool winnings kept our grocery budget firmly at a notch above ramen noodles, so we came here as often as we could.

I tried not to pay much attention to our goalkeeper, Kyle, who was arguing with his girlfriend, but they were hard to ignore. It was an hour after a victory, so their fight was right on schedule. Last time their clash was over him kissing her too hard, and smearing her Barbie pink lipstick. That had been one long night.

"I saw you looking at that skank!" Melanie's voice was shrill, which was the only tone I'd ever heard on the girl. I idly wondered what it would sound like if she ever whispered.

Kyle's indignation was so faked, *I* didn't even buy it. "Who? Women come to our games sometimes, Mel. They're half the population. I wasn't looking at anyone in particular. Just playing the game."

"Three times you laughed at a joke that girl told after the match. You think I didn't see it?"

Kyle scrunched his nose. "Who, Rosie? She's my teammate. Jeez." I was the only girl on the soccer team.

Melanie huffed, her arms akimbo. "I don't care if you joke with the ugly girl. It's the one in the halter top who you couldn't stop grinning at that I have a problem with."

My movements stilled as I leaned on my pool stick. Judah hadn't heard, because he was still being an obnoxious winner, dancing as he counted our take. It was just me who could stand in my defense, only I never wanted to in these situations. Melanie was right. I'd gone through many painful chiropractic treatments to try and straighten my hump, but scoliosis wasn't one of those things that went away with a simple crack of a spine. No matter how many times I went to the dermatologist, a heavy smattering of acne covered my cheeks, chin and forehead. I knew no guy ever looked my way, and over the years, I'd become okay with it. It helped me find out who my true friends were, and who not to waste my time around. Still, Melanie's words punched me in the gut. I wanted to believe the best in humanity, but sometimes it was a struggle.

Kyle's genuine displeasure at Melanie's slam made me stand a little taller, though he didn't say, "No, Rosie's not ugly," but rather, "Hey, she's my friend, and you need to cool it with that kinda talk."

I swallowed down the bad spot on an otherwise awesome night, working up a grin for Judah, who'd finally come down from his gloating. "You ready to go, Ro?" Judah asked, tucking our winnings into his pocket.

I put on my best fake smile and pounded my fist in the air. "I'm super way pumped to study!"

The crowd was thickening, hitting the point in the night where, if you hadn't already secured a chair, you were nursing your beer standing up for the rest of the evening. I held onto Judah's hand so we didn't get separated as we weaved through the college students who'd come to celebrate the end (or near end) of the semester.

I was starting to feel claustrophobic right as someone bumped into me from behind, knocking my hand out of Judah's. The bulky body bumped me forward into a woman, who turned to scowl, and then reared back with the infamous grimace when she saw what I looked like.

I held up my hands like claws and hissed, as if I was a hag who was about to put a hex on her, cursing her into decades of unending slumber. If I was going to be gawked at like I was hideous, I wanted to really earn the part.

Judah snorted a laugh at the girl's horrified expression. He gripped my hand tighter so we didn't get separated as we slipped through the crowd, finally making our way out onto the cracked sidewalk. The neon from the bar's sign lit Judah's smile just enough for his levity to migrate to me. "Did you see her face? I thought she was going to pee herself. I love when you do that. And if I didn't say so in there, good game."

I bowed under the streetlight to my adoring fan, grinning as I righted myself. The smell of exhaust and semi-fresh air was a welcome reprieve from the peanut shells and bottom-shelf beer I'd been breathing in all night.

Judah did a doubletake, his brows furrowing in confusion as if I was wearing a weird hat or something. He took three steps back, and then two forward to squint at me, pushing his Buddy Holly glasses further up on his nose. "Rosie, your face! Did you... Are you wearing makeup or something?"

My nose crinkled. "Huh? Why would you even ask me that? I don't even own any makeup. You know that."

For the first time in his life, Judah pointed at my face in distaste. "Your acne is gone. Like, you were normal just a minute ago, but now your skin is all... I dunno. You don't look like you."

"Who do I look like, then?" I challenged, hurt that he would point at me like the circus freak I often felt like.

"You look like your Aunt Lane! I mean, the similarities were always there, but now..."

My hand went to my throat to play with my necklace. I often did that when I wanted to soothe myself after being looked at like I wasn't pretty in a world where things like pretty mattered a little too much. My fingers touched the naked skin of my neck above my blue jersey, fumbling around for the chain that should've been there, but suddenly wasn't.

As if trying to pat down a fire, I felt all over my collar and my shirt, a panic rising up in me at losing the one precious thing I owned. "Oh, no! Judah, where is it? My necklace is gone!" I blinked rapidly as my left eye started to twitch while I searched around me for the sentimental treasure.

Judah frowned and turned on his phone to use as a flashlight, searching the concrete from where we stood all the way back to the bar. "I'm not seeing it. You sure you didn't take it off?"

I threw my hands in the air after shaking out my shirt and still coming up empty. "In all the years you've known me, have you ever seen me without that necklace? I never take it off! Lane made me promise to keep it on forever. Oh, she's going to flip." My vision started to swim, making the cars passing by look blurry, and then unnervingly detailed, disorienting me enough to take a step back. Rapid blinking made things clearer, but still didn't reveal my necklace anywhere in sight.

"I can't picture Lane getting pissed that you lost something. I can't picture her mad at you, period. It's an honest mistake, Ro. We'll come back in the morning and check the lost and found. It's probably on the floor in there. Chain was bound to break one of these days."

I groaned at the thought of people squashing the locket that had belonged to my long-deceased mother. My aunt had taken the locket from my mother's meager belongings and passed it down to me. "It's the only thing of my mother's that I have! Judah, we have to find it."

"Alright, alright. Don't worry. I'll help you."

My left eye started to itch as if there were phantom spiders running all over it, so I ran my index finger across my eyelid. I grimaced when I felt heat radiating out in a circle around that whole section of my face. I started blinking rapidly to clear away the foreign sensation, willing myself not to lose my cool and smack myself in the head to make the tingling stop.

When my gaze fell on Judah after my vision finally focused, he jumped back in horror. "Gah! What's wrong with your eye?"

It was the hurt that had never come from him until this moment. All the other kids in school had blanched at my lazy left eye, but Judah never cared that I looked different. Now he was acting like the woman who'd cringed in the bar when she'd gotten a good look at me. To have him comment on my wonky eye in the same minute he was acting all horrified by the rest of my face was a double whammy that made me take a step back. Anger welled up inside of me and spewed itself all over my best friend. "Are you just now noticing that I look like this? What's your deal, Judah?"

He seemed to remember himself and cleared the gap

between us, hands raised. "I don't mean it like that. Your skin is totally as clear as a baby's, and your eyes are pointing in the same direction! It's freaking me out! How are you doing that?"

I felt my face and, sure enough, my skin was devoid of pockmarks. There wasn't even any of the scarring I'd acquired from acne gone rogue throughout the years. "Wha... Are you serious?" My optometrist swore up and down that my vision hadn't been affected by my lazy eye, but I began to notice that even though it was nighttime, I was able to see a little clearer – the edges of everything were a bit crisper. "Judah?" My voice came out in a pinched bleat of panic.

"I'm sure there's a totally logical explanation. Maybe it's a trick of the moonlight?" he suggested, though I could tell he didn't believe his conjecture.

I shook my head, feeling all turned around and border-line emotional. "A lazy eye doesn't just fix itself in a blink!"

"Okay, let's go home where there's actual light. Then we can see what we're dealing with. Maybe I'm wrong."

"Are you ever wrong?" I asked, incredulous.

"No," Judah replied apologetically. It was true. Judah was always at the top of the curve in school, but was blessed with the grace not to lord it over the dummies like me who were barely hanging on. His shoulders deflated when he took in the effect his unfiltered words had on me. "Come here. I freaked you out with my pointing. I wasn't thinking. I'm sorry."

Judah held out his arms, and I didn't hesitate to crash into them, resting my trepidation on his shoulder in hopes it would evaporate there. "Don't point at me like that anymore," I said quietly, letting him know that he was my safe place, and taking that away would be a devastation I wouldn't recover from. "Everyone else can, but you? You're my..." I fished around for the right word, but landed on shtick. "You're my pimp daddy."

Judah snorted into my hair. "You're totally right. I'm sorry, hot mama. Are you okay?"

"I lost my necklace, so no. Everything else can take a backseat to that. My acne is really gone? I saw myself in the mirror after the soccer match, and I was still me."

"Not a trace of it, Ro. And your left eye is pointing straight now. It wasn't that way when we were playing pool in there just a few minutes ago."

I was about to crack a lame joke to ease the seriousness, but a sudden ache in my back forced me to roll my shoulders through our hug. A gust of air thrust out of me when it felt like something suddenly shoved me from inside my spine. The push held enough of a punch to catch me off-guard, changing the most basic things about my appearance, and freaking me out when I was already on the brink. "Oof!"

Judah scrambled to hold onto me as my legs gave out. I whimpered pathetically when my back decided to be a total wuss and start spasming. "Hey, what's wrong? What's happening?"

"My back hurts! Oh, man! Super way painful. Give me a second." I tried to stand on my own, but my spine was in full-on contortion mode. Judah held me, despite my protest and my torso bending away as it tried to center itself.

A terrifying crack sounded, rippling down my spine. Judah and I cried out in alarm as one voice, but he held me until I was finally able to find my footing. I slowly stood with a bit more stability, rolling a kink from my shoulders.

Judah hopped back with alarm clear on his face. He lifted his finger to point, but remembered himself and lowered it. Instead I followed his eyeline and patted my shoulders in fear.

The noise from the college kids passing by blurred into the background when my fingers reached over my shoulder and landed on... nothing. I pulled in a deeper breath than I'd ever managed before, my lungs expanding with extra room that came from standing up straight.

Only I'd never stood up straight before.

"My hump," I whispered, amazed and terrified. My mouth fell open when I realized that I was seeing the world from a vantage point of about two inches higher than usual, due to not being stooped anymore.

Judah shook his head, his hand over his mouth. "Rosie, your hump is gone!" He looked like he was about to say something else, but the newfound air that dragged inside of me was pushed out in a forceful gust.

Something heavy pulled at my chest, making the

whole area feel bruised and unsteady. Discomfort mutated to pain as I moved my arms over my chest. I'd always had a flat chest, with no breasts to brag about. That, I'd been grateful for, though. Having immobile A-cups meant you could run faster on the field without being bogged down by weighty body parts.

My mouth fell open as dread colored my cheeks. Beneath my banded arms, I could feel my chest growing at an alarming rate. The whole area ached so bad I had to bite down on my lower lip to keep from screaming. Inches and inches expanded faster than I could conceal them, my skin stretching grotesquely as the elasticity of my sports bra was tested to its limits.

And then both straps snapped.

Never in all of our years as friends who'd seen each other through puberty had Judah ever glanced at my chest. He gawked like a teenager with no thought of social propriety as I scrambled to hide my spontaneous breasts. "Did those just... Are your..." He couldn't say the word "boobs" to me, which was good, because I might've imploded on the spot from mortification if he did.

"I'm going to go look for my necklace!" I shouted, horrified and utterly drenched in confusion. I worked the tattered remains of my bra over my hips and discarded the sad fabric in the nearest garbage can, flummoxed and a little terrified that I was morphing into something... not me.

I didn't wait for him, but barreled back into the bar,

holding my bosom in place with my arms crossed. Goose-bumps were covering my arms, and tears of angst threatened to spill out of me. My shoulders and my chest felt like someone had taken a baseball bat to them, but the terror at the suddenness of it all hurt far worse. I pulled out some cash in my haste to find my necklace, and slapped it on the bar top. I rarely drank more than a beer or two, but my back ached, and my chest felt like the skin might tear at any moment. Frankly, I was surprised it hadn't. I slammed the shot in hopes it would be my pain reliever.

I'd never cried in a bar before, and was firm that tonight wouldn't break that trend. I didn't know what was going on with my body, so I decided I would deal with all of that later when I had a mirror and, I dunno, a sedative or something. My nerves were on the brink of a total breakdown.

My necklace. I have to find it and get out of here.

I renewed my focus, determined that I wasn't leaving until I had the locket around my neck once more. I was great at finding things. I was always the kid who had the most Easter eggs in my basket. I'd never lost my car keys. Not once. I was a human GPS who could find true North blindfolded. I followed my gut, and it led me to whatever I needed to find. It was how I landed so many flawless shots. My gut told my pool stick where to aim, and I never had a problem. I inhaled the stench of beer that stank like it had been soaked into the walls, warning my gut that it was go time. Judah came in a few minutes later, shaken but ready to be helpful in my quest to find my locket and get the crap out of there.

Three hours later, the bar was closing and we were being pushed out on to the street with a promise that the owner would call if they found anything.

Judah didn't say a word, but kept his arm around me as we walked, my eyes on my shoes and my hands blackened from running them over every inch of that disgusting, sticky floor. I had one family heirloom. One. My Aunt Lane salvaged one thing off my mother's body before it had been cremated. The locket was gone now, and though I had no memory of my mother, the fragile connection I had to my roots was gone with it.

Read *Ugly Girl* by Mary E. Twomey today!

ABOUT THE AUTHOR

USA Today bestselling author Mary E. Twomey lives in Michigan with her three adorable children. She enjoys reading, writing, vegetarian cooking, and telling her children fantastic stories about wombats.

While she loves writing fantasy, dystopian, and paranormal tales for her readers, Mary also writes romance under the name Tuesday Embers, and cozy mysteries under the name Molly Maple.

Visit her online at www.maryetwomey.com, and sign up for her newsletter, so you never miss a new release.

www.ingramcontent.com/pod-product-compliance
Lightning Source LLC
Chambersburg PA
CBHW010316100726
47906CB00006B/1017